Praise for The Amoveo Legend series

"Sizzling sexual chemistry that is sure to please... I really can't wait to see where we go to next."

—*Yankee Romance Reviewers*

"A moving tale that captures both the sweetness and passion of romance."

—*Romance Junkies*, 5 Blue Ribbons

"A well-written, action-packed love story featuring two very strong characters."

—*Romance Book Scene*, 5 Hearts

"*Unleashed* earned its Best Book rating in spades... The characters haunted my dreams and I thought about this book constantly."

—*Long and Short Reviews*

"I loved this book. A paranormal top pick, and I'm looking forward to many more in this series."

—*Night Owl Romance* Reviewer Top Pick, 5 Stars

"Awesome... captivates the reader with action and romance."

—*Rom Fan Reviews*

"The love scenes are steamy... the plot is intriguing and... the reader will be entertained."

—*Fresh Fiction*

The Amoveo Legend

UNTAMED

SARA HUMPHREYS

sourcebooks
casablanca

Published by Sourcebooks Casablanca, an imprint of Sourcebooks, Inc.
P.O. Box 4410, Naperville, Illinois 60567-4410
(630) 961-3900
FAX: (630) 961-2168
www.sourcebooks.com

Printed and bound in Canada
WC 10 9 8 7 6 5 4 3 2 1

"A sibling may be the keeper of one's identity, the only person with the keys to one's unfettered, more fundamental self."

—Marian Sandmaier

For Megan, Charlie, and Kate...
keepers of the keys.

Chapter 1

WHY WOULDN'T HER LEGS GO ANY FASTER? HER LUNGS burned with effort, and sweat dripped down her back as she stumbled blindly through the fog-laden woods. He was right behind her. Always. His energy signature, the spiritual fingerprint that was so distinctly his, rolled around her in the mists. Behind her. Above her. In front of her.

He was everywhere.

His energy enveloped her, but still—she couldn't see him.

Layla's breath came in heavy, labored gasps, and a bare branch caught in her long, curly red hair as she tripped over a log. She pulled the tangled strands away, swore softly, and ducked behind the trunk of a giant old elm tree. Layla pressed herself up against it, praying he wouldn't see her. In response to her silent plea, the fog in the dream realm thickened and provided additional shelter from her relentless hunter.

She'd been able to avoid him so far, but tonight it felt as if he was dreadfully close to finding her—and claiming her. His powerful energy swamped her and stole from her lungs what little breath she had left. She squeezed her eyes shut and prayed that the tree and the fog would swallow her up. Could she do that? Could she control the environment of the dream that much? Just as she was about to try, an unfamiliar voice tumbled around her.

Why do you run from me? The smooth, deep baritone

flooded her mind and filled every ounce of her being in a shockingly intimate way. The sharp pang of desire zipped through her and made her breasts tingle. The sudden onslaught caught her off guard and had her head spinning.

Layla froze.

He'd never spoken to her before. She could barely hear him above the rapid pounding of her heart and wondered for a moment if she'd imagined it.

You did not imagine it. *His voice had become irritatingly calm.* Please answer my question. Why do you run away from me? *That distinctly male voice rumbled through her. It reverberated in her chest just like the deep bass beat of one of her favorite songs.* Why are you afraid of me? *Amusement laced his voice and floated around her in the fog.*

That did it. Now she was pissed. He was laughing at her? First he haunts her sleep every night for the past two weeks, and now he's making fun of her? Oh, hell no! Layla's eyes snapped open, and she expected to find him—whoever he was—standing right in front of her. However, she was met only with the thick fog she'd created.

I'm not afraid of you. *She placed her hands on her hips and looked around at the swirling mist. Layla tilted her chin defiantly.* I just don't want anything to do with you. So why don't you piss off!

Rich, deep laughter floated softly around her. You make it sound as if there is a choice in the matter.

You bet your bossy ass there is. *Layla shouted boldly into the gray abyss.* I decide my fate. Me. Layla Nickelsen. *She pointed at her chest with her thumb.* Me. Not you or anybody else.

She waited. The beautiful sound of silence encircled her. Was he gone? She sharpened her focus and found him quickly. No. His energy still permeated the dream but had lessened. He had backed off? Interesting.

Layla stepped away from the tree, and the fog retreated in response. She steadied her breathing as her heartbeat slowed to a normal pace. A victorious look came over her face as she found herself gaining control. She pushed her hair off her face and watched the familiar woods where she had grown up come slowly into focus. A satisfied smile curved her lips; she nodded and made a hoot of triumph. Fate can kiss my ass.

The words had barely left her mouth when two strong arms slipped around her waist and pulled her against a very tall, hard, and most definitely male body. Stunned and uncertain of what else he might do, Layla stayed completely still and glanced down to discover that her hands rested on two much larger ones. She could feel his heartbeat against her back as it thundered in his chest and thumped in perfect time with hers.

He dipped his head, and warm, firm lips pressed an unexpectedly tender kiss along the edge of her ear. Luminous heat flashed through her with astonishing speed, making her breasts feel heavy, and sending a rush of heat between her legs. It took every ounce of self-control to keep from sinking back into his strong, seductive embrace. Her body's swift reaction was positively mortifying. She shivered, bit her lower lip, and fought the urge to turn around and kiss him. Why, and how, could she be turned on like this? Layla stiffened with disgust at her lack of self-control and her body's obvious attraction to his.

You cannot outrun your destiny. *His surprisingly seductive voice dipped low, and his breath puffed tantalizingly along the exposed skin of her neck. She closed her eyes and tried to fight the erotic sensations, but it was like trying to stop the tide as it throbbed through her relentlessly.* And for future reference, Firefly, the only one kissing your ass—or anything else on your beautiful body—will be me. *He released her from the confines of his embrace and disappeared with the mist.*

The shrill ring of the motel's wake-up call tore her from sleep. Without even looking, Layla picked up the receiver and slammed it down harder than necessary. For the first time in a long time, she hadn't wanted her dream to end. That was a switch. She pushed herself up onto her elbows and blew the bed-head hair out of her face. She looked around the cheap motel room and squinted at the sun that streamed so rudely into her room.

"Why can't the damn curtains ever close all the way in these places?" Her sleepy mumble echoed through the empty room. The memory of last night's dream was still fresh and raw, which was painfully evident by the heat that continued to blaze over her skin. Layla flopped back down and threw her arm over her eyes. It looked like her bossy stalker was right.

There was no escaping fate.

"Shit."

"Something's different about you," Kerry said with a suspicious look in William's direction. She cocked her head and studied him intently from across the dining room table of her spacious apartment.

"I'm not sure what you're implying," William said coolly. "I simply came by to see how the two of you are doing now that you're married."

He folded the newspaper neatly and placed it on the mahogany table, exactly in the spot he'd found it. He sipped the cold orange juice and checked his watch, hoping to keep Dante's irritatingly perceptive mate from knowing just how much her intuitive nature unnerved him.

"On the surface... you look exactly the same." She waved one manicured hand at him. "Three-piece suit. Hair tied back and not a smile in sight. You seem to be as uptight as ever, the cold bastard most of us have come to know and love."

"Charming," he murmured. "What exactly do you mean?"

"I mean," she said, lowering her voice to conspiratorial levels. "You're uncharacteristically distracted, and if I didn't know better, I'd say that your unannounced visit this morning has more to do with *you*, than it does with Dante and me."

"Really?" He glanced out the large picture window, pretending to be interested in the New York City skyline as opposed to her observations. "And why would you think that?"

"Well, for starters"—she laughed as she buttered her toast and prepared the rest of her breakfast—"most people don't just pop in on newlyweds for a visit first thing in the morning, let alone you. I mean, let's be honest, William. You're emotionally anorexic, and in the brief time that I've gotten to know you, you've rarely shown concern. In fact, the only emotion that I think I've ever seen you exhibit is anger, but you *had* been stabbed at the time, so that was certainly understandable."

"I wasn't angry," he said humorlessly. "I was irritated."

"Forgive me." Kerry took a bite of her toast. "You were annoyed that you got stabbed, not angry."

"Hey," Dante interrupted. Clad in his bathrobe and toweling off his wet head, he sidled up to his mate and gave her a kiss. "I thought you weren't pissed about that anymore," he said as he helped himself to some juice. "You know it was an accident. I was trying to kill that crazy Purist bitch Pasha, not you."

"He wasn't pissed." Kerry elbowed him. "He was irritated," she said in a tone that William assumed was her best attempt at mimicry.

He liked Kerry and appreciated her directness. It was, in his opinion, her finest quality, but he wasn't in the mood for jokes. Then again, he was rarely in the mood for joking around.

"Ah yes, it's a feeling I'm familiar with again," he said pointedly to Kerry.

"See? Something is definitely up with you. A few weeks ago, it took getting stabbed to ruffle your feathers, but now, a little teasing, and you're already annoyed. Ever since we left New Orleans, you've been just a bit… off." She extended her hand to William and smiled. "C'mon, fork it over."

He flicked a glance to her outstretched hand and back to a pair of mischievous brown eyes. He knew what she wanted him to do.

Kerry was a hybrid—half human and half Amoveo

from the Panther Clan. In addition to the Amoveo abilities inherited form her father, her human mother had passed on her gift of second sight. With one touch she could see inside of people and the secrets they buried deep.

William shook his head. "There's no need for that." He turned his attention to Dante. "Your mate is quite perceptive, even without using her second sight."

"Ha," Kerry shouted. "I knew it." She clapped her hands. "What is it?" Her eyes grew wider, and she leaned both elbows on the table as she peered at him. "Wait just a minute. It's not a *what* at all... it's a *who*... isn't it?"

"You found your mate?" Dante said with a wide grin. "That's wonderful news. Is she a hybrid, like Kerry and Samantha?"

"Not exactly." William stood and straightened his vest.

He walked to the window and looked out over the sea of tall buildings, longing to shift into his gyrfalcon form. He wanted to fly and soar over the world, away from his doubts, because for the first time in his life, he was unsure of himself.

"She *is* a hybrid." He kept his back to them, for fear of revealing his uncertainty. "However, there is one very large difference between my mate and yours."

"What? Is she from some unknown Hamster Clan or something?" Kerry asked with her usual teasing tone.

"No," William bit out. He kept his hands clamped firmly behind his back and struggled to keep his growing frustration at bay. "She knows what she is." He finally turned to face them and found them looking as shocked as he had when he realized the truth. "She knows that she is half Amoveo."

"Wait." Dante's brow furrowed with obvious confusion as he looked from William to Kerry. "She knows that she's a hybrid?"

"Yes." He nodded in Kerry's direction. "You were correct about New Orleans. That's where I found her. It's Layla Nickelsen."

"The photographer from my shoot." Kerry slapped Dante on the arm. "I knew there was something up with her, but I just couldn't put my finger on it."

"Well"—Dante winked—"you were a bit distracted with your own… issues."

"Hot damn! Way to go, William!" She wiggled her eyebrows at him. "If memory serves, she's one spirited chick. Something tells me that you're going to have your hands full with her."

"You have no idea," he mumbled. "Although, the thrill of discovering her has been rather short-lived." He ran a hand over his face and paced back and forth by the windows, almost forgetting the two of them were even there. "I assumed that she knew nothing of her Amoveo heritage, just like you and Samantha, but when I connected with her in the dream realm… she ran from me. At first, I thought it was because she took the connection for an unusual or unsettling human dream, but last night… she confronted me."

"Confronted you—how?" Dante asked.

"I've connected with her in several dreams over the past few weeks, and she continued to elude me, but last night she stopped running." William adjusted his tie and smoothed it down, as if it could calm his growing confusion.

"What did she say?"

"She told me to get lost and called me a stalker."

Kerry laughed long and hard, and Dante tried to suppress a smile, but to no avail.

"What on earth are the two of you laughing at?" William asked, openly bothered by their reaction. He stood ramrod straight as he watched their blatant amusement at his conundrum. "I don't find this the least bit funny."

"Oh, William." Kerry wiped at the tears that were streaming down her face as her laughter subsided. "I'm not sure what's more amusing. Your reaction to her, or the fact that you just don't understand why a woman—whether she's a human, an Amoveo, or a hybrid—wouldn't want to be stalked?"

"Well, what on earth am I supposed to do?" William's brow furrowed. "You know that the dream realm connection is crucial to our mating process."

"How about introducing yourself to her in real life? What do you know about her aside from the fact that you *think* she knows she's a hybrid."

"I don't *think*," he snapped. "I *know* that she's aware of her Amoveo heritage."

"Fine." Kerry sighed and folded her arms. "If she knows what she is, then who the hell raised her? It can't be an Amoveo, right?" She looked at Dante. "Wouldn't other Amoveo know about it? I mean, where in the hell has she been all these years?"

"I'm not sure of anything anymore," William murmured. "You know that the prince informed the rest of the Council members that Purists like Brendan and Pasha wouldn't be tolerated. He has publicly embraced the idea of humans mating with Amoveo, and he wants any other hybrids found and brought into the fold and protection of their clan."

William couldn't help but notice Dante flinch at the mention of his father's name; his betrayal was still raw, a wound that would never heal. Brendan and the rest of the Purists wanted Kerry and Samantha dead, as well as anyone who would encourage the cross-mating of humans and Amoveo.

"I know she was raised in a rural area of Maryland by a human woman," William continued. "I do not believe that the woman who raised her is a blood relation, but she must know about the Amoveo."

"Hey," Kerry said brightly. "I have a crazy idea. Why don't you actually go and introduce yourself? Y'know? In person—as opposed to dream-stalking the poor woman."

William blinked in surprise. "I am not stalking her. I'm solidifying our connection via the dream realm," he said adamantly.

Kerry looked at him as if he were a complete moron.

"Yeah, *you* were raised by two Amoveo, but you're telling me that you believe *Layla* was raised by a human, so how much does she really know?" She looked from William to Dante and shrugged. "Sometimes a small amount of information is more frightening than none at all."

William nodded in agreement. Kerry was absolutely right. All he knew was that she had some idea that she was Amoveo and could control certain aspects of the dream realm. The cold, hard truth was that he didn't know much of anything, and he found that to be the most uncomfortable feeling of all.

"You may have a point," William said quietly.

"You'll notice that he didn't say I was right," she said to Dante, laughing.

"Thank you for your assistance with this matter," he said with a nod.

"You're not gonna wear that are you?" Kerry asked through a grimace.

"Of course." He glanced down at his suit as he straightened the vest again. "Why do you ask?"

"I only met Layla briefly… but she didn't strike me as an I-love-a-guy-in-a-suit kind of girl." She cocked her head and looked at him intently. "You might want to try a pair of jeans and a sweater, or at least ditch the tie."

William made a face of disapproval, and Dante nearly choked on the toast he was eating.

"That'll be the day," Dante said through a coughing fit.

"Fine." Kerry held up her hands in defeat. "It was just a suggestion. Maybe I'm wrong, and your three-piece-suit lawyerly hotness will knock her socks off."

"Thank you." William bowed his head in deference. He turned his attention to Dante. "I can call on you and Malcolm if I'm in need of assistance? The Purists don't seem to be aware of her existence, but I would be more comfortable approaching her if I knew I could count on you both… considering your experience," he said with a glance to Kerry.

"You don't even have to ask—consider it done," Dante said as he and William shook hands over the table. "Have you told the prince that you found Layla?"

"No," William said grimly. "I want to find out more about her before I approach Richard and the rest of the

Council. She's remained safe all of these years, and I'd like to keep it that way."

"But the prince told everyone that the *Purists* are the enemy, *not* the hybrids." She looked from Dante to William. "Why keep Layla a secret? Even if it's just for a little while longer?"

William thought for a moment, wanting to choose his words carefully. "Let's just say that I suspect not all of the council members share Richard's welcoming feelings about interbreeding with humans."

"Are you sure?" Dante took Kerry's hand and linked her fingers with his. "If there are Purists on the Council, there could be a shit-storm of epic proportions."

"Let's take things one step at a time. First, I have to convince a woman who hates me that I am her life mate."

"You better find some patience and a sense of humor." Kerry squinted, inspecting him closely. "You have any squirreled away under that nifty suit?"

"Thank you for your *help* as well, Mrs. Coltari." He bowed regally and ignored her comment. "I'll be taking my leave."

"Anytime, Iceman," she said with a wink.

William shot her a look of disapproval at the use of her nickname for him, uttered the ancient language, and vanished into the air.

Kerry smiled as he disappeared and murmured, "I bet a hundred bucks she gets him to ditch a lot more than that tie."

Chapter 2

LAYLA SWUNG THE OLD JEEP INTO THE DRIVEWAY OF Rosie's farm and instantly felt safer. The tension headache that had been eating at her since she left New Orleans began to ease, and she let out a long slow breath. The drive from New Orleans to Maryland had been relatively smooth but seemed to take forever. She desperately wanted—no—needed to be home, now more than ever.

The tires crunched along the winding dirt driveway as the old Jeep bounced along and rattled her around, but she barely felt it. A huge smile cracked her freckled face the moment that the old farmhouse came into view. It looked exactly the same as it had all those years ago, when she had first seen it.

Layla slowed the open-air Jeep to a halt at the bottom of the hill and pulled the hand brake. She grabbed the roll bar, stood in the seat, and closed her eyes. A gust of wind blew strands of long red hair off her face as she took a deep breath and reveled in the crisp, sweet, familiar scent of the farm. The cool fall air filled her nostrils and encapsulated each individual smell, allowing her to pinpoint every one. The sweet scent of the hay and the freshly mowed grass mixed with a hint of manure from the stables. The combination of the weather and the aroma instantly brought her back to the day she'd first arrived.

The first twelve years of her life had been spent being bounced from her mentally ill mother to various foster homes. She always tried to fit in, to keep her mouth shut, but sooner or later, she would let a secret slip. After that, it was only a matter of time before the foster parents asked that she be relocated. Layla grimaced. The last home she was placed in had been particularly unpleasant.

If it hadn't been for an unexpected visit by a new social worker, she would likely have wound up dead. The horrid memories threatened to creep in and steal her serenity, but the wind brought a reprieve, and the familiar scent of Rosie's apple pie. She smiled and opened her big green eyes to gaze upon the only place that had ever really been home.

Layla plopped her butt back into the beat-up leather seat, released the brake, and threw the Jeep into first gear. Woodbine farm was a safe haven for her, just as it had been for her foster brother and sister. No one and nothing could hurt her here. Not her mother, not the crazy people she photographed, and not her dream stalker.

The Jeep came to a shuddering stop in front of the house, and within seconds Rosie came lumbering through the screen door to greet her. Her salt-and-pepper braids hung all the way down to her waist, and the plaid shirt and overalls were stained from gardening. With arms wide open and a huge grin on her tanned face, Rosie practically flew down the stairs. Layla barely had time to get out of the car before Rosie tackled her in a welcome-home bear hug. Her big, soft form enveloped Layla's much smaller one with minimal effort.

"Layla Nickelsen," she bellowed into her ear and

rocked her back and forth. "You are a sight for these old eyes." She pulled back and eyed her at arm's length. "What the hell have you been doing, girl? You are skin and bones! You're swimmin' in that damn jacket."

Leave it to Rosie to point out the obvious. Suddenly self-conscious, Layla pulled the big cargo jacket closed. She had always been thin, but the sad fact was that lately she was downright skinny. Stress from the last job in New Orleans had really rattled her cage, and nightmares haunted her sleep every night since then. The combination of bad dreams and stress had killed her appetite.

She shrugged her slim shoulders. "Hey, I've been working like crazy. What can I tell ya?" Layla looked away quickly, and grabbed her duffel and camera bags out of the back of the Jeep. She couldn't look Rosie in the eye and lie to her. Never could. Why would time have changed that? The hard truth was that she might be almost thirty years old, but around Rosie, she was always that little girl looking for a safe haven.

For the first time in a very long time, she was scared. Layla gritted her teeth and shut her eyes against the long-forgotten feeling. Years ago, she'd promised herself that she would never allow herself to be afraid again. Ever. Fear was a dangerous, weakening, and self-defeating feeling. Monsters could smell fear, and that's how they picked their victims. Victims were weak, and she would never be a victim.

She was home, and she was safe.

Rosie took Layla's now quivering chin in her hand and forced her to make eye contact. Those familiar warm, blue-gray eyes softened, and her voice dipped low. "You can't lie to me, girl."

Layla nodded almost imperceptibly as the tender sound of Rosie's voice threatened to push her over the edge. She swallowed hard and fought the pathetic urge to cry. No tears. She hadn't cried once since she'd arrived at Woodbine, and she wasn't about to start now. No matter how freaked out she was, there would be no more tears.

"Everyone else may buy your tough-girl routine, but I know better." Rosie gave her cheek a pat. "Now, why don't you come on inside and get settled in your old room. We'll talk about whatever is botherin' you over some pie and coffee."

She winked and wrapped her arm around Layla's shoulders, which immediately loosened the knots in her stomach.

"Come on. Your brother should be back soon. You know that boy." She sighed loudly and looked over her shoulder. "One whiff of my apple pie, and he comes runnin'. Too bad he don't come runnin' like that when it's time to muck out the barn." She chuckled.

Layla walked up the steps wrapped in the safe shelter of Rosie's embrace. Even the familiar creak of the old steps helped to put her at ease. She threw a glance across the rolling fields, and her gaze slid to the barn looking for any sign of her brother Raife. The horses grazed lazily, and the chickens clucked loudly in the distance, but no sign of Raife. She smirked and shook her head. Raife loved the farm and had stayed on to run it, but what he really loved was to roam in the woods that surrounded it.

She and Raife's twin sister Tatiana used to tease him relentlessly about it. Raife and Tatiana were Rosie's niece and nephew and had been raised on the farm since they were babies. For all intents and purposes they were her siblings—blood or not, they were the only family she ever knew. Once Layla arrived at the farm, it didn't take her long to realize that the universe had thrown them together for a reason. It turned out that they had a lot in common. They were all orphans, they were all damaged, and they were all hybrids.

—◦◦◦—

That first forkful of cinnamon-spiced apples and buttery crust burst in Layla's mouth with explosive sweetness. Eyes closed, she savored the comforting flavors and made a shamelessly loud, yummy noise of satisfaction. Rosie's hearty laugh bounced through the country kitchen, and she clapped her hands. That rich, familiar sound warmed Layla's spirit as much as the steaming coffee warmed her body.

She shrugged sheepishly and swallowed the mouthful of pie. "You still make the best apple pie on the planet, Rosie." Layla sat back and wiped her mouth with the red-checkered napkin from her lap. "Believe me. I've tried apple pie in every single town I've been to, all over the world, and none of them hold a candle to yours," she said, smiling.

Rosie nodded and stared at her through doubt-filled eyes. "That's fine and dandy. But you and I both know that you didn't come all the way home, after all this time… just to have my pie."

She pulled out one of the wooden chairs, and the sound of it scraping on the floor brought back memories of various lectures Layla had gotten at this table. Most of them were for getting into fights at school. Tough Girl Talks—that's what Rosie called them.

"He found me," she whispered.

She snapped her mouth shut, as if she couldn't really believe she'd said it out loud, because she'd barely been able to admit it to herself. The only thing that she had truly feared happening—had finally happened.

She drew in a shaky breath and forced herself to look Rosie in the eye. "My mate found me."

Rosie didn't flinch.

"Did you hear me?" Layla said quietly. "My mate found me."

"I heard you just fine." Rosie nodded and stirred her coffee. "I'm just wondering why you're acting like someone just tinkled in your lemonade."

"Rosie," Layla asked with surprise. "How can you act like this is all okay?"

"Young lady, you are running away, and that's not okay." She sipped her coffee and made that tsking sound that instantly sent Layla back to her childhood. "I thought I taught you better than that."

"You did," she sputtered.

Guilt tugged at her because she'd never want Rosie to feel that somehow she was to blame for any of this. She looked down at the mug in her hands and bit her lip to keep from crying. She couldn't add disappointing-the-woman-who-raised-me to her list of screw-ups.

Rosie read her like a book, as usual, and gave her arm a reassuring squeeze.

"I spoke to you a few weeks ago, and you were about to start some modeling shoot in The Big Easy. Next thing I know, you're hightailing it back here." She served up another piece of pie onto Layla's plate. "Now why don't you quit running and start talking."

"God, you're right." Layla laughed, rubbed at her tired eyes, and sucked in a deep breath. "I've been doing nothing but running away from him since he found me." She shook her head at her own foolishness.

"Well, now." She sighed heavily. "Don't beat yourself up over it. The important thing is that you're not running anymore."

"He's been trying to connect with me in the dream realm ever since New Orleans, and at first I tried ignoring him. I thought maybe, if I didn't give him any attention, that he'd give up and go away. But no such luck."

"I see." Rosie made a sound of understanding. "What's he like?"

"I don't really know a whole hell of a lot." She smiled at Rosie. "Except that he's persistent."

"Has he been cruel to you? Has he threatened you or been violent and tried to intimidate you into being with him?"

"No." Layla shook her head adamantly. "Not at all. Nothing like that... I just..." she trailed off, uncertain how to verbalize her feelings. "He's been... nice... cordial even. And bossy, extremely bossy."

"Mmm-hmmm." Rosie peered at her over the steaming mug of coffee. "Sounds like a real cad."

"Rosie—" Layla laughed in spite of the situation and shook her head. "You're oversimplifying it."

"Maybe." She shrugged. "Or maybe you're making it more complicated than it needs to be. He may be Amoveo, but he's a man, too." Her warm eyes twinkled brightly. "Is he handsome?"

"Yes," she said quietly. Layla shifted in her seat and avoided Rosie's probing gaze. He wasn't just handsome. He was the sexiest man she'd ever encountered, and she hadn't even seen him. "Well, I think he is. I haven't seen him yet... exactly."

"Girl," Rosie said with exasperation. "You are writing him off before you even lay eyes on him? That just seems silly. You should at least find out if this fella can melt your butter."

"Come on." Layla chuckled. "That's not all that important."

"The hell it isn't," Rosie exclaimed. "If a man can't flip your switch, then you're just livin' in a dark, dark world. Uncle Ernie may not have looked like much. God rest him," she said, making the sign of the cross over her ample breasts. "But that man turned me on like no one I ever met, and we may have fought like hell, but the makin' up made it all worthwhile."

Layla's face heated with embarrassment at the very idea of Rosie and her late Uncle Ernie knocking boots. She plugged her ears. "Okay, no more sex talk about you and Uncle Ernie, please."

"Oh alright, now." She tugged Layla's hand out of her ear and held onto it. "What I'm telling you is that you can't make any decisions until you have all of the information. I realize that you're not keen on the idea of having some predestined husband or whatever, but you can't run away from it. You have to face him and this whole thing head-on. Then you can make your choice."

"I think that's the part that really bothers me," she said softly.

"Which part, darlin'?"

"I feel like I don't have a choice. He's going to drag me off like he owns me."

"Hold on one damn minute." Rosie leaned in and grabbed both hands. "You may be half Amoveo, but you're half human too. Last time I checked God gave man free will." She lowered her voice to just above a whisper. "Our lives are the sum of the choices we make. Don't let some legend determine your future. Don't give anyone or anything that kind of power over you or your life."

"You're right." Layla nodded firmly. "I'll meet him face-to-face. Then I can tell him that I'm not interested in being dragged off and mated like a prize cow."

"We'll see." Rosie chuckled. "You just never know what the future has in store. You know what they say, darlin'… While you make plans, God laughs."

A brisk gust of wind whipped through the rust-colored leaves and fluttered over his white and brown speckled feathers, but William barely noticed it. The diminutive redhead with the big personality ruffled his feathers more than anything else ever could. He'd been searching for her for years to absolutely no avail, and then two weeks ago—boom—there she was. She appeared seemingly out of the blue, but his relief at finding her was quickly replaced with frustration and confusion. She baffled him because she *knew*. She knew what she was. She knew who *he* was, and she rejected him. He'd come to her every night in the dream realm since then, but each time she ran.

She feared him.

He shook his feathered head and adjusted his position on the thick branch. Frustration filled him, and his sharp talons dug into the rough bark because this was a far more complicated and messy situation than he'd planned on. William was used to getting what he wanted and getting it with minimal fuss. He'd been certain that once he found his mate, whoever she was, that things would fall into place.

Apparently not.

Perplexed, William remained perched on the thick branch of the oak tree and watched Layla through the kitchen window. In his clan form, as a gyrfalcon, his vision was incredibly acute, and at this particular moment he was very grateful for it. Even from this distance high up in the tree he could see her delicate form perfectly. She was tiny and couldn't have been much more than five feet tall, and although she was petite, she most definitely was not weak. She radiated strength, and as he'd recently experienced, had a significant stubborn streak.

Her creamy skin was sprinkled with caramel-colored freckles, and he couldn't help but picture himself lapping at each and every one. Perhaps what he loved most was her fiery red hair. He wanted to bury his face there and inhale her distinctly spicy scent directly from the source. He'd captured her unique energy signature that day in the bayou, and it hadn't left him since. The intense aroma of cinnamon and spice permeated his dreams and haunted his days.

He'd known who she was the second he'd laid eyes on her, and he thought for certain that Dante would notice her too, but he'd been far too concerned about Kerry to pick up on it. William had openly criticized both Malcolm and Dante for their lovesick foolishness because he didn't understand how the two of them had become so twisted up over their women. Clearly he owed them an apology. He cringed. He hated to admit that he was wrong, and he knew they'd never let him hear the end of it.

That day in the bayou, Layla's energy signature had slammed into him with a voracious intensity that took him completely by surprise… and William was not accustomed to being surprised. He prided himself on his innate ability to always remain calm, keep a cool head, and maintain a sense of order.

All of that changed the second he found her.

It was as if he'd been asleep his entire life, and she had awakened him. The world seemed brighter, louder, sharper, and more chaotic. This woman had turned his world upside down and had him spinning. The only thing that could quell the stark need in his gut was connecting with her.

His mate.

He had suspected that his mate could possibly be a hybrid like Malcolm and Dante's. After what had transpired over the past few months, after all that had been revealed, it wouldn't have been a surprise. However, he expected her to be unaware of her roots, just as Kerry hadn't known about her Amoveo heritage. The hybrids were being hunted by an underground network of fanatical Amoveo Purists, and as a result, they had been kept hidden from their people.

However, Layla *knew* she was a hybrid, and so did the human woman she was speaking with. This was where she'd grown up, that part he'd figured out. Rosie was human, but apparently knew that Layla was half Amoveo. The entire situation was highly irregular because there were only a handful of humans who knew about their existence, and they were closely watched by the Council.

William shifted on the branch and attempted to shake off the sense of dread, but this scenario was confusing and unexpected.

Movement to the right of the house caught William's eye and broke his concentration. A blur of black slipped around the side of the house, and the energy signature with it just about knocked William out of his tree. His eyes glowed brightly as the potent combination of fear and anger took hold. It was an Amoveo male that he had never encountered before: Wolf Clan. Why would any other Amoveo be here? He hadn't even told Dante and Malcolm about Layla. The unfamiliar hand of panic gripped his heart. Purists? No other answer came to mind.

Anger flared hard, and William zeroed in on the intruder's location. Whoever he was, he'd shifted from wolf to human form and was about to go inside the house. William whispered the ancient language, vanished with the wind, and within moments was standing on the ground behind Layla's would-be assassin. With unnatural speed he grabbed the man's right arm, twisted it behind his back with one hand, and put him in a choke hold with the other.

"Who sent you?" William barked into the man's ear.

"Fuck you," he bit out and stomped his steel-toe boots into William's instep.

William grunted at the pain, and it was the only opening his opponent needed. He struggled as William grimaced at the smell of him, a rancid mixture of dirt, sweat, and farm animals. Slick with sweat, he slipped out of William's grip, and the two men slammed into the side of the house in a blur of arms and legs. As William pinned the man up against the wall by the throat, he wondered fleetingly what kind of assassin dressed like a farmer.

The man's human eyes shifted into the glowing blue eyes of his clan as he grabbed William by the lapels of his pinstripe suit. They stood there locked in a stalemate—eyes glowing, muscles straining, and neither willing to retreat.

William knew if he squeezed just a little harder, he could break his neck and be done with it.

The man's blue eyes glowed brightly, and anger carved deeply into his features. His lip curled back with disgust. "You're not laying one finger on my sister, you asshole," he growled.

William froze. Sister? He was Layla's brother? William held the man's intense gaze and looked for any sign of deception, but found none. He was about to start questioning him, when a familiar voice sliced through the air—straight to his heart.

"He's right," Layla fumed. "You are an asshole."

Chapter 3

THE CLOCK ON THE WALL TICKED LOUDLY AND ECHOED through the kitchen as the four of them sat around the kitchen table awkwardly staring at each other. Layla stole a sidelong glance at William, who was busy attempting to remove sweat and dirt stains from the lapels of his blue suit. He made a face as the dirt merely smudged, but didn't actually come off.

She stifled the urge to giggle. A suit? Her mate hangs out every day in a suit. *Yeah, right. That's the guy for me. Not.* Oh, he was handsome, as she suspected he would be, but she would be damned if her life was going to be left up to the fates.

Raife glowered at William while he ate his apple pie with a vengeance. Layla gave Rosie a look that screamed for help. If someone didn't say something soon, she was going to completely freak out.

Rosie watched William making a bigger mess of his jacket and shook her head disapprovingly. She finally broke the deafening silence with a sound of frustration.

"Take off that damn thing, and give it to me," she huffed. Rosie walked around behind William and pulled the jacket off his shoulders before he could stop her. "You're gonna rub a hole in it." She took it back to the laundry room. "I'll get it cleaned up."

"It's really quite alright, madam," he sputtered after

her. Rosie, as usual, got her way which left William looking completely befuddled.

Layla's lips quirked at his discomfort; this man was not used to being told what to do. Her gaze slid over his hulking form, and she couldn't help but admire his broad chest and shoulders. He was over six feet tall—a bit bigger than Raife, and that was saying something. They were about the same height, but William was bulkier.

His large muscular frame dwarfed the wooden chair he sat so stiffly in. The man looked ridiculously out of place in the country kitchen. She had to admit he was hot. Hot? Hell, that didn't cover it. He was… exquisitely unique, strikingly beautiful.

Shoulder-length blond hair, streaked with brown, was tied in a tight ponytail at the nape of his neck. Having his hair pulled back allowed his fiercely handsome face with its chiseled features to take center stage.

Her gaze landed on his mouth, and for just a moment, she wondered what his lips felt like. *I bet they're firm and warm. Just like in the dream realm.* His dark gaze flicked over and locked with hers. Layla's heart fluttered because he didn't just look at her… he *saw* her, and she bet a million dollars that he just heard her too.

A faint smile played at his lips. *Damn it.* She looked away quickly. She'd have to remember to guard her thoughts around him.

"Now," Rosie began as she sat back down at the table, "Let's start by cutting the madam crap. It's Rosie."

He bowed his head. "I am William Fleury. It is a pleasure to meet you, Rosie." His voice remained calm, cool, and collected.

It was easy to tell that it took quite a bit to rattle

this guy. He'd lost control outside with Raife, and it definitely irked him. She deduced that he was not a man who liked to relinquish control. The ferocious look in his eyes, and the energy waves that pulsed off him when he struggled with Raife, were completely different from the man who sat next to her now.

How could the universe pair her with him? She spent most of her life feeling out of control. She lived moment to moment, went from job to job, and thrived on the organized chaos of her life. Something told her that William would take issue with that.

"Yes, well, you already met Layla's brother, Raife." Rosie jutted a thumb without looking at Raife.

"I did not know who you were, Raife." William cleared his throat. "You'll have to pardon my outburst, but I was concerned for Layla's safety."

Raife grunted. "Yeah, well… now you know. You're not taking my sister anywhere or doing anything else against her will."

William's face remained a calm mask of detachment. "I have to admit that finding *you* here was quite a surprise, Raife." His attentions returned to Layla. "In fact I've had several surprises today."

Layla scoffed. "You're not a big fan of surprises are you?" Her gaze skimmed his suit-clad body. *He probably sleeps in that thing.*

"No. I'm not." He eyed her intently. "Layla, I must admit, you are the biggest surprise of all." He continued to inspect her thoughtfully and leaned back in the farmhouse chair, which creaked in response. "I did not expect you to know who or what you are," he said quietly.

Layla's cheeks burned with anger and embarrassment

because she knew he was referring to the fact that she was a hybrid. She wasn't stupid. She, Raife, and Tatiana were told that they'd been hidden here for a reason. They knew that the rest of the Amoveo thought of hybrids as nothing more than birth defects. Raife's mother had laid everything out in black-and-white in her diary, and none of it sounded very good.

"Just what the hell does that mean?" Her eyes narrowed, and her nostrils flared, as she felt the heat creep up her cheeks. "I guess it came as a pretty rude awakening to find out that your mate is just some half-breed, huh?" Layla's chin jutted out defiantly as she waited for him to confirm her suspicions.

His dark stare didn't move from her face, and his mouth was set in a grim line. "Is that what you think of me?" His voice dropped to a hoarse whisper. "I *did* realize that you were a hybrid. However, I didn't think you would be *aware* of it," he bit out. Anger undulated off him in thick waves, and he turned his attention to Rosie. "What have you been teaching them?"

Rosie shook her head and laughed loudly, obviously unfazed by his response. William's face belied his surprise at her reaction. He probably expected Rosie to submit and shy away at his anger. His energy waves subsided slowly as he looked from Rosie to Layla and straightened his tie. *Surprise, surprise.*

"Typical Amoveo man for you." Rosie sighed and wagged a finger at him. "You remind me of Raife's daddy. My sister Lucy fell for him like a ton of bricks." She smiled and let out a soft, almost sad laugh. "Run off and married him after knowing him only a couple of weeks. I didn't see her again until she showed up here at the farm with Raife and his twin sister Tatiana. Lucy said her man had been killed and that the children were in danger." Rosie shrugged. "No one ever came around looking for her or the kids." Her smile faded. "I thought it was all a lot of horseshit until puberty hit this house. Then all hell broke loose." Rosie's eyes rimmed with tears as the memories reopened old wounds. "Lucy never saw any of that, of course." She sniffled. "She died about a year after she came home. Raife and Tati were just two years old."

"I'm sorry," William said somberly. His eyes, almost ebony, filled with sympathy, and the anger that had laced his energy signature moments ago was gone. Layla's brow furrowed as she started to examine this stranger through a different lens. Maybe he wasn't quite the jerk she thought him to be, but at the very least, he wasn't going to be as easy to figure out as she had originally thought.

"Yeah, me too," Rosie said and wiped at her eyes. "You know, in that year she was living with me, she shared some pretty interesting stories. Like I said, I thought they were big, fat whoppers. Fish tales." She sat back and regarded William through serious eyes. "But as soon as the twins hit puberty…"

William switched his attention to Raife. "You shifted?" he asked with genuine curiosity.

Raife nodded curtly. "Yeah, telepathy too." He sat up a little taller, clearly proud of his abilities. "Tati and I could always communicate that way, ever since we can remember." He glanced at Layla and smiled broadly. "Then when Layla showed up, she joined right in. It was as if she'd been doing it all her life."

Layla looked fondly at her brother and winked. *You always know how to make me feel better, big brother.*

He's not taking you anywhere, Red. His thoughts came through strong and steady, but he didn't take his blue eyes off their visitor.

William cleared his throat and shot Layla a look of disapproval. *Damn.* He'd heard them. She'd have to tell Raife about this annoying new development later. They never had to worry about anyone else intruding on their conversations before.

Amusement flickered briefly across William's face before he turned his attention to her brother. "Raife, do you know which one of the wolf clans your father was from?"

He nodded confidently. "I have my mom's diary. It's got everything in it."

"There's a diary?" William's eyebrows lifted. "May I see it?"

"No, you may not," he barked. "You don't need to see it, because it looks like you already know everything. She said he was in the Timber Wolf Clan. What about you? Huh? What clan are you in?" he asked in a challenging tone.

William's energy waves rippled faster and washed over Layla with surprising speed. His face hardened, and he straightened his back as if he was readying for a fight. Not again. She'd had about as many testosterone-laden moments as she could handle.

"I am a member of the Falcon Clan—the Gyrfalcon Clan to be specific." His large dark eyes locked instantly with Layla's. He breathed deeply, as if he was breathing in her very essence. "And you?" he asked in that smooth seductive tone that tickled the most intimate part of her. "Do you know which clan you are descended from?"

Layla gripped the mug in an effort to steel herself against the erotic effect he was having on her body, which had developed a mind of its own. "Cheetah," she breathed softly and tore her eyes from his.

The truth was that she hadn't ever shifted. She'd walked the dream realm in her clan form, but had never been able to shift the way Raife and Tati had. It bothered her. She knew it shouldn't, but it did, because she always felt second-rate or handicapped. She certainly didn't want William to know about it, and have him discover that she wasn't as gifted as she apparently should be.

"Yes," he murmured as his gaze wandered over her. "I suspected you were a member of one of the cat clans."

"Oh yeah?" Layla kept her eyes trained on the coffee in her hand. "Why?" It took significant effort to keep from staring at him and drooling like some sex-starved teenager. *Ugh.* She needed a cold shower and a beer.

"The way you move," he said in quiet, almost reverent tones. "There's a fluidity and a quickness to the way you handle your body. That's a common trait for members of the cat clans." He studied her quietly for a moment and said, "Do you have any idea which of your parents was Amoveo?"

Layla's face heated with anger as the mere mention of her father sent her to a very dark, primal place. "Oh, I'm well aware of my parentage." She struggled to keep her temper under control. "My father was apparently a member of the Cheetah Clan, and my mother was human. From what I gather, she fell in love with him hard and fast *before* she found out what he was. Once she did…" She shrugged, and her voice trailed off. "She couldn't handle it."

Layla flicked a glance to Rosie, hoping to gain some strength from her, and with a quick nod and a wink, the desired effect was achieved. She smiled back and took a deep breath before continuing. "My mother lost it, went completely off the deep end. Drugs. Alcohol. You name it—she did it. It's amazing I was born healthy," she murmured. "The little time I did spend with her, in-between being bounced around foster families, she babbled on about how he was a devil and turned into a cheetah right in front of her. As you can imagine, I thought she was freaking insane… but once I got here, I realized that she was telling the truth."

She looked him straight in the face.

"She was still nuts. Although I think the drugs are really to blame for that. She obviously couldn't process what he told her, and it pushed her right over the edge into loony-land. She died of a drug overdose. Hence, my childhood spent in the foster care system."

"Foster care?" he asked with concern. "What about her family?"

Layla snorted. "That's making the arrogant assumption she had any. She didn't," she bit out. "At least none that I know of. And as you probably know, hybrids aren't exactly held in high regard by *your* people, so dear old Daddy never showed his face." Her voice quivered, and tears pricked the back of her eyes as she held his gaze. "Which is just fine by me," she said. "So you'll forgive me if I don't fall at your feet and beg to be carried off. Hooking up with one of you didn't work out well for my mother, or for Raife and Tati's mother, for that matter." Her challenging gaze held his, daring him to deny it. "Did it?"

Silence pulsed thickly between them, and the energy waves in the room swirled violently around the kitchen, but William's gaze didn't falter.

"No, I don't suppose it did," he began slowly. "But I am not the enemy. Your father abandoning you is unacceptable, and I promise you I will help you find out who he is and exactly what happened."

Layla shook her head furiously. "No. Absolutely not. I don't want anything to do with him. I don't even care who he is," she added quickly.

William was silent for a moment. "As you wish," he said evenly. "I would never do anything to intentionally upset you. I want you to trust me."

"In her diary, my mother also said we shouldn't trust *any* of the Amoveo," Raife interrupted, his voice laced with irritation. "She said that my father was probably killed by his own people because he mated with her—a human. She made it pretty clear that we were in danger and should avoid the pure-blooded Amoveo like the plague—mate or no mate."

Layla and Rosie looked back and forth between the two men as they silently glowered at one another. It was like some stupid game of alpha-male chicken.

William nodded and looked at Raife as though he was choosing his words carefully. "I can certainly understand your wariness," he began slowly. "Your mother was partially correct. There are some members of our race who are a danger to you. The Purists were likely the ones responsible for your father's death,

Raife. We recently discovered their..." He paused for a moment, taking the time to find just the right word. "Mission."

William folded his hands on the table and regarded them with consideration. "We are aware of at least three other deaths that they are responsible for." His mouth set in a grim line, and he turned his intense gaze to Layla. "To be very honest, Layla, your father may not have abandoned you."

"Oh really?" she asked skeptically.

"Well, not in the malicious way you are thinking," he said tentatively. "All of the Amoveo parents of the hybrids we've discovered so far either allowed their children to be adopted, for their own safety, or—"

"Or they were murdered," Raife finished.

Layla felt the bile rise in her throat. Murdered?

It never occurred to her that her father may have been killed because of *her*. Let alone the idea that he stayed away from her for her own good. Guilt crept into her heart. Could it be true? Could her father, whoever he was, actually have loved her all these years and stayed away to protect her?

She swallowed the lump in her throat and thought about the offer William made about finding her father. She hadn't ever entertained the notion of finding him, and the idea of it still had her uneasy. But maybe...

"Yes, Raife." William nodded somberly, interrupting her private debate. "Your mother was right to hide you and keep your existence a secret. However, you should know that the majority of our people are not as close-minded. Over the past several generations, we have been hunted to the brink of extinction by the Caedo family.

Therefore, the ability to mate with certain humans is a gift not to be squandered."

"Who?" Layla asked with a questioning look to Rosie and Raife.

Rosie shrugged. "Don't ask me. I don't know more than you do."

"The Caedo family members are one of only two sets of humans who know of our existence. They've made it their mission to hunt us down and exterminate us," William said bluntly.

"One family has almost wiped you all out?" Raife made a sound of disbelief. "My mother didn't mention anything about the Caedo family in her diary. The only enemy she mentioned were the pure-bloods."

"Well, the Caedo are real and have killed hundreds of us over the years. We are actually a rather fragile race," William said. He glanced at Layla for a moment, before looking back at Raife. "We can have children only with our life mate. When our mate dies, we lose all of our abilities, and ultimately, we die as well. For all intents and purposes, we become human. We age as a human would and live out the rest of our lives just as you would," he said to Rosie. "In fact, when I first arrived today, I thought you might be a member of the Vasullus family."

"Nope." Rosie shook her head. "Never heard of them."

"When the change takes place, it's very difficult, as you can imagine. Everything you've ever known and the life you had has been ripped away. Within a few years of our mate's death we are void of our Amoveo abilities, and the aging process begins. Amoveo who suffer this fate are all considered part of the Vasullus family. It is a way to stay connected with our people and focus on keeping the rest of us hidden from our enemies. When one of us is killed, the ramifications to our race have a much larger ripple effect." His serious sable eyes latched onto Layla's, and her heart skipped a beat. "No life mate. No children."

She held his gaze, meeting his challenge. "You came to collect me so that we could do our duty and breed?"

"No," William said in a tone that hovered between confusion and annoyance. His light blond eyebrows furrowed above his large brown eyes. "It goes far beyond—"

"What if I don't want children?" Layla interrupted. A dark cloud flickered briefly over his features but was swiftly replaced by his usual calm demeanor. She raised one eyebrow. "Well?"

Layla's gaze wandered over that devastatingly handsome face, and when those big dark eyes locked onto hers, her heart fluttered like a rabbit's. A slow burn crept up her belly and flared brightly over her skin as his voice flashed into her mind. *I find it very difficult to concentrate with you so close to me. This talk of children isn't helping either. Now all I can do is picture myself making babies with you.* His deep baritone brushed her mind, and her nipples tingled. For Christ's sake, they actually tingled. One touch of that voice, and she had the insane urge to jump his bones right there at the table.

Layla's face burned with mortification. What the hell was going on? Had she completely lost her senses? Her body reacted to the sound of his voice with embarrassing speed. For a moment, it seemed as if everyone else in the room fell away, and it was just the two of them. *Later, Firefly.* The sinful promise lingered along the edges of her mind. He looked away, and the spell was broken. Layla shot him a look of doubt and shifted in her chair. *Don't hold your breath.*

"I had always hoped that my mate would want children, but I wouldn't want to do anything that would bring you unhappiness," he said firmly.

Layla's stomach dropped. Her happiness? He didn't even know her. Why would he be worried about her happiness? Layla didn't trust people easily, and she certainly wasn't ready to trust this man or *his people*. No matter how sexy he might be.

William turned his attention back to Raife, who was still scowling at him. "You might take some comfort in knowing that you are not the only ones. Two other hybrids have recently been discovered and have successfully connected with their mates."

"The photo shoot in New Orleans," Layla said softly, without taking her eyes off William. "Kerry Smithson is a hybrid, and that bodyguard of hers is Amoveo, isn't he? I'm betting he's a pure-blood like you."

William nodded slowly, and his eyes smiled back at her. "Yes. You are correct." He cocked his head and regarded her curiously. "What gave them away to you?"

Raife put up his hands to silence them. "Wait a minute. That sexy model chick is a hybrid like us?" he asked with genuine awe. "The busty beauty that's in all the magazines?"

"Yes," William confirmed. "Kerry is a hybrid, and my friend Dante is her mate. However, unlike you, Kerry was unaware of her heritage."

"I'll be damned," Raife said quietly. He sat back in his chair and crossed his arms over his chest.

William turned his attention back to Layla. "How did you know?"

Layla cleared her throat and took another sip of her coffee. She wondered just how much she should tell him. How much of herself should she reveal? The silence in the room hung heavily, and all eyes were on her.

She looked up at Rosie, who gave her that go-ahead-and-say-it face. Layla forced herself to look William in the eye again.

"My pictures," she said. "I can see things… get impressions of the people I photograph." She sat back in her chair. "One of the foster families I lived with when I was little was actually very nice, and the lady there gave me an old camera. I was about eight. It wasn't long after my mother died," she murmured, and her eyes took on a faraway look as the memory crept in. "It frightened me at first, but mostly, it fascinated me. It gave me an advantage too. The first thing I did when I got to a new foster home was take their picture. That way I knew what I was getting into."

Her back straightened as more unpleasant memories threatened to surface. She shook her head and looked back at William, who continued to study her intently. "Anyway, when I took Kerry's picture I saw a panther. That's her clan, right?"

"Yes." William nodded and puffed up with pride. "You have a very interesting gift. I've never heard of any of our people who are able to do that. Kerry is a powerful psychic and can read thoughts by touching another person, but this is the first I've heard of anyone getting psychic impressions from photographs." His admiring gaze searched hers. "Can you gain insight from *any* photos or just the ones that you actually take?"

"Nope," she said with a shake of her head. "Just mine. That's why I generally prefer the wildlife jobs. Photographing people always brings more baggage than I want. Although, I gotta tell ya, that shoot in New Orleans takes the freaking cake," she said sharply. "I was taking some test shots for light and caught one of that bodyguard, Dante. I saw a fox. The impression of his animal was much stronger than Kerry's, and it overpowered his human image. Kerry's clan animal came through the same way Raife and Tati's always has—it was kind of blurred or blended with her human image. Makes sense, I suppose." She lifted one shoulder. "Since we're a blend of two races."

"I see," William murmured. "What about me? How did you know that I was there?"

Layla's heart skipped a beat as she looked into those dark chocolate eyes again. She nodded almost imperceptibly. "Your energy signature," she said in barely audible tones. "I sensed it in the bayou that first day. It was one of the oddest moments of my life, and considering the life I've had, that's really saying something. It was the biggest déjà vu moment ever, because it was foreign and familiar at the same time." She studied his face and found recognition. He knew exactly what she was talking about, which was oddly comforting. "And then, in the dream realm, of course."

"Can't even give the girl a moment of peace, can you?" Raife mumbled. "Harassing her in her sleep seems a bit much, don't you think?"

William turned his serious face to Raife, giving him

his full attention. "The life mate bond is both physical and metaphysical, so the dream realm and telepathy are crucial to completing a true connection." His expression softened. "I assure you that my intentions with your sister are honorable. She is my mate, and I would give my life to protect her."

"Whatever, man," Raife said dismissively. "You can't just show up here out of the blue and drag her off like you own her," he shouted. His eyes had shifted to their clan form and glowed bright blue. "She doesn't even know you."

Layla put her hand on Raife's arm and sent him soothing waves of energy. Even though he was just a few months older, he had always played the role of overprotective big brother, but before today, she'd never really needed it. Layla prided herself on her innate ability to fend for herself, and normally, she would be slapping him upside his head, telling him to mind his own damn business.

However, today was not a normal day.

She caught his eye and smiled as his eyes shifted back to their human state. "It's okay, Raife. I'm not going anywhere." He sat back in the chair without taking his eyes off William. Layla squeezed his hand briefly and then turned her attentions to the man who claimed to be her mate.

"So, what's your deal?" She pulled her legs up under her in an effort to get more comfortable. "Did you just expect me to hop in bed with you and start mating?" She laughed and sipped her coffee.

William didn't take his intense gaze off her. "Actually, I thought we could start with dinner." He arched one eyebrow. "But if you'd prefer to go right to the sex, then I'd be more than happy to accommodate you," he said with mild amusement.

Layla's mouth fell open, and she sputtered like some ridiculous, prudish old maid who had just been propositioned for the first time in her life.

Raife stood up and slammed his fist down on the table. "Hold on, just one damn minute!" William didn't flinch and kept his sights on Layla.

Rosie, of course, remained the calm in the storm. She stood and whistled loudly to silence the chaos. Hands raised, she shot them all a scolding look. "All of you, just *shut up*."

Raife fumed quietly and sat back in his chair. He ran one hand through jet black hair that was as rumpled as his overalls. Layla continued to stare at William, who was looking up at Rosie with an annoyingly calm expression.

"That's better." She placed her hands on the table and glared sternly at each of them. "Now… we knew that this day might come."

Layla opened her mouth to protest but was immediately silenced by one glance from Rosie. She swore to herself, crossed her arms under her breasts, and struggled to keep quiet.

"As I was saying, this was a long time in coming." She turned her attention to William. "You." She narrowed her eyes. "If you plan on trying to court our girl," she said with a nod to Layla, "then I imagine you'll need a place to stay. You can settle yourself in the guest bedroom. Luckily, it's not being rented at the moment, and this will give you and Layla here a chance to get to know each other and figure out if this mate business is the real deal or not."

"Rosie, this is crazy," Layla protested.

"It's crazy bullshit," Raife seethed.

Rosie smacked him on the back of his head. "Don't cuss in my kitchen," she said, pointing her finger at him.

Raife rubbed the back of his head. "Sorry," he mumbled like a scolded little boy. He stood up from his chair and took his empty pie plate to the sink. The dishes clattered loudly. "I have to tend the horses," he grumbled as he stalked out of the kitchen.

Layla looked helplessly at Rosie, who had started gathering things from the table. She was serious. This wasn't a joke. Rosie expected William to move in. What in the hell was going on?

"Rosie," she said pleadingly.

Turning to Layla with a softer tone she said, "Crazy or not. It is what it is, and you will have to decide for yourself. Don't leave it up to fate, and no more running. You gotta take the bull by the horns." She glanced at William and winked. "Or the bird by the beak." She chuckled, but her smile faded when she saw the look on Layla's face. "You can't run away, girl. You, better than anyone, should know that."

Looking into Rosie's sympathetic eyes, Layla knew she was right. Her mother tried to run from the truth, and look where it got her—a one-way ticket on the crazy train.

Breaking the silence, William cleared his throat and stood up from his chair. "As long as it's not too much trouble, I would appreciate the opportunity…"

Rosie responded with her usual brusque manner. "If

it were too much trouble, then I wouldn't have offered." She glanced at Layla. "Well?" Rosie barked. "What are you waiting for? Take William upstairs to get settled. Shouldn't take too long," she said, eyeing his lack of luggage. "You obviously travel light." She pushed the chair in and scooped up the rest of the debris on the table. "By the way, once y'all are done with that you can go into town before it gets too late and pick up some things at the grocery."

Rosie looked back at the two of them, who simply sat there staring at her. "Well, get outta my kitchen. I have things to do, and so do you," she said as she tended to the sink full of dirty dishes.

"Come on." Layla reluctantly pushed herself out of the chair. "We better do as she says, or we'll never hear the end of it." She made her way into the front hall. "The woman gets as ornery as a billy goat if she doesn't get her way," she mumbled.

"I heard that," Rosie shouted.

Layla turned to shout an apology, only to run into William. She let out a yelp and probably would've fallen on her butt, if he hadn't reached out and grabbed her. His strong hands encircled her slim biceps and steadied her with minimal effort. Layla found herself pressed up against his hard body and realized that her hands had somehow found their way to his chest.

His heartbeat thrummed strong and steady beneath the crisp white shirt. The fabric whispered cool and smooth under her fingertips, but the heat of his skin quickly seeped through, causing her fingers to dig involuntarily into the unyielding muscles of his chest. Her gaze wandered up his throat, which worked as he swallowed. She had the overwhelming urge to kiss him just beneath his jawline.

What the hell was she thinking?

Sex. That's what. Hot, sweaty, tear my clothes off, pin me up against the wall, and make me lose my senses kind of sex. Layla squelched a groan, squeezed her eyes shut, and let out a slow breath.

"I didn't mean to startle you," he said gruffly.

He relaxed his grip, but didn't release her. Eyes still closed, she nodded and shivered as his thumb brushed a soft stroke along the exposed skin of her arm, just below the edge of her rolled up sleeve. Layla bit her lip and struggled against the urge to moan.

Her eyes tingled, and she knew they had shifted. *Dammit.* That only happened when she got really mad—or really turned on—and at the moment, she was feeling an intoxicating mixture of both.

Her shirt and jeans felt two sizes too small, and all she wanted to do was get naked and climb this guy like Mount Everest. Her body reacted to him on an animalistic level, and based on the rock hard erection pressing against her stomach, it was blatantly obvious that she was having a similar effect on him. This was ridiculous. They were standing in the front hallway plastered to each other like white on rice.

Layla grit her teeth and pushed against the firm planes of his chest. He didn't move. She swore and forced herself to look him in the face. Mustering courage, her eyes flew open and instantly latched onto his.

Big mistake.

His had shifted as well, and she found herself staring into the most compellingly beautiful eyes she had ever seen. Like two large, glittering black diamonds, they entranced and ensnared her, and she didn't think she could look away if she wanted to—and she didn't want to. They reminded her of the nighttime sky, when the moon glows through the clouds and illuminates the dark. The enthralling and seemingly limitless depths pulled at Layla, and something primal called to her.

His expression was a mixture of lust, desire, and restraint. She sensed his need to conquer her. Take her. And he could've. Not only was he three times her size, but her body was sending all the right signals, in spite of what her brain was saying.

Yet he didn't.

His fingers pressed deeper into the soft flesh of her arms, and he drew in a shaky breath. Her tongue flicked out and moistened her lips, but his gaze didn't waver. The strangest image went through her mind of a massive, feathered raptor zeroing in on its prey.

She was in big trouble.

"We should really go up to your bedroom," she said in a lusty voice she didn't recognize.

His eyes widened, and he arched one knowing eyebrow at her. "Really?"

Layla just about died. Her face burned with lust and embarrassment because it sounded like she was propositioning him, which she most certainly wasn't. *Liar, liar pants on fire*. Somehow that childhood chant took on a whole new meaning.

She shoved at his chest, and this time he released her. Layla took another step back, needing to increase the space between them as cold replaced warmth with disappointing speed. She half expected him to come after her, but he didn't. He remained stone still, while clearly tracking her every move. *Oh yeah, prey in the predator's sight. Shit.* She blinked, breathed in deeply, and willed her eyes to their human state. Thankfully, it worked.

When she opened her eyes, she did her best to keep her voice even and act like she didn't want to jump his bones. "What I meant was we should go upstairs, so you could get settled in your room—not what you were thinking," she said, wagging an accusing finger in his direction.

His now human eyes crinkled with amusement. "I wasn't thinking anything."

"Whatever," she said briskly.

William followed her up the staircase, and she could feel his eyes on her the entire time. His energy signature was thick and strong, and his distinct scent surrounded her. He smelled like a crisp, snowy winter night. Cool, clean, and vital.

Ever since that day in the bayou, she would catch his scent now and again, a lingering phantom that flirted dangerously along the edge of her senses. Not anymore. Now that she had met him in person, there would be no escaping it. No escaping *him*.

Layla turned right at the top of the stairs, opened the first door on the left, and gestured for him to go in. "This is your room. Towels are on the dresser, and if you need more, they're in the closet at the other end of the hall. The bathroom is there." She pointed to a door on the right-hand side of the bedroom.

William stepped through the doorway, and Layla couldn't help but notice that he looked as good from the back as he did from the front. You could probably crack walnuts on his ass, and she suspected he was all sinewy, thick muscle underneath that suit.

Her eyes tingled and shifted again. *Dammit*. She squeezed them shut, took a deep breath, and willed them back to their human state. Done. "Thank God," she said softly.

Standing stiff as a board, hands behind his back, he turned slowly and surveyed the room. She half expected him to break out a white glove and give it the dust test. She leaned against the doorjamb because there was no way she was stepping foot in his bedroom.

"This is very nice. Thank you," he said with a bow of his head.

"Well, okay." Layla stepped back into the hallway and waved. "I'll let you settle in." Although, she wasn't sure what he had to settle, since he didn't have anything. She grabbed the glass doorknob and began to close the door.

"Where is your room?" he asked pointedly.

She swung the door back open and gave him a tight smile. "On the other side of the bathroom," she said with a dismissive wave.

Her eyes wandered down the length of him and back up again. The clothes he wore seemed to be in complete contradiction to the body underneath. He looked more like some kind of Nordic warrior, and he should be wearing anything but that buttoned up shirt and tie. Her eyes locked with his, and the now all-too-familiar warmth flooded her body. Layla concentrated on keeping her eyes from shifting.

A smile played at his lips as if he knew exactly what

she was struggling with. "So, we're sharing a bathroom." He said it as a fact, not a question.

Layla tried to stop from smiling back. Too late. "Yes, so be sure to knock before you come in there. I like to take a bath at night, and I wouldn't want to put either of us in an awkward position."

She blushed as soon as the words came out of her mouth, because she immediately pictured them in the tub in various positions. Heat crept up her cheeks as William's eyes locked with hers, while he loosened his tie and undid the top button of his collar. She registered the fact that he was undressing, and since there was no luggage, if he continued, then he would be naked. Her mouth went dry.

Must. Leave. Now.

Layla gave him a quick smile and shut the door before he could say anything else. She let out a long slow breath as she walked down the hallway to her room. Okay, so he was sexy. Crazy sexy. Confident. Cool. Self-assured. However, she knew that beneath that calm exterior was something far more savage, and her stomach fluttered at the thought.

Her hand latched onto the doorknob, and his enticingly sexy voice floated into her mind.

Oh, and don't worry, Firefly. I don't think you and I will find any position awkward.

Chapter 4

HER SPICY SCENT LINGERED IN THE ROOM LONG AFTER she left. William closed his eyes as he breathed in the intoxicating aroma, his gut clenched with need, and his eyes shifted. A low growl rumbled in his chest as he struggled to get his body under control. It had been all he could do to keep from ravaging her in the hallway downstairs. He almost came apart the moment her silky skin connected with his, and that fair, freckled flesh cried out to be tasted.

When her petite frame pressed up against his much larger one, he immediately sensed her desire for him. Her body had reacted as swiftly as his, and he knew it caught her completely off guard. When he looked into her eyes—in their clan form—something clicked. It was akin to a lock slipping into place. That elusive sense of belonging that he'd been straining and struggling to find was finally here. Looking into those glowing, exotic eyes, he knew he was home. Reason left him, and all he could think of, see, or hear was her. Layla. Her happiness and well-being was all that mattered.

Layla's human eyes were emerald green and beautiful in their own right, but her clan eyes were a mesmerizing combination of gold and green. He'd never seen anything like it. He'd met other members of the Cheetah Clan, and they all had the traditional golden eyes. Not one of them possessed the prism of colors that glowed brightly in the eyes of his mate. The mere memory made him hard as a rock.

He cursed, whipped his tie off over his head, and tossed it over the wrought iron bedpost. He needed a cold shower to calm his raging hormones and clear his muddled brain. He caught a glimpse of himself in the mirror above the antique dresser and shook his head at his disheveled state. His long hair was coming loose from the leather strip, and his clothes were rumpled. If his friends could see him now, they would have a quite a laugh at his expense.

Layla was right. He did look out of place in the suit and tie, but he had nothing else with him. He would have to do some shopping in town. His visualization abilities had been waning steadily over the past two years, so he needed to conserve his energy, and visualizing clothing was not a priority. He knew that once he and Layla completed the mating rite, their powers would be stronger than ever. In fact, just being near her had energized him, but he didn't want to use his energy on frivolous things. William closed his eyes and let out a long, slow breath of frustration that nagged at him in a most irritating manner. It still remained to be seen if she would even accept him.

The sound of a car starting outside captured his attention. He went to the window and pushed aside the lacy white curtain, only to find Layla pulling down the driveway in her Jeep. Alone. Tension immediately settled in his neck, and his brow furrowed with worry, as an unreasonable wave of panic came over him. She was leaving? Wait. Didn't Rosie say something about running errands for her this morning? He swore softly and ran a hand over his face. What the hell was this woman doing to him? He'd never been this irrational before.

He watched the Jeep bounce down the dirt driveway. Her red hair whipped wildly around her. Oddly enough, the image of that cartoon character the Tasmanian Devil came to mind. The woman was a spitfire, and quite frankly he didn't know quite what to make of her. She clearly didn't ask him to accompany her, and she'd likely be upset if he just invited himself along, but that was just too damn bad. She wasn't going anywhere without him, and although it was unlikely that the Purists even knew about her, he wasn't willing to take any chances.

William closed his eyes and sent his energy signature in search of hers. His eyes shifted as Layla's vivacious energy linked with his own. His body tensed, and every nerve ending lit up the instant her life force merged with his. A fresh and unexpected surge of power jolted through him as he joined with her. Energized by this intimate connection with his life mate, William whispered the ancient language, "*Verto*," and vanished.

———

Within seconds he was sitting in the passenger seat next to a very startled and pissed off woman.

"What the hell?" Layla shrieked. She slammed on the brakes and brought the Jeep to a skittering halt at the bottom of the hill. She gaped at him through a cloud of dust. Her green eyes looked back at him wildly with a mix of anger, surprise, and awe. "How the hell did you do that?" she sputtered through shuddering breaths.

William cocked his head and gave her a questioning

look. "You are not familiar with our visualization abilities?" *Interesting*. She knew only pieces of information about their people. His mind immediately went to the diary of Raife's mother. From what Rosie said, she had only been with her mate for a couple of years, and it was anybody's guess what this man had told her. He had to get his hands on this diary.

Embarrassment flickered briefly across her features but was soon replaced with a look of disdain. "I didn't say that," she huffed. Layla tucked her long red hair behind her ear and put the car back into gear without looking at him. "You shouldn't do shit like that. I could've crashed the car and killed us both."

"Apologies," William said quietly. "It was not my intention to upset you."

He kept his attention completely focused on her, hoping she would forgive him for startling her. It seemed that he couldn't keep from making her angry. This whole mating business was like trying to walk through a field of land mines. One wrong step—and boom you're dead.

Layla let out a slow breath. "What are you doing here anyway?" She gripped the steering wheel with her diminutive hands and stared straight ahead. "I don't recall inviting you into town with me."

"Well, as you may have noticed, I do not have any of my belongings with me. I thought perhaps I could purchase some more appropriate attire." She looked at him out of the corner of her eye. "With your help, of course," he said politely.

She glanced at him sideways and gave him the once-over. "Well, you do look more suited to an office than a farm." She laughed, and the sound wafted over him like a summer breeze. She leaned her elbow on the window and adjusted the side mirror. "What do you do, anyway? I mean besides stalk a woman you barely know?"

She wanted to know more about him. William took this as a positive sign and couldn't help but grin. Good Lord, he'd never smiled this much in his life. "I am a corporate attorney. My clients are mostly Amoveo, but I do have some human clients as well."

Layla laughed loudly, slipped on her Ray-Bans, and threw the Jeep into first gear. "A freakin' lawyer? I should've known."

William braced himself as the Jeep continued its bumpy journey to the sun-dappled road. "Why is that funny?"

"You and I seem to be about as opposite as two people can be, that's all," she shouted above the wind and passing traffic. "I'm a photographer. You're a lawyer. I'm as small as you are big. You seem to be pretty uptight, and I live life by the seat of my pants." She looked at him quickly before focusing back on the road. "And I imagine that's just the tip of the iceberg."

William said nothing because she was right. They were opposite in just about every way imaginable, except for one. They were destined for each other.

They made it to town alive. Although, there were several points when he thought Layla's driving might very well kill them both. The woman drove like she was in some kind of *Dukes of Hazzard* car chase. Stop signs were apparently optional, and she seemed to view the speed limit as more of a guideline than a rule.

Layla whipped the Jeep into the shopping center,

flew into a parking space, threw the hand brake, and hopped out without even bothering to open the door. She stood on the sidewalk simply staring at William, who remained in the passenger seat, attempting to regain his bearings.

"Are you coming in, or what?" she asked as she popped a stick of gum in her mouth and impatiently waved for him to get out of the car.

"Yes," William said as he opened the door and exited the dusty vehicle. "I was just taking a moment to recuperate," he mumbled under his breath.

"Is that supposed to be some kind of jab at my driving?" She put her hands in the back pocket of her jeans. Her stubborn little chin tilted up at him, daring him to give her grief.

William was about to launch into a litany of examples of her reckless driving, but that stony look in her eyes gave him pause. The little devil was looking for a fight and trying to get him riled up. Nice try. Small, but mighty—the phrase that came to mind every time he laid eyes on her.

Layla wasn't going to get a fight, but he was happy to give her a challenge.

"Not at all." He stepped onto the sidewalk and closed the distance between them easily. Her sweet, bubble gum breath filled his nostrils and mixed deliciously with her naturally spicy scent. His felt himself stir in response, sensed her heart rate increase, and shivered as her energy waves rippled over him with increasing speed.

Layla didn't flinch. Her lithe body remained motionless, and those sparkling green eyes stayed locked with his. It was a stalemate. Who would blink first? William positioned his body closer still, just a breath away from hers, but refrained from touching her, even though he could think of doing nothing else.

"I like a woman who moves fast," he said seductively. Her eyes widened as he pictured himself licking those succulent, bubble gum lips. It was all he could do to smother the groan of desire and torment that threatened to boil over and reveal him for the horny bastard he'd become.

"We'll see about that," she said through a knowing giggle. Before he could respond, she turned on her heels and sauntered toward the store. "Come on, counselor," she called over her shoulder. "You've got to get more appropriate duds."

After what felt like forever, they finally left Epstein's clothing store, and not a moment too soon. William allowed Layla to pick out the clothes for his stay at Woodbine, and much to his dismay, she selected things that he would never purchase on his own: jeans, T-shirts, sweaters, sneakers, and a pair of shoes that strongly resembled construction boots.

He drew the line at the flannel shirt. There were just some things he wouldn't wear. Although, truth be told, if she had pushed hard enough, he would've done it. He was beginning to realize that this diminutive woman would probably be able to get him to do just about anything for her. And she knew it.

At her request, he left the store wearing some of his new "duds," which consisted of a white T-shirt, black sweater, jeans, and the clodhopping boots. She looked pleased, but he felt completely off his game. Maybe that's why she was pleased?

A native of Alaska, clothes like these were very similar to what he wore every single day growing up, and if he was back home with his parents and sisters, he'd be wearing something similar and feeling quite comfortable. But that was the problem. He couldn't afford to get complacent right now. He had to stay sharp. Focused. Until he knew exactly where he stood with Layla and was assured that there was no looming Purist threat, he couldn't let his guard down for one minute.

He'd worked his ass off to earn a reputation as a smart, tough, and sometimes ruthless member of his clan, not to mention a vicious attorney. When he wore a suit, it helped him believe that he was that man. As ridiculous as it may seem to someone else, it helped him feel in control and keep everything in line.

She looked him up and down as he walked next to her. "You look good, counselor. Much better than that stuffy old suit." She winked and handed him the bag with the rest of his purchases. "Come on," she said with a nod toward the car. "Let's put these in the Jeep, and then we'll hit the market at the end of the strip to get Rosie's stuff."

The mouthwatering scent of freshly baked bread filled the store. William's stomach rumbled with hunger the instant they stepped inside, and he realized that he hadn't eaten anything since the night before. He'd been so preoccupied with Layla that he'd forgotten to eat. He rubbed his stomach and scanned the store for the source of the flavorful aroma.

Layla laughed and passed him the shopping basket. "Hungry?" she asked with a big grin.

He looked into her smiling face and couldn't help but smile himself. "Well, yes, actually I am."

"I know." She laughed. "I think the entire store just heard your stomach growl."

She grabbed him by the arm and pulled him down the first aisle to the bakery counter. He imagined that he must look like quite a sight, being dragged through the store by this sprite of a woman, but he didn't care. He'd follow her anywhere.

Layla stopped at one of the refrigerated cases, scooped up a premade sandwich, opened it, and handed him half.

"No sense in standing around with a growling stomach in the middle of a grocery store," she said before taking a generous bite of her half.

"No," William said as he followed her to the deli counter. "No sense in that at all." He ate his half in a few bites, which didn't go unnoticed by Layla.

"You eat like my brother," she said with a smirk. "Hi, Ralph." She waved to the older man behind the counter.

"Well, well. If it isn't Layla Nickelsen!" The man behind the counter was about six feet tall but was the skinniest man William had ever seen. His long, thin face was weathered and wrinkled, and a shock of white hair covered his head. He looked fondly at Layla and gave her a big toothy grin. "How've you been young lady? Still traveling all over creation and taking pictures?"

"Yes sir." Layla looked around behind the counter. "Where's Ginny?"

"She's up at the front register." His raised his eyebrows in surprise. "Didn't you see her?" But before Layla could answer, he shimmied his way between the wall and the end of the counter. "Ginny," he called, while wiping his hands on his stained apron. "Come on back here, woman." He winked at William. "Women — never are where we tell 'em to be, are they? May as well try and control the seasons."

The scarecrow-like man disappeared down one of the narrow aisles, presumably in search of the woman he was referring to.

"I couldn't agree more," William murmured and looked pointedly at Layla.

Layla ignored him, picked up a loaf of olive bread, and popped it into the basket that dangled from William's hand. He kept his gaze on her as she perused various concoctions behind the glass of the deli case. Her springy curls fell over her shoulders as she gathered a jar of something yellow, and the wave of red practically swallowed her delicate form.

He wanted to tangle his fingers in those silky locks in the most urgent way. He cleared his throat in an effort to steel his resolve and stuffed his other hand in his pocket to keep from touching her. Layla looked up at him, and he must've looked as uncomfortable as he felt, because her brow furrowed with worry.

"You okay, counselor?" she asked in a voice tinged with genuine concern.

Before he could answer her, a high-pitched feminine shriek pierced the calm of the store. A short, rotund woman came barreling down the aisle toward them with her arms wide open. She grabbed Layla and hugged her with vigor.

"Well, hell's bells," she shrilled and rocked her back and forth. "I am so happy to see you." Layla smiled and glanced briefly at William over the eager woman's shoulder.

"For heaven's sake, Ginny. Let the poor girl go. I don't see how she can breathe with you squeezing her like that," Ralph said with a pat on her arm. He shook his head and turned his attention to William. "I swear this woman is the biggest drama queen around."

Ginny shot Ralph a look of disapproval, but quickly looked back at Layla. "Oh shut up, you old bugger." She pushed Layla away and held her at arm's length. "You are just as cute as ever." She grabbed a handful of red curls, and William couldn't help but be jealous. "Still have this gorgeous head of hair. When did you get back into town?" She released Layla from her grasp and crossed her arms under her large breasts as she continued her inquisition.

"Just got back today, actually." Layla smiled and let out a slow breath. "It's really good to see you guys." She laughed. "How's Anna? Is she still in town, or did Hollywood finally call her away?"

Ralph pulled Ginny into the crook of his arm. They were quite a sight. He was as tall and skinny as she was short and fat.

"No way! You think we'd let our little girl run off to Hollywood?" Ralph shook his head adamantly. "Hell no!"

"Oh Ralph, stop it." Ginny elbowed him playfully in the ribs and giggled. "She's doin' great. Got married last year and is expecting a baby next month. Our first grandchild, can you believe it?" She giggled and clapped her hands but stopped abruptly when her gaze landed on William.

She'd been so wrapped up in her greeting with Layla that she'd barcly registered his presence. William was wondering how long he would stand there before she said something. Her eyes grew wide as her gaze flicked from William to Layla. She smoothed her brown hair, tucking the stray hairs back into her bun.

"Well, my stars. Who is this big fella?"

Layla blushed. "Oh, I'm sorry. I um—should've introduced you—um… this is…"

William watched her fumble over her words, clearly unsure about how to introduce him. He smirked, and for a moment, considered letting her flounder. Part of him was quite curious as to how she would explain who he was, but he decided to let her off the hook.

"I am William Fleury, an old friend of the family," he said with the most charming smile he could muster. "I'm an attorney, and I'm in town handling some business for Rosie."

"Really?" Ginny's eyes grew wider still, and her voice dropped to just above a whisper. "Oh, are you here to handle the sale of the farm?"

Layla's face screwed up tightly with confusion, and her energy waves shot off in rapid fire. "What are you talking about?" Her startled gaze flew from Ginny to Ralph and back again. "Rosie's not selling the farm. She can't! She wouldn't," she sputtered.

"Oh honey, I'm sorry," she said quickly, as her plump hand went to her chest dramatically. "It was just a rumor that I'd been hearing around town. I wouldn't have said anything, but when William said he was a lawyer…" She sighed. "Well, I just assumed that's what he was here in town helping her with." Her apologetic eyes rimmed with tears, and she wrung her hands nervously. "I'm so sorry, honey. I didn't mean to upset you."

William could see that Layla was trying to keep her fear at bay. He was surprised at his reaction to her discomfort, and he had an intense urge to wrap her in his arms and console her. He would've tried, if he thought she'd accept it, but that was hoping for far too much.

He subtly shifted his body closer and reached out with soothing energy waves. Her concerned green eyes flew to his, and recognition flickered briefly over her features. She sensed his efforts to help her and didn't kick him in the shin. It was a small victory, but he'd take it.

Layla took a deep breath and turned her attention back to Ginny. She shrugged in an attempt to play off her concerns. It was ridiculous to take her frustration out on Ginny. "No worries. I overreacted," she added quickly.

Ralph let out a loud grunt. "Now you see, woman? You know what they say about assuming things. It makes an ass out of you and me!" He squeezed her tightly, made a tsking sound, and tossed the dish towel over his other shoulder. "Well, truth be told, you just made an ass out of you." He winked at Layla.

Ginny's round cheeks tinged with red. "Oh, now hush," she simpered. "Everyone knows that Frank Clark has been trying to get Rosie to sell that place for years." She looked up at William, obviously attempting to fill him in, but lowered her voice to a loud whisper. "Frank has been buying up old farms in the area and turning them into housing developments."

"Yeah, well, he's not getting Rosie's place. That's for damn sure. He's not turning our home into more of his suburban sprawl."

Without thinking about it, William inched closer and placed one hand on the small of her back. She stiffened briefly, but to his surprise, did not move away from him. He stroked the curve of her back with his thumb and sent her subtle, steady pulses of reassuring energy. *I'm sure Rosie would've told you if she were planning on selling the farm, Layla.* Her body relaxed, and that sweet voice slipped into his mind with an odd familiarity. *I know, but why do I have the sinking feeling that there's some truth to this?*

His breath caught in his throat as she completed the telepathic connection. William knew it had been a risk to try and speak with her this way, but he *had* to. The desire to be linked with her in mind, body, and spirit had become an all-consuming need, and he was as dumbfounded by it as anyone. He glanced down at her for some further reassurance, but she kept her attention fixed on the older couple.

Ginny patted her arm sympathetically. "I'm sure it will all work out." She gave William a polite smile. He could tell she didn't quite know what to make of him. This woman was a gossip and likely had her nose in everyone's business. He had a sinking suspicion that before the day was over, everyone in town would know about his presence.

"Well, it's nice to meet you, Mr. Fleury. I don't know how I could be so rude and just ramble on like that." Her eyes narrowed a bit. "You're an old friend, you say?" she asked on another fishing expedition.

Layla smiled tightly and shoved her hands in the pockets of her jeans, her tense reaction confirmed William's suspicions. His fingers fluttered along her back and wandered to the edge of her jeans. The tails of her shirt that stuck out from under the short sweater were riding up, and without meaning to, his thumb slid along the strip of exposed flesh. A sizzle of electricity flared through him, and his heart beat like a jack hammer in his chest from that one stroke of skin-to-skin contact. Layla sucked in a deep breath and threw him a scolding look. *Easy there, big guy, you're walking a fine line between being supportive and being a creeper.*

William quickly put his hand in the pocket of his own jeans. Never in his life had he exhibited such lack of self-control. He cast a contrite look to Layla, expecting her to give him the look of death. To his delight, her lips curved into a smile as she turned her attention back to Ginny.

"Yup," Layla said with a nod to William. "Old friend from New York. We worked together on some projects a few years ago," she said casually and with such ease that William almost believed it.

"Well, any friend of Layla's is a friend of ours," Ginny said with a glance to her husband. "Right, Ralph?"

"That's the ticket," Ralph said with a wink. "Now, did you need something from the deli counter, or did you just come in here to see my handsome face?"

Before Layla could answer him, the bell at the front of the store rang impatiently. Ginny grunted a sound of displeasure. "Oh, for goodness sake, I have to get back up front. I'll tell Anna you're home. She's going to be positively tickled." The bell shrilled with impatience, and Ginny let out a huff. "Oh, I'm coming. Keep your panties on," she shouted abruptly and marched down the aisle.

William watched her short, round form disappear and

had a momentary pang of sympathy for whoever was ringing that bell. Something told him that she was going to give them an earful for interrupting her reunion with Layla and her interrogation of him.

"That woman is so excited about being a grand-mother, she can't contain it," Ralph said quietly. He laughed and shook his head as he slipped behind the counter. "Now, what can I get for you, young lady?"

They finished their shopping quickly, and when they got to the counter, Layla didn't dawdle. She clearly didn't want to get peppered with more questions from Ginny. As they piled the groceries into the backseat, he looked across the way and watched Layla. The wind blew her curls off her face, and he noticed how young she looked.

Her skin was free of lines. Based on her complex-ion, he doubted that she spent much time in the sun. He imagined she'd burn easily. She was a natural beauty and didn't wear a speck of makeup. She didn't need it. Thick, dark red lashes framed those huge green eyes in a strikingly beautiful way.

Layla shoved the last package into place and lev-eled her gaze to William. He held it. She pushed her windblown hair back self-consciously. "What are you looking at?" she asked with a short laugh.

"You, I'm looking at *you*, Layla." She stilled as his penetrating stare wandered slowly over every visible inch of her. William concentrated on keeping his eyes from shifting; he didn't want to do anything to spook her or send that defensive wall back up. He took his time, committing every freckle to memory. Finally, after sev-eral minutes, his dark eyes locked with hers once again. "You are exquisite," he said softly.

Chapter 5

Was it possible to have an orgasm simply by having a man look at you? No. Not just look. *Devour*. He was devouring her with his eyes, and it was, without a doubt, the biggest turn on of her life. His fierce gaze locked onto hers with a piercing intensity that impacted every inch of her being.

For most of her life she'd worked hard at being invisible and flying under the radar. She loved being behind the camera and taking pictures of the beautiful and unusual, but *she* never wanted to be either. Layla avoided male attention like the plague, so as a result, her high school boyfriend and a couple of lovers over the years were the sum total of her adventures with men.

However, when William looked at her, it turned her on more than anyone ever had. No one had ever looked at her so intimately. It was as if he stripped her bare, saw straight to her very soul, and cut through all of her bullshit, which unnerved and fascinated her.

Her heart hammered in her chest as she held his powerful stare and nibbled on her lower lip. Those dark brown, almost black eyes, looked back at her unwaveringly. His skin was fair, not as fair as hers, but most people weren't. Long strands of his unusual whitish-blond and brown hair blew free from the confines of his ponytail and danced around that insanely handsome face.

He didn't move, didn't flinch or try to brush them

back, but kept his attention fully focused on her. His massive frame looked poised and ready to pounce on her at any moment. She was grateful that there was a Jeep between them, because if he'd been within reach, she probably would've tangled her fingers in that long hair.

"Oh-my-Gawd!"

Another familiar shrill voice came from behind and split the air, bringing Layla back to reality with irritating speed. William, clearly annoyed at the interruption, looked past her for the source of the outburst. Layla cringed and gave the old Jeep tire a kick. She'd know that fingernails-on-a-chalkboard voice anywhere. Sylvia Clark. She was the only child of Frank Clark and the town's mean girl. Layla hadn't seen her in a few years, and their last encounter hadn't exactly been a pleasant exchange.

Layla grit her teeth and turned to face her, all the while hoping she'd gotten really fat. However, the moment she latched eyes on her, all hopes were dashed. Nope. Still tall, blond, gorgeous, and dressed to the nines.

Where the hell was the justice in that?

The woman was like a walking Barbie doll—if Barbie had an evil twin. A flowing black wrap was draped dramatically over what was undoubtedly a designer, top-of-the-line ensemble. Shopping bags were dangling over both arms, and she looked like she'd just come from the beauty parlor. Hair done. Makeup perfect. She may be a bitch, but she was undeniably gorgeous. All these years later, Layla still felt second-rate around her.

To Layla's surprise, Sylvia grabbed her by the shoulders and gave her the double-air kiss on both cheeks.

She took her hands away quickly, as though she might get dirty if she touched her for too long.

"Well, my, my, my," she breathed. "Don't you just look exactly the same as you did last time I saw you?" This was obviously not meant as a compliment.

Sylvia removed her large black sunglasses and flicked her light blue eyes over Layla from head to toe. She smirked briefly, before turning her sights on William. Her eyes grew wide, and a smile slithered over her preserved face. "Well, this is new," she simpered. "And who might you be, handsome?"

William stepped around the Jeep and moved in next to Layla. Sylvia didn't take her eyes off him. Layla couldn't read her mind, but she could read her energy, and it screamed sex.

Sylvia wanted to fuck William's brains out.

Anger, jealousy, and an instinctive urge to protect what was hers flashed through her brutally. She clenched her fists and froze. What was hers? What the hell? She didn't want him. He wasn't hers. He was a stranger. Why should it matter how any woman looked at him? *Dammit*.

Layla took her aviators out of her pocket and shoved them on, afraid her eyes would shift. She crossed her arms under her breasts and wrestled with the urge to punch Sylvia's lights out and throw her in the nearest body of water.

William shook Sylvia's hand and politely introduced himself. "I am William Fleury," he said as he draped his arm casually over Layla's shoulders. "I'm an old friend," he said with a warm look in her direction.

Layla's heart flip-flopped. He didn't look at Sylvia that way. He looked at *her*.

She stilled as he pulled her against his warm body. She should've been pissed that he took such liberties, but frankly, she was having too much fun watching Sylvia get snubbed. This rich, beautiful woman, her entire life, had been playing with men and having them fall at her feet, including her brother, Raife. The bitch had toyed with him and teased him all the way to the altar, before she dumped him.

William, however, barely paid her any mind. She'd have to be sure to thank him for putting on such a good show, and it *was* just for show, she reminded herself.

"Old friends," Sylvia asked suspiciously. Her gaze moved suspiciously from Layla to William as she nibbled on the end of her sunglasses. "Well, we're old friends too. Aren't we, Layla? Yes, sir. We go way back." Her big blue eyes sparkled with something that would've looked like mischief on a nice person, but on her it screamed troublemaker. Her bright red lips curved into a phony smile. "You know, you two should come on over to the Rustic Inn tomorrow night. Tyler's band is playing, and you'll have a chance to see old friends." She winked at William. "And make new ones."

Layla shrugged. "I don't know if we can. We just—"

"We'd love to," William said, cutting her off.

Her face heated with anger, and William just lost any points he'd earned. The man was so damn bossy she wanted to scream. She didn't want to go anywhere that Sylvia was going to be, but she didn't want to have a fight with William and give her any fuel for her fire. So instead of screaming, *hell no*, she plastered on a tight smile and managed to squeak out, "Sure. We can probably come by for a little while."

Sylvia laughed and slid her oversized sunglasses back on. "Well, that's just fabulous." Then quicker than a snake, she slipped over and planted a kiss on William's cheek. "It was very nice to meet you, handsome." Then she turned on her heels and flounced away. "See y'all tomorrow evening," she shouted as she disappeared around the corner. "Eight thirty sharp."

Once Sylvia was out of sight, Layla shoved William away from her and muttered several unflattering comments about him as she got into the Jeep and slammed the door. She watched as William calmly got into the passenger seat.

"What the hell is wrong with you?" Layla snapped as she started the engine.

"I don't understand why you're so upset," he said in that all-too-calm tone.

She shook her head and backed out of the space. "I guess it doesn't matter," she muttered and pulled onto the street.

"What doesn't matter?" William shouted above the din of traffic.

"Human or Amoveo." Layla shot him a look, shook her head, and threw it into high gear. "Men are dense."

They drove back to the farm in silence. She knew that he wanted to talk and fix things, but she wasn't in the mood. The truth was that she was as confused as he was, and on top of everything else, she couldn't stop thinking about what Ginny had said about Rosie selling the farm.

When they got home, Layla didn't say more than a word or two to William. Rosie was nowhere in sight, so she dropped the groceries in the kitchen, mumbled vague directions about where to put things, and went upstairs. All she wanted to do was to take a hot bath and be alone. She needed time to clear her head and think.

Ever since William had come around, everything was all topsy-turvy. Nothing made sense. She couldn't think straight because her hormones kept getting in the way and muddying up the waters. A nice hot soak in the tub could cure almost any ill, and right now, that ill was a six-foot-two-inch hunk of bossy hotness.

Layla went into her room and closed the door. She leaned against the cool painted wood and shut her eyes. She savored the familiar smell of her childhood bedroom, a combination of cedar chips, clean cotton sheets, and a hint of jasmine, all of which conjured up feelings of peace, comfort, and safety.

Layla glanced at the clock and realized that it was almost dinnertime, but she was too tired to eat. A long hot bath was first, and then maybe a chat with Rosie. She'd sensed something going on with Rosie when she'd gotten home earlier today. She, Raife, and Tati had always made a concerted effort to respect Rosie's privacy, but sometimes her energy was so strong, she couldn't block it out.

Layla had gotten a whiff of concern and worry from Rosie when she got home, which she originally chalked up to Rosie's concern for her—but not anymore. She knew that there was some truth to what Ginny said, and she was damn well going to find out.

Layla shed her clothes and wrapped herself up in a soft white towel. She sat on the edge of the old claw-foot tub as it filled with piping hot water, and generously poured in her favorite bath salts. Within seconds, the scent of gardenias filled the steamy bathroom.

Layla removed the towel and caught a glimpse of herself in the fogged up mirror. She wiped at the slick surface so she could better see her reflection and clipped her hair up off her neck. She inspected her naked body with a woman's typically critical eye and went down the laundry list of things she didn't like about herself... too thin, breasts are too small, and way too many freckles.

Layla sighed audibly as the steam gratefully fogged up the mirror and obscured her reflection once again. "Not exactly a Barbie," she mumbled. "More like Raggedy Ann."

She submerged her body in the soothing, fragrant water and laid her head back on the bath pillow as her mind wandered to William. She hated to admit it, but he was beginning to grow on her, and it had definitely impressed her the way he jumped right in with Ginny and Ralph. The man didn't miss a beat.

She'd been cold to him from the moment he'd found her. She wouldn't have blamed him if he'd let her fumble through that introduction, but he didn't. He even came to her rescue. She giggled and lathered up the bar of soap between her hands... he'd rescued her from a socially awkward moment.

She ran the slippery bar up her arms and thought about the way he did it again when Sylvia showed up. Her brow furrowed. It was a rescue up until the point he'd agreed to go to the Rustic tomorrow.

Layla tensed at the memory of the way Sylvia looked at William. That trollop wanted to sink her claws into him and have him for dinner. She figured that William, like every other man she'd ever known, would fall all over himself to impress her, but he didn't. In fact, he barely paid her any attention and kept his focus on her, *not* on Sylvia.

Layla ran the slippery bar of soap over her breasts and down her belly. She closed her eyes and couldn't help but picture William and his broad shoulders, strong arms... and that face, Sweet Jesus, that handsome face could melt butter... just like Rosie said.

Her eyes tingled and shifted harshly. Her heart raced, and for the first time, she allowed herself to feel it... to feel the rush of desire that the mere thought of him provoked.

She wanted him.

There was simply no denying that her body craved his. A contented sigh escaped her lips as she pictured him there washing her body with his strong hands. Trailing those long, nimble fingers over her breasts, down her stomach, and finally finding her most sensitive flesh, and... *I like to think of myself as a gentleman.* His gruff, seductive voice rushed into her mind with zero warning.

Layla shot up to a sitting position as water sloshed out of the tub. She covered her naked breasts and looked wildly around the empty bathroom. He wasn't physically there, but his mind was firmly linked to hers, so at this point... it was just geography... for all intents and purposes he was in there with her.

His voice dropped low and tickled her intimately. *However, if you keep this up, Firefly, I'm going to come in there and actually do all of the things you're thinking about.*

Layla let out a shuddering breath. *Stay out of my head.* She waited for his response. The seconds ticked by loudly from the antique clock on the wall. His voice, softer, laced with disappointment, floated gently into her mind. *As you wish.*

Silence followed, but so did something else that was completely unexpected… emptiness. When he withdrew his mind from hers, it was as though he had disappeared, but she knew he hadn't. He was still here on the farm, yet his connection with her had been severed, leaving a horrible void where his energy signature had been only moments ago.

Layla's heart sank, and tears pricked at the back of her now human eyes. Tears? She sniffled and wiped at her eyes. What the hell was going on? William had some serious explaining to do.

Layla got out of the bath and into her pajamas. What she needed now, more than ever, was familiarity and some alone time.

She knew that she had to talk to Rosie and that she would be expected downstairs for dinner, but she had to lie down and close her eyes. Just for a little while. Maybe a nap would help her get her bearings back, she thought as she snuggled under the soft, familiar quilt that covered her bed. Her eyes fluttered closed, and as she was gently shrouded by sleep, she mumbled, "Lots of explaining to do, William."

The hint of a smile played at her lips as his voice drifted into her mind. *See you soon, Firefly.*

Immediately after they'd returned from the store, Layla had escaped up to her bedroom. He knew she was upset with him, and he wasn't exactly sure why, but suspected it had something to do with the woman they'd met earlier, Sylvia Clark. Based on Layla's reaction, he deduced there was a rather cantankerous history between the two women, and now he felt stupid for not realizing it earlier. He let out a loud sigh of frustration and ran his hands over his face.

Would he ever get anything right where Layla was concerned?

Left to his own devices, William took the opportunity to wander through the downstairs of the house and couldn't help but notice the various photographs that lined the walls of every room. There were several of Layla, Raife, and another young woman he could only assume was Tatiana, but some were landscapes that had most definitely been taken by Layla. Almost all of the framed photos in the house had been taken by Layla. Her energy signature emanated from each one. It was nothing more than a ghost, a whisper of her left behind, but it was more than enough for William to know they were hers.

The first floor was made up of the kitchen, a formal parlor that looked as if no one actually went into it, the front hall, and an enormous family room that cried out for a gathering. A well-worn leather sofa and chair reminded him of a bomber jacket he'd had in his youth. He felt immediately at home in this room and imagined that most people did. It was an open, welcoming space with several windows lining the far wall. The early evening sunlight streamed in and bathed the room in a warm, amber glow.

At the center was a massive stone fireplace with a pitted wooden beam that served as a mantle, and a large

black-and-white photo hung above it. He paused, captured by the starkness of it in such a cozy room. It was
of a broken down cottage, or possibly an old farmhouse,
sitting amid barren trees that held the distinct mark of
winter. Slowly, he moved in to get a closer look and was
amazed at the crisp, black-and-white details throughout.
It was a haunting photograph.

He recognized Layla's energy signature immediately
and could tell that it was likely taken somewhere on the
property, but there was something else about it that he
couldn't quite put his finger on. He imagined that the
cottage in the photo had some significance for it to have
such a prominent place in the room.

In the midst of his art appreciation, and without any
warning, wicked images of a naked, soapy Layla filled
his mind. His eyes snapped to their clan form when a
soft moan filled his mind. He squeezed his eyes shut
and leaned one hand on the wood mantle as one wicked
image after another flashed through his head in a porno-
graphic slide show.

A moment passed before her curt voice cut abruptly
into his mind. *Stay out of my head.*

His heart sank at the sound of her request, and the
heat left his body as quickly as it had come.

Emptiness crept in as he severed the connection to his
mate. Before he found her, loneliness had become a way
of life, and he'd grown accustomed to feeling detached
from the world. He'd lived with it for so many years that
it shouldn't bother him, but it did, because now he knew
exactly what he was missing.

He let out a growl of frustration and shoved himself
away from the fireplace. How on earth was he going to

be able to win her over and convince her that he wasn't here to drag her off and dominate her? He had to find something to do with all this pent up frustration. Sexual frustration he could handle. It didn't thrill him, but he could handle it. It was the emotional cost that he was finding more uncomfortable than anything else.

William wandered back into the kitchen. With neither Rosie nor Raife in sight, he decided to make himself useful and put the groceries away. It took a bit of investigating and several wrong cabinets being opened, but by the end, he felt satisfied that he'd put things in their proper place. William gave one last look around to be sure he didn't miss anything, gathered his packages from their shopping excursion, and headed upstairs.

Rosie's now familiar bark stopped him just as he reached the top of the stairs. "Looks like you had a successful shopping trip today?"

William leaned over the railing and held up one of the bags. "Yes. She's a very efficient shopper."

Grabbing the ever-present dish towel from her shoulder, she looked around quickly. "Where's Layla?"

"She's taking a bath, I think," he said, trying not to think about the erotic images she sent him. He cleared his throat and quickly changed the subject. "I put the purchases from the market away. I hope everything is in the right place."

Rosie raised her eyebrows and made a sound of approval. "Nice gesture, putting the groceries away. You're a good houseguest, and it's not a bad move when trying to woo a woman either."

"Happy to help," he said with a nod. "Would you like me to get Layla for you?" He hoped he didn't sound as transparent as he felt, because he was looking for any excuse to go to her room.

"Hmmm," she murmured and shook her head. "No. If I know her, she's about to crawl into bed." She made a tsk-ing sound. "That girl needs to eat something. She's skin and bones." She sighed. "Well—" She patted her ample backside. "As you can see, no one has to twist my arm to eat. It's dinnertime. Are you gonna come have somethin'? I don't know where Raife has gotten off to, and I hate eating alone," she said with a twinkle in her eye.

"I would like that. I'm almost as hungry as I am tired." William's face heated with embarrassment, and he looked away quickly. He suspected that she knew he wanted to connect with Layla in the dream realm. "It's been a big day for all of us. I think a good night's sleep is exactly what we need to move things along."

"Sounds good," she said with a wave. "Put your things away, and I'll make you a plate. It's leftover night, so I hope you aren't too picky."

William put both bags into one hand and grasped the mahogany newel post with the other. "Thank you, Rosie. I'm quite hungry and could eat a horse."

"You may be from a bird clan, but it sounds like you don't eat like one. Good. I like a man with a healthy appetite."

"Yes. My mother always said that there must be some trace of her wolf clan in me, and it is revealed every time I eat. Leftovers sound perfect, and I'll be down shortly. Perhaps you could give me a tour of the farm tomorrow morning? Show me the ropes, so to speak?" he said, hoping she'd get the hint.

He really wanted to learn more about Layla, and

he knew Rosie was the one who could give him a clue as to how to figure her out. Raife wasn't likely to be much help at all, at least no help getting to know Layla. The only thing he would probably do is kick his ass out the door.

"You betcha." She nodded and winked. "Tonight you c'mon down for something, and then tomorrow morning after breakfast you're gonna get schooled." Laughing heartily, she made her way back toward the kitchen. "I'm too damn old and tired to drag your ass around the farm tonight. Now put that crap away and get down here and eat something."

"Yes, ma'am," he said.

His hand had barely touched the doorknob when Layla's vibrant energy signature latched onto his, re-opening their connection. William stilled. His body hummed with the power of their combined energies, barreling through him like a freight train. Past the buzzing, dynamic charge whistling through his body, he heard her soft voice tenderly utter his name. "William." It sounded like a prayer... a promise. Any reservations he had about trying to connect with her in the dream realm disappeared.

Steeling himself and struggling to maintain control, delicately he touched his mind to hers. *See you soon, Firefly*.

Chapter 6

THE PEWTER MISTS ROLLED AROUND WILLIAM LAZILY as he walked through the as-yet-undefined dream realm. Reconnecting with Layla's energy signature before he fell asleep had allowed him to find the path to her dream with surprising ease and was another encouraging step in the right direction.

Making his way through the fog, he hoped she would call to him, whisper his name and light the way, but so far she remained shrouded from his sight. At least she wasn't running away from him as she had been. She was there. He could sense her watching him, tracking his every move, and since it was her dream that he tuned in, she held all the control.

His impatience rising, he decided it was time to rattle the cage a little bit and draw her out of the shadows. I'm relieved that you've stopped running away from me, he shouted into the swirling haze with his hands held securely behind his back. But you're still hiding from me and hiding from a challenge doesn't strike me as your style. He tried to keep a smile out of his voice, but to no avail. He didn't know why, but he found it amusing to tease her. He'd seen Malcolm and Dante banter this way with their mates and never understood it—until he found Layla. I thought you had more guts than that. A low growl rumbled around him in response, and the mists dissipated to reveal the moonlit woods of the farm.

Bingo.

As he suspected, she didn't shrink from any challenge, and that was a major turn-on. He always admired women with guts, like his sisters and mother. His father had always said that it was his mother's unwillingness to retreat and her unwavering tenacity that he found most attractive. His mother and two sisters were descended from the Arctic Wolf Clan; most women of the wolf clans were known for their fierce determination and loyalty.

William searched the woods for the red-headed minx, and as he wandered along the path, he had to admit that Layla's stubborn streak was one of the most appealing things about her. He scanned the surrounding area with painstaking slowness, but still didn't see her. *Come out, come out, wherever you are,* he sang.

What's the matter, counselor? Her teasing voice tumbled into his mind. *Can't find what you're looking for?* Her words were immediately followed by another growl that reverberated through him.

William froze—she was in her clan animal.

His heart quickened with excitement at the mere thought of seeing Layla in her cheetah form. Standing on the carpet of fallen leaves mixed with pine needles, he called up the sharp eyesight of his falcon and scanned his surroundings in search of her. A high-pitched chirping sound just above him caught his attention; he stilled and zeroed in on the vaguely familiar sound. He'd heard members of the Cheetah Clan utilize various growls, chirps, and hisses to communicate with each other in their clan form, much like cheetahs in the wild. The chirping sound stopped and was immediately followed by a soft rumbling in his ear.

She was in the tree behind him.

He turned to his right and found himself staring into the glowing gold and green eyes of his mate. She must've been lying in wait with her eyes closed, because there was no way he would've missed those glowing orbs—the sight of them were imprinted on his brain. It was no wonder he had difficulty finding her. Layla's spotted coat blended perfectly with the moonlit golden-bronze leaves that clung to the sprawling branches of the enormous beech tree.

Layla's lithe spotted body was stretched out on a low branch; her head rested on her front paws, which were crossed casually under her chin. Those exotic eyes were rimmed with black and inked a trail along the sides of her nose and around her muzzle. She was the most beautiful creature he'd ever laid eyes on in either form.

What's the matter? *Her voice purred into his head, and those eyes of hers twinkled back mischievously.* Cat got your tongue?

Not yet, but then again, I just got here. *He inched closer, and she raised her head, forcing him to look up at her. Her fur-tufted ears pricked up, and she kept her laser-sharp gaze locked firmly with his. His fingers twitched at his sides, itching to stroke that spotted coat.*

You have an answer for everything, don't you? *She stood on the branch, her claws digging firmly into the flesh of the tree.* What are you doing here anyway? *She said with mild annoyance as she leapt past him and landed soundlessly on the ground.*

William watched her sleek body move gracefully as she loped over to the moonlit path that ran along a gurgling stream. Well, this is your dream realm, *he said, moving in next to her.* You tell me. I wouldn't be here if you didn't want me to be. *She sat on her haunches and looked up at him with curiosity—or annoyance—he wasn't sure which.* I think it's very interesting that you're here with me in your clan form, Layla.

She huffed, and a soft growl rumbled in the back of her throat as she started walking down the path again. Yeah, well, I can kick your ass pretty easily in this form—dream or no dream—so I figured it would be safer this way. Easier to negotiate. *Layla stopped when they reached a break in the trees, which opened up to an enormous field with tall grasses that fluttered in the wind. The moon shone down on the flickering grass, giving the illusion of a sea of liquid silver stretching endlessly before them.* Wait a minute. You said that you couldn't be here if I didn't want you to be?

Yes. *William knew where she was going with this.* If you'll recall, *he began slowly.* When I came to you in the other dreams, you couldn't see me—or wouldn't see me—I'm not really sure which it was. *He squatted down so that they were eye to eye and lowered his voice to just above a whisper.* However, it would seem that we've surpassed that particular hurdle. *Elbows resting on his jean-clad knees, his fingers laced together in front of him, he fought the urge to touch her.* So now that you have me here, what do you plan on doing with me? *he asked suggestively.* I hope you're up for more than just negotiating. *His brow furrowed at the idea of negotiating.* What exactly do you want to negotiate?

First things first, *she cut him off with a snarl.* As for the dreams, I didn't want to deal with you or the idea of giving my life, my future, or my choices to you. *She sat completely still and kept those glowing, golden eyes locked with his; only her black-tipped tail flicked slowly, almost hypnotically, behind her. The purring grew to a low growl as William's heated gaze wandered over her body from head to tail, until he finally locked eyes with her once again.* My life is mine, William. I decide my future. Not you or some stupid legend. *Her voice softened and breezed through him with a hint of sadness.* I was not merely put on this earth to be yours. *Her energy pulsed with determination, and the growl continued to rumble and permeate the dream realm.*

His eyes snapped to their clan form as he fought the flash of anger. This is what she thought of him? That he was here to dominate and control her? To take possession of her? William had never been so insulted in his life. I never said you were, *he said quietly. He stood slowly, giving her the space he instinctively knew that they both needed.* My intention is not to take over your life, Layla, but I would like to be a part of it. We are mates, *he said definitively.* I am not interested in controlling you because I suspect that would be as successful as trying to control the cycle of the moon. *He turned his back on her, shoved his hands through his shoulder-length hair, and let out a frustrated sigh as he looked out over the silvery grasses.*

Well, you're right about that. *She laughed, and he couldn't help but notice she was purring again.* Just ask Rosie.

The silence hung between them as they both stared out over the moonlit field. He'd never felt so completely out of sorts in his life, because he was as confused and thrown off by their mating as Layla was. The strength of his feelings for her and the pulsing need to claim her were startling, foreign, and all-consuming. He knew there were certain animals that imprinted on mates, and he imagined that's what had happened to them, although he'd never heard any of his people refer to it that way.

He couldn't help but wonder if it was this confusing for all Amoveo when they found their mates. He crossed his arms over his chest and shook his head. Probably not, he mused. It was probably just him. He never was good with emotions. They were too intangible and confusing, and they did nothing but cloud people's judgments or decisions. William had always prided himself on his ability to remain cool and detached, but Layla evoked the exact opposite in him.

She was fire to his ice.

He glanced down at her, and any anger or irritation he felt floated away with the breeze. If he was this confused, what must she be feeling? She had heard nothing but horror stories about the Amoveo, so how could he possibly expect her to welcome him with open arms? If his friends were here, they would tell him he was acting like a dick… and they'd be right.

He had to show her that he was not the monster she thought he was… and that she was everything he had hoped she would be.

He cleared his throat, and she glanced up at him briefly before looking up at the inky, black sky. The dream realm you've created is beautiful, he murmured.

This is home, she mused softly. Her voice touched his mind with almost painful tenderness.

Her spotted coat, dappled with moonlight, called to him. Keeping his eyes on her, watching for any sign of *discomfort as his energy mingled with hers, he reached over to touch her. Fingers outstretched and hovering just above her head, he threw a silent prayer to the universe and stroked her fur as gently as possible. He let out the breath he was holding when she didn't bolt or break their connection. Her fur was surprisingly rough against his fingers and the friction only served to entice him further. All he could think was that if touching her felt this good in the dream realm, how spectacular would it be in reality? He rubbed behind her ears and grinned as she leaned into his hand and encouraged his attention.*

That feels wonderful. *She purred and stood on all fours as he continued his exploration. William ran both hands along her sleek back. She was an exotic combination of silk and steel, strength and beauty, all rolled into one as she rubbed against his legs and almost knocked him over. Layla walked past him as his fingers trailed along her tail, which she yanked from his grasp playfully. He watched her walk away from him a few paces, and she crouched low with her long tail twitching behind her.* So you say that you don't want to possess me, right? *she challenged.*

Yes, *he said hesitantly. He narrowed his eyes.* What are you up to?

Well, you see, counselor... *She crouched lower, and her lips curled back to reveal a mouth full of sharp white teeth.* You'd have to catch me first. *Then in the blink of an eye, she burst into a run and exploded across the field like a rocket.*

You're not the only one who enjoys a challenge, *he shouted after her.*

William's eyes flicked to their clan form and glowed brightly in the night as he broke into a run, whispered the ancient language, Verto, and shifted into his gyrfalcon. The warm, familiar ripple of the shift washed over him, and within seconds he was soaring high above the field, gaining on his mate. He tracked her as she sprinted through the tall grasses and with a loud shriek, he swooped down low and fast, matching her speed.

Looks like I could catch you after all. *He touched his mind to hers and heard her laugh in response.*

Really? *She chuckled as she ran at a breakout pace.* Look out for the lightning.

He was about to ask what she was talking about, when a white bolt of lightning shot down in front of him, blackening the grasses, and almost cooking him along with it. He shrieked loudly, banked to the right, and lost sight of his mischievous mate. She may not know everything there is to know about being Amoveo, but she sure seemed to have a solid handle on controlling the dream realm.

Layla burst out of the grasses and slowed considerably as she entered the forest. Breathless, she trotted over to a giant pine tree and flopped down on a bed of needles at the base of the trunk. I won. *Her victorious voice panted happily into his mind.*

William soared in, shifted, and stood next to her in his human form once again. Built for speed, but not for distance, Firefly? *He shoved both hands in his pockets and leaned against the neighboring tree.* I suppose that's why you resorted to cheating. *He sighed.*

Layla snarled, and before William could say another word, she shimmered and shifted into her human form.

William's mouth went dry at the sight of her. She was wearing a white tank top, which molded perfectly to her small breasts and topped the most miniscule pair of white shorts he'd ever seen. Oh yeah, she knew exactly how to use the dream realm.

It wasn't cheating. *She rose from the bed of needles and leaves.* I was simply using all of my resources. That's not cheating. *She closed the distance between them until she was standing just inches from him.* It's resourceful. *She breathed the words softly and seductively as her eyes wandered over him, boldly appraising him.* I thought, as an attorney, you'd appreciate ingenuity like that.

Those sparkling green eyes met his and her hands rested on slim hips, daring him to argue with her. He definitely had no desire to confront her. He felt like their entire relationship so far had been one sparring match after another, but looking into that heart-shaped face, quarreling was the furthest thing from his mind.

He took a curly strand of her hair between his fingers and found it was softer than the fur of her cheetah. I've been dying to touch your hair since the day I first found you. *He wrapped the smooth strands around his finger and rubbed his thumb over the coiled lock.* It's even silkier than I'd imagined, *he murmured.* Did you know that it glints like fire in the rays of the sun and burns like embers in the glow of the moon?

She'd moved closer, and he didn't know if he'd pulled her there, or if she'd done it on her own. Her breasts brushed his rib cage, and she let out a light sigh as her hands found their way to his waist, and she hooked her thumbs into the loops of his jeans. He tangled both

hands in her lush curls and reveled in the feel of it laced
through his fingers. His eyes snapped to his falcon as her
hands found their way under his shirt, and she slipped
her fingers just beneath the waistband of his pants.

The glowing eyes of her clan flared brightly at him
from under thick eyelashes, and her lips tilted suggestively. Is that the only thing you've been dying to get
your hands on? The moon burned brighter in the night
sky, and the winds of the dream realm blew hotter as
their energies mingled and tumbled around them.

William brushed his thumbs along the curve of cheeks,
wishing this moment was happening in the flesh and not
just in the dream realm. Those spectacular glowing eyes
stared at him, filled with stark need to connect, to discover if everything they felt was valid. Or was it all just
exacerbated by the dream? William uttered a curse into
the rushing wind and closed the distance between them.
Although, he wasn't sure if he bent to claim her, or if she
rose to meet him—perhaps it was a bit of both.

She tasted like bubble gum, and he wondered fleetingly if she tasted this sweet in reality. His fingers
tangled in her hair as he devoured her tender lips. To
his delight, Layla sighed contentedly and sank into the
kiss as her arms wrapped tightly around his waist. Her
lips parted, and she welcomed him into the warm darkness of her mouth. He angled her head to delve deeper
and discover her. The intensity increased swiftly as she
swept her tongue along his and grazed her teeth temptingly, before she nibbled at his lower lip.

You taste as good as you look, and that's saying
something. He murmured the words against her lips
and rubbed handfuls of her hair between his fingers.

He moved his attentions to the smooth skin of her cheek, whispered his lips along her jawline, and blazed a trail along her neck. Layla's whole body trembled against him, and she moaned as she brushed her palms deliciously along the small of his back.

You are gorgeous in both forms. *He kissed his way back up to that succulent mouth and tasted them briefly.* I can't wait to shift with you in the material plane, to race with you through that field in reality. *She stiffened in his arms, and within seconds thunder and lightning broke out violently around them.*

It would seem they were sparring once again, except he had no idea what he'd done. William pulled back and found her staring at him with a stone cold look in her eyes that he'd unfortunately seen before— the same look she'd given him when she found him fighting with Raife.

Her eyes burned brightly, anger carved deeply in her features, and those lips that he'd been drinking from just moments before, were set in a frown. She slipped out of his embrace and shook her head as she backed away from him slowly.

No. *Layla shouted it above the howling wind and thunder as her curly hair blew wildly around her.* Good night, William.

With genuine confusion he watched helplessly as she moved further and further away. What in the hell had he done? Frustration flooded him as he felt all of their progress slip through his fingers like sand. Layla, wait. *He reached for her, but before he could say another word, the fog bank rolled in and swallowed her from his sight.*

—⁓—

Layla woke up the next morning feeling more rested, but no less confused. The shared dream with William was the first thing on her mind, and her conflicting emotions were the culprit for her mental exhaustion. She knew she had no one to blame but herself. After all, *she* had let *him* into her dream and allowed him to find her, and the whole goddamned thing backfired on her. She foolishly thought that if she would be able to maintain control and perhaps find a way to make him see how nuts this whole "mate" thing was. She scolded herself and pushed the sheets off her bare legs. Oh sure, she controlled the environment, but not her damn hormones.

She stretched her arms over her head, loosening her sensitized body, and her mind went right to that crazy-ass kiss, which was all-consuming—and frightening. She had no desire to give any credence to this whole predestined mate nonsense. However, it was what he said that set her nerves on edge more than anything else. He wanted to shift with her in reality, and that would be just fine if she could actually figure out how to do it.

Layla swore under breath in frustration, feeling like nothing but a half-breed freak.

She haphazardly fixed the bedding, as Rosie always wanted her to, and fluffed the pillows more violently than necessary. She hated that she'd never been able to shapeshift outside the dream realm, because it made her feel defective, and reminded her time and again that she wasn't normal in either world.

Gooseflesh rose on her arms as a cool breeze whisked into the room from the open window—at least she told herself it was from the wind. Layla rubbed her arms and hurried over to close it as she reminded herself that Rosie would tell her that being cold was her own damn fault for wearing hardly anything to bed. William didn't seem to be bothered by it. An image of his desire-stamped gaze filled her mind, sending warmth flaring through her body hard and fast. He didn't disguise his need for her; in fact, he'd been fairly open and seemingly honest with her so far. Guilt tugged at her as she realized she'd been anything but that with him. Maybe she wasn't giving him a fair shot. Perhaps he wouldn't be as appalled by her shortcomings as she was.

"Yeah, right," she mumbled to the empty room.

Layla tugged the old window down with a thud, and as usual, white paint chips flaked off in the process. She reached up to draw the curtains, but her eye was caught by movement to the right. William and Rosie were walking along the edge of the horses' corral and making their way up to the barn.

Rosie was talking in her usual animated manner, and William walked serenely next to her with his hands clasped firmly behind his back, clearly hanging on every syllable she uttered. Layla rested her forehead against the chilled glass. She could only imagine what tales Rosie was telling. She loved to tell stories—especially embarrassing ones.

Layla dressed quickly in a comfortable pair of old jeans and her faded RIT hoodie sweatshirt. She loved this old thing. She had gotten it her first day on campus, and it was broken in from so many years of wear. It wasn't pretty, had some stains on it, and was frayed along the edges, but it was the most comfortable piece of clothing she owned, and right now, she could use all the comfortable she could get. She trotted down the steps quickly, eyeing the pictures along the wall of the staircase, and smiled because she had taken all of them. Rosie had hung her photos all over the house and would brag about her to anyone who would stand still and listen.

Layla came into the kitchen and found Raife seated at the table, scarfing down yet another piece of Rosie's apple pie. He shoveled the last forkful into his mouth and chased it with a glass of milk. Layla couldn't help but chuckle and swat him on the back of his head as she made her way to the fridge.

"You may be a part of the Wolf Clan, but you sure do eat like a pig," she teased as she grabbed a glass from the cupboard.

Raife responded with a loud belch.

"I rest my case," Layla said with satisfaction as she poured herself a glass of iced tea. She closed the door of the fridge with her foot and made her way to the table.

"Eating apple pie for breakfast?" She made a tsking sound and wagged a finger at him.

Raife let out a short laugh. "Breakfast? Check your watch." He nodded toward the clock on the wall. "It's after noon, sleepyhead."

Layla's mouth fell open. "Oh, my God! I haven't slept this late in years. I must've been tired. I only meant take a nap before dinner last night, and I ended up sleeping for over twelve hours."

Raife eyed her with suspicion over his glass of milk. "Uh-huh, wonder why that is?" he asked before downing the rest of his milk.

"Must be because I'm home," she said quickly, knowing it was a lie. Layla gave a cursory glance out the window, but didn't catch sight of Rosie or William.

"They're up at the barn," Raife said curtly.

Layla rolled her eyes and sat across from him. "I wasn't looking for him," she said in a tone that even she didn't believe. She cringed at how transparent she had become when it came to William.

"Yeah, right." Raife tossed his napkin onto the empty plate in front of him. He leaned back in his chair and regarded her with a look of complete disbelief. "You haven't been able to think about anything else since he showed up." He crossed his arms over his chest. "How was your little trip into town yesterday?"

"Actually," she began slowly, "it was a bit off-putting."

"Why?" he asked, sitting up straighter in his chair. "What did he do?"

"Nothing." Layla shook her head quickly and sat across the table from him. "No, no. It wasn't William. He's been…well, he's been a perfect gentleman, actually."

He had been. He hadn't tried to force himself on her or drag her off like the caveman Raife accused him of being, or she expected him to be. He'd been a gentleman, even in the dream realm. He'd only stolen that one, knee-buckling kiss, and that one didn't really count.

Dream kisses didn't count, did they?

She made a face and took a sip of her iced tea. She frowned as she realized it was a much more disappointing fact than she'd expected it to be. Layla pulled her feet onto the chair and wrapped her arms around her knees. She hadn't felt this unsure of herself since she was a kid.

"Good." Raife relaxed his posture and sat back again in his chair. "He better be, or I'm going to kick his feathered ass."

Layla gave him a doubtful look. "Whatever." She took another sip of her drink. "We went to the grocery and saw Ralph and Ginny yesterday afternoon. Ginny mentioned something about Rosie selling the farm to Frank Clark. Can you imagine? I mean, I totally freaked out and practically ripped Ginny's head off for suggesting such a thing." She rubbed her chin on her denim-clad knees. "Actually, William was the one who calmed me down." Her brow knit together in concentration. "He used his energy to soothe me. Just like you, me, and Tati have done for each other for years." She shrugged as if she had to explain his kindness. "I guess it's a pretty common Amoveo thing."

Raife stayed stone still and kept his blue eyes on his sister. It dawned on her that he didn't seem surprised at all by what Ginny suggested about the sale of the farm. A sick feeling settled in the pit of Layla's stomach.

It was true. Rosie was selling the farm.

"Raife," she said hesitantly. "It's not true, is it? Rosie isn't selling the farm… is she?"

Raife looked away from her. His jaw clenched, and he let out a long, slow breath. "She's been thinking about it," he said quietly.

"What?" Layla sat up, and her feet hit the floor hard. "She can't sell this place, Raife. This is our home." Her voice rose and sounded an awful lot like that scared little girl she swore she'd never be again.

Raife's nostrils flared and anger carved deeply into his features. "You think I don't feel the same way? I still live here, Red. This is my home. I don't just come back and visit once a year like you and Tati," he said with a sharp wave of his hand.

Anger and frustration rippled off him as his words stung with the sharp twang of truth. He was right. She and Tatiana only came home to visit once or twice a year, but Raife lived and worked here. She was being a selfish brat and hadn't considered his feelings or Rosie's at all.

Her eyes softened. "I'm sorry. You're right." She was quiet for a moment, wanting to choose her words carefully. "Is it final? I mean, has she signed anything yet?"

Raife shook his head. "No. She's met with Frank a couple of times at his office in town. He's offering her a crazy amount of money for the property."

"Thank God," Layla breathed. "So there's still a chance we can talk her out of this?"

"I don't know." He sighed loudly and ran his hands over his face. "I can't blame her, Red." He rested his elbows on the table. "This place isn't cheap to run, and most months we barely break even. Rosie's been renting out the extra bedrooms from time to time to help make ends meet. I even got a gig bartending a couple nights a week at the Rustic Inn."

"Really? Well, I'm going to talk to Rosie about this. There's got to be something we can do." Layla was quiet for a moment as she regarded her brother carefully. She felt the need to change the subject. The last thing she wanted to do was upset Raife more than she already had. "Guess who else we ran into yesterday?" She wrinkled her nose.

Raife shrugged. "I dunno know. Who?"

"Your ex-fiancée, Sylvia Clark," she said with clear disdain. "She's still phony."

A big smile cracked Raife's face and created the two familiar dimples that he was famous for. The girls loved his dimples. "Did you deck her again?"

Layla threw her head back and laughed loudly at the memory of when she'd hauled off and slugged her at Tyler's party. The bitch had been toying with Raife off and on for years, but the last straw came when she called off their engagement a month before their wedding and instead ran off with David Garrity—who became ex-husband number one.

Layla's smile faded when she recalled the broken look on Raife's face when he'd told her what happened. Sylvia didn't even have the decency to do it herself, but instead, let her father do it. Good old Frank Clark happily told him that Sylvia had gone on a weekend excursion with a young man of her social caliber and would not be marrying some *farmhand*.

The memory of it still made her blood boil, but was also tinged with guilt. Layla had sensed Sylvia's less than honest feelings in some photos she'd taken for their engagement, and she'd tried to tell Raife that she was hiding something, but he wouldn't listen. Layla always thought she should've tried harder to convince him.

"No. I try not to go around decking other women, but believe me, I wanted to knock her lights out," she said firmly. "She's still as cold as ever. How many husbands is she up to, anyway?"

"She just divorced dummy number three."

"I figured as much." Layla reached over and grabbed Raife's fork. She peeled back the saran wrap and scooped up some of what was left in the pie plate in the middle of the table. "He was probably a rich dummy though."

"Not anymore," Raife said with a satisfied smile.

"You seem happy that she took yet another man for all his dough." She ate the sugary goodness in one bite.

Raife shrugged. "Hey, if they're stupid enough to marry her, then they deserve whatever they get. I'm sick and tired of rich, entitled assholes getting everything they want, and the little guy getting screwed."

"Agreed." Layla nodded and swallowed her mouthful of pie. "Which is just one of many reasons we need to keep Rosie from selling this farm. *Especially* to Frank Clark," she said, pointing her fork at him.

"Speaking of rich, entitled assholes... what does William do for a living?" Raife asked as he stood and gathered his dishes from the table.

Layla had to bite her tongue to keep from coming to William's defense. He was rich. At least he seemed to be. The man pulled out a huge wad of cash at Epstein's yesterday and didn't blink at the bill, but he wasn't an entitled asshole like Frank Clark. The very idea of comparing William to a man like Frank was ridiculous, because the man she was getting to know was not a selfish asshole.

Bossy and pushy? Yes.

She smiled at the drink in her hand. But selfish? Not that she'd seen, at least not yet. The chivalrous way he came to her aid and his sole concern for her well-being... these were not the makings of a heartless jerk.

She cleared her throat and flicked her gaze back up to her brother. She wasn't going to defend him to Raife, at least not yet. "Well, if you must know," she said reluctantly, "he's a lawyer."

"Ha!" Raife tossed the dishes in the sink. "Even worse than I thought."

Layla smirked and drained the rest of her iced tea. She knew her brother wasn't going to give William an inch. She watched him as he rinsed his dishes in the sink. For all his stubbornness, her brother was the kindest man she'd ever known, and he had a heart of gold. Any woman who landed him would be treated like a queen—she glanced at the sink with a smile—and have really clean dishes.

"Oh, I should mention one more thing about William," Layla said tentatively.

Raife didn't turn around. He just kept washing his dishes and putting them in the drying rack. "Yeah? What's that?"

She squeezed her eyes shut. "He can hear our conversations," she said a bit too quickly, bracing herself for his reaction.

The telepathic communication between the three siblings had always been something sacred, and she worried that this latest development would just piss him off more. The dish clattering in the sink ceased, and the rush of the water seemed louder than ever. Layla cracked open one eye and saw Raife standing perfectly still, his body stiff with tension.

"Raife? Did you hear what I said?"

Raife shut off the water and grabbed a dish towel from the counter. He turned slowly to face her as he dried his hands. "I heard you," he said in a voice tinged with sadness. "Look, I know that there are others like us, and I'm well aware that William is your mate." He made a loud sound of disgust. "Shit, the sexual chemistry between you two is palpable, and to be quite honest, it grosses me out because you're my sister."

Layla opened her mouth to protest, but he shot her a look that kept her quiet. Her face burned with embarrassment at the mention of the chemistry between her and William. *Awkward*.

"Listen, Red. I want to learn as much about him and the rest of the Amoveo as I can. Look, until yesterday, as far as we knew, there weren't any others around." He tossed the dish towel back on the counter and leaned against the sink. "Shit. I'd even half-convinced myself that they were extinct, and we were the only ones left. So you'll forgive me if I'm a little uncomfortable with all of this."

"I don't know if they're all the boogeymen that we've been afraid of all these years." Layla peered at her brother through sympathetic eyes. She knew exactly how he felt. "William hasn't given me any indication that he wants to hurt us, and I don't know about you, but I want to learn more about them. Knowledge is power. Right?"

Raife nodded and sighed before looking away. "Right."

"He did something else yesterday," she began slowly. Layla didn't want to overload her brother with too much at once, but she knew he needed to know about William's other abilities. "Something that I didn't know we could do."

Raife's body tensed, and the muscles in his jaw clenched. "What?"

"He materialized out of thin air in the passenger seat of my car," she said with genuine awe. "He called it part of the visualization skills." She shrugged and let out a loud sigh. "Whatever that means."

"Really?" Raife's eyebrows flew up. "You mean he just appeared?"

Layla nodded, and a smile spread over her face. "Yeah," she said slowly. "I have to admit it was pretty cool."

Raife murmured a sound of understanding and pushed himself away from sink. "I wonder what other surprises he's got up his sleeve."

Layla held her brother's serious gaze and lifted one shoulder. "I have no idea."

He cast a glance out the window. "Looks like Rosie's been giving him the full tour of the farm. What's next? A night on the town?"

Layla laughed as she rose from her seat at the table. "Actually, we're supposed to go to see Tyler's band play tonight at the Rustic Inn."

"Really?" His eyebrows raised, and that dimpled grin cracked his face. "That's perfect. I'm working tonight, so it'll give me a chance to get to know good old William and keep an eye on him at the same time." Before Layla could protest or say a word, Raife placed a kiss on the top of her head, grabbed a banana from the fruit bowl, and headed upstairs. "Something tells me you two need a chaperone."

A chaperone? Great. That's all she needed was to have Raife watching their every move tonight. How was she supposed to figure William out with Raife in the background? *And* to top it all off that Barbie-doll-from-hell was going to be there. "Wonderful," Layla said with a growl of frustration.

Are you alright? William's smooth, seductive voice

slipped gently into her mind. Relief washed over her, and to her surprise, she instantly felt more at ease. The connection with him was back with shocking intensity, and it energized her physically and mentally. *I'm sorry. I know you have asked me to stay out of your head, but I can tell you're upset.*

Layla smiled. *Well, you're right on both counts. I did ask you to stay out of my head, and I am a bit upset.* Her smile faded. *Rosie really is thinking about selling the farm to that asshole Frank Clark.*

I'm sorry, Layla. It seems clear that this place is very important to you. His voice dipped low, to an almost contrite tone, and rolled through her in soothing waves. *And I'm sorry if you feel that I have invaded your privacy by connecting with you, but I had to be certain you were alright.*

It's okay... I guess it'll just take some getting used to. She cleared her throat and fought the surprising flood of emotions. Life was changing at an alarming pace, and she hoped she'd be able to keep up.

Chapter 7

LAYLA WALKED TOWARD THEM FROM THE HOUSE AS HE caught her scent on the wind. Her cinnamon spice was tempered by the enticing perfume of gardenias, and when mixed with the crisp fall air, it created a delicious, intoxicating fragrance. Memories of their shared dream had been flirting along the edges of his mind all morning, and seeing her now brought them to the forefront.

His brow furrowed as he recalled how abruptly she had severed their connection and thrown him out of her dream. The only thing that gave him hope was that she seemed receptive to him again this morning, and he sent a silent prayer that she would remain that way.

He drank in the sight of her as sunlight cast golden rays over that curly red hair, making it burn brightly like firelight. Her petite form was completely enveloped by an enormous sweatshirt, which many women would look dowdy or dumpy—but not on Layla. On her it was intriguing and created a shroud of mystery that sparked the desire to discover every curve she hid underneath. His cock twitched in response. He'd never wanted anything or anyone so badly in his life.

"You know, boy," Rosie whispered. "That girl doesn't trust easily."

William turned his attention to Rosie, and his face heated with embarrassment, because he'd almost forgotten she was standing there. Thank God she couldn't read minds, or she'd likely want to slap him silly. He cleared his throat and clasped his hands behind his back in a pathetic effort to keep his raging hormones at bay.

Rosie's gray eyes glared sternly up at him beneath salt-and-pepper eyebrows, and for a moment, he thought that maybe she *could* read his mind. He was about to assure her he meant no harm, but before he could get out a sound, she slapped one weathered hand over his mouth, while pointing at him with the other.

"Just shut up and listen." William nodded his acceptance, but Rosie kept her hand over his mouth. "I mean it. You're going to have to work your ass off to get her to trust you and open her heart to you. First of all, the thought of having some Amoveo man come and carry her away has been hanging over her head her whole life." She sighed loudly and looked him up and down. "But it seems pretty clear to me that you aren't of a mind to do that... are you?"

William shook his head slowly, but she didn't remove her hand from his mouth.

"Good," she continued. "Now, that girl has been through hell and back. Her Mama was bat-shit crazy, and after that woman died, she bounced around from place to place until she finally landed with me." Rosie narrowed her gaze and dropped her voice to just above a whisper as tears rimmed her eyes. "Layla acts tough—but it's just that—an act. That girl is still broken inside, but I think you might be just the person to help her mend." She sniffled and finally removed her hand from his mouth. "You get me?"

"Yes," William said quietly. "I believe I do."

Rosie had confirmed his suspicions. He knew that

there was much more to Layla than met the eye, and he was determined to discover it all, even if it would take him the rest of his life.

"Good," Rosie said with a good firm smack to his cheek. William blinked with surprise, and simply nodded his understanding. Rosie winked at him and patted him on the arm as she walked away. "Don't forget what I said," she shouted over her shoulder.

"Forget what?" Layla asked breathlessly. She'd jogged the last several yards up the hill to meet them by the barn.

"Nothing," Rosie said dismissively. William watched with genuine interest as Rosie quickly took charge of Layla the same way she'd taken charge of him. "Well, I see you finally woke up. Since I am not a lady of luxury," she said with a teasing lilt to her voice, "I've gotta get some paperwork done. Why don't you take William around the outskirts of the farm?" She gave a quick nod toward him without looking. "Y'know, show him all the places you kids loved to roam when you were growing up here."

Layla looked from Rosie to William and back again. She crossed her arms and focused all of her attention on Rosie as nervous energy waves fluttered from her and buzzed over William in rapid-fire succession.

"Paperwork, huh? This wouldn't have anything to do with Frank Clark and selling the farm would it?"

Rosie sighed loudly and shoved her hands into the pockets of her overalls. "No, it wouldn't."

"Really?" Layla eyed her suspiciously. "Well, would you mind telling me why you're thinking about selling the farm to Frank Clark? The same man you have repeatedly referred to as *the slimiest bastard around*," she said, making air quotes with her fingers.

"Yes, actually." She laughed. "I believe I would. However, more importantly, you're being rude. You have a guest. Now, quit worrying about things that don't need to be worried about. The farm isn't going anywhere today."

"But Rosie—"

"Bye." Rosie walked away and waved without turning around. "You two have a nice walk. I'll see you back here for dinner." She looked at the darkening sky. "Better not be out too long. Looks like a storm is coming."

"That woman is the most infuriating piece of work," Layla muttered as she watched Rosie walk away and ignore her question. "Shit."

William fully expected her to run after Rosie and force the conversation, but to his complete surprise, she turned and brushed past him toward the barn.

"I'm pissed, and a walk isn't going to cut it." Her green eyes glittered with determination. "Come on, counselor. We're going for a ride."

She'd saddled the horses with the ease of experience, and in no time they were on horseback and headed along a well-worn trail. William was riding a massive gelding with a chestnut coat named Mudpie, and Layla led the way on a brown and white-spotted mare she referred to as Freckles. The irony was not lost on him. They walked at a steady pace along the narrow path through the dense woods, and the horses seemed to know the path by heart.

Layla glanced over her shoulder at him, the reins comfortably held in one hand. "How you doin' back there?"

William smirked. "Quite well. Mudpie is a good, strong horse. He reminds me of one of the horses we had when I was growing up. I enjoy a ride in the woods, but riding in the snow is my personal favorite. It's invigorating."

She hadn't even asked him if he could ride a horse and had been visibly surprised when he put one foot in the stirrup and swung his leg over with ease. He liked that he wasn't the only one getting a surprise or two.

"You had horses?" she asked as she ducked under a low hanging branch. "Where did you grow up?"

She wanted to know more about him. This was a good sign.

"On the outskirts of Nome, Alaska." William watched for her reaction, but she kept her back to him. Her energy waves remained calm. So far, so good. "As you know, I am a gyrfalcon. My father is as well, and my mother is in the Wolf Clan—the Arctic Wolf Clan." He shrugged. "We are partial to cold weather, and the remote area allows us to roam in our clan form. It's quite liberating really. I am always fascinated by Amoveo who choose to reside in cities." He furrowed his brow. "It seems to me it would be quite stifling to have to limit being in one's clan form so often."

She agreed absently. "I guess."

William sharpened his focus. Something wasn't right. Layla seemed detached, as if she had no idea what he was talking about. She must know that feeling of freedom to run in clan form. It was when they felt most alive—most connected to who they really were under the skin.

"Don't you think so, Layla?" he asked. "You must love running through these woods in your cheetah form." He looked around the woods, and recognition crept in. "This is the place you have been creating in the dream realm. I would imagine you shifted and indulged in these woods often."

Layla said nothing, but her energy waves skittered subtly, and William's senses went on high alert. Even her posture on the horse had gone from relaxed and easy to stiff and on high alert. She was wound as tightly as he'd ever seen her. She was clearly bothered by the mention of shifting. But why? Why would it bother her to—?

Realization washed over him as he put the pieces together.

Layla had never shifted before.

Last night in the dream realm she cut him off as soon as he mentioned shifting in the physical world, and now the mention of shifting pissed her off. He suspected she'd never been able to shift and didn't want him to know, or at the very least, didn't trust him enough to tell him.

He kept his focus on her as they approached an opening that led to a wider path in the woods and noted that her energy waves pulsed nervously. William heard the ripples of a stream flowing nearby and felt her energy in perfect time with the sounds of the water in the distance.

Her connections to this property were yet another aspect of her Amoveo heritage. She had imprinted on this place the same way he had imprinted on his home in Alaska. It was this psychic muscle memory that allowed them to use visualization for travel, among other things, but given the latest revelation, he suspected she didn't realize the extent of the power she held.

Lost in his own thoughts, it took him a minute to

realize Layla was staring at him over her shoulder. Her green eyes twinkled mischievously, and a challenging smile spread over her peaches-and-cream face. "Try to keep up, counselor."

Before he could ask what she meant, Layla clucked loudly at Freckles, and the two took off at a gallop. William watched his mate ride away as her red hair flew wildly behind her, and laughter peppered the air. He reached out to her with his mind, and his body hummed the moment he connected his energy signature with hers. *No problem, Firefly.*

"Yah," William barked loudly, kicked, and urged his horse forward.

The gelding did as commanded and took off like a shot after Layla and her mare. He caught up to her quickly, and with the wider path, was able to gallop alongside her—but not for long. Layla threw him a wicked grin, kicked the mare, and shot out ahead of him again. William laughed and maneuvered his horse directly behind Layla's, looking for the first opportunity to get next to her again.

The path narrowed, curved to the left, and the trees gave way to a rippling stream, which ran next to the path. The horse's hooves thundered loudly through the quiet woods, and William felt his excitement rise.

There was nothing more exhilarating than the chase.

The path and stream curved to the right just as Layla cast a glance over her shoulder, looking for William. As a result she didn't see the enormous oak tree that had fallen and blocked the path. What happened next happened in a split second.

William pulled back hard on the reins and barely

kept Mudpie from running into Freckles. He watched in horror as Freckles came to a screeching halt, and Layla was thrown head over feet through the air, before landing with an audible grunt on the other side of the log. William's heart pounded and dread swamped him as he lost sight of her.

He jumped off his horse, and with unnatural speed, scrambled over the enormous tree trunk. He landed on the ground next to Layla's motionless form, squatted, and pushed the mass of curls off her face. Dirt smudged her fair skin, and blood trickled down from a cut on her left eyebrow. His heart hammered in his chest, and he linked his energy signature instantly with hers— scanning her life force, searching for other injuries she might have suffered. To his great relief, she seemed to be relatively unharmed, and he let out the breath he didn't realize he'd been holding.

He slipped his arms beneath her, and as he scooped her up with minimal effort, she mumbled something inaudible and grimaced in pain. William sat down as gingerly as possible and leaned back on the fallen tree trunk with Layla's delicate form cradled safely against him. Her soft bottom nestled in his lap, and her spicy scent surrounded him. William kissed the top of her head as it rested against his shoulder, and she moaned softly in response.

"Layla," he said in a shaky whisper. "Please wake up."

He studied her face and sent out a silent prayer that she would awaken unscathed. He was furious with himself for being so reckless. It was not like him to be this careless and throw all caution to the wind, which only further proved that this woman had him completely off his game. In the middle of scolding himself, those big green eyes fluttered open and latched onto his.

"You know," she breathed. "There are easier ways to get me on my back." Her pink lips curved into a weak smile. She laughed softly but winced from the pain and tried to touch the cut on her eyebrow, but he took her delicate hand in his. Her warm fingers felt like silk as they tangled with his.

Holding her gaze, he pressed her hand to his chest and shook his head. "Don't touch it," he said gently as he inspected the injury. "We'll clean it up back at the house." William's gaze slid over her lovely face, and his heart thundered in his chest. "I'm sure Rosie has something that will do, and you should heal quickly," he whispered hoarsely.

It was pure torture to have her body against his and not claim her. Wrestling with his desire, he squeezed her hand tighter and stroked her arm with the other. Layla's eyes widened. She squirmed in his lap, which only served to make every inch of him harder than a rock.

He'd never wanted anyone with such intensity, and it took every ounce of self-control to keep from throwing her on the ground and ravaging her like some kind of crazed animal. Struggling against the driving need to devour her, he held her tighter, and his heart skipped a beat as Layla's fingers dug into his chest in response. Silence hung heavily between them, their energy signatures mingled in the air, and the rapid thrumming of their heartbeats tumbled in sync with one another.

Layla's tongue darted out, moistening that sinful-looking mouth seductively. The instant William's heated stare zeroed in on those luscious lips, his eyes tingled and shifted, causing every part of him to harden to the point of pain.

Memories of their kiss in the dream realm battered him as he let his gaze wander over the beautiful landscape of her face, wanting to commit every inch to memory. The tiny, upturned nose, the creamy skin with caramel freckles, and those glorious, high cheekbones that looked to be carved from the finest china.

However, nothing compared to the mesmerizing eyes of her clan, which glowed brightly at him with the intriguing prism of colors so distinctly hers. William cradled her in his arms, but when their eyes met, he was the one held captive. He had to taste her. It was no longer a matter of want. He *had* to. Trapped by those glowing pools of gold and green, his last shred of restraint snapped.

A low growl rumbled in this throat as his mouth crashed onto hers. White-hot desire blazed brighter as she opened that succulent mouth and touched her tongue to his. She tasted like honey, bubble gum, and spice. Their lips melded. She moaned and clutched him closer to her. Teeth nibbling. Tongues tangling. Tasting. Touching.

He couldn't get close enough.

Lips firmly fused, Layla reached up and removed the leather tie holding his hair back. His long blond hair fell over their faces, and he felt for a moment as though they were hidden from the world. That's what he wanted—to take her and hide her away from anyone or anything that could harm her.

William sighed into her mouth when she tangled her fingers in the pale strands and pulled him close, deepening the kiss. It was an erotic and intimate sensation to have her fondle his tongue with hers, urging him to the brink of madness.

He almost came apart right then and there.

William took her head in both of his hands and devoured her mouth with his. She sat up, and in one swift motion, she straddled him. He smiled against her mouth. *Someone is feeling better.*

She grabbed fistfuls of his hair and suckled his lips. *Better? I'm way beyond better.* When her lusty voice breezed into his head, it intensified the entire experience, and desire swamped his body and mind.

William reveled in the handfuls of curls that flowed through his fingers, while he paid thorough attention to the velvety cavern of her mouth. She was fire to his ice, but somehow, they fit... perfectly. Her tongue stroked the roof of his mouth, and her sweet lips fused exquisitely with his.

Food? Sleep? Not necessary. He knew now that kissing this woman and holding her in his arms was all the sustenance he would ever require. He could kiss her forever.

A deafening crack of thunder shattered the silence of the woods, and within seconds rain poured down and soaked them to the bone. The horses whinnied and shuffled nervously at the sudden change in the weather. Layla suckled his bottom lip and held it between her teeth for a moment before releasing it.

"That's not me this time. It's good old Mother Nature," she said. Laughing, she threw her head back and caught the cold, pelting rain in her open mouth. Those were some lucky raindrops.

He ran his hands down her slim back and rested them

on her hips, which were nestled snugly against his. He
smiled as she reveled in the rain, but his happiness was
short-lived when he saw the rivulets of water tinged with
red that marred her lovely skin. The cut above her eye
was still bleeding, and the blood was now running down
her cheek.

He cursed silently. The woman had just been thrown
from her horse, and he was mauling her like some kind
of beast. Shame washed over him as Rosie's words of
warning rang through his head. He needed to earn her
trust and her heart, before he tried to get in her pants.

God, he felt like a jackass.

"We should go," he said above the thunder and rain.

Layla stopped laughing and gave him a look that
hung somewhere between hurt and confusion. Her hands
rested lightly on his broad shoulders, and her body stiffened beneath his hands. "What's wrong?"

"You're bleeding." William's mouth set in a hard
line, and his eyes shifted back to their human form.
"You were just thrown off a horse for Christ's sake, and
I'm molesting you, instead of helping you." His fingers
dug into her hips through her soaked sweatshirt. He held
her tighter, afraid she would disappear.

Layla's lips curved into a lopsided smile, and her
eyes glowed back at him brightly. She slid both hands
up his neck and did that tantalizing thing with his hair.
She leaned into him, her mouth hovering temptingly
above his. "You were helping," she breathed the words
against his lips.

She licked rainwater from his mouth with her satin
tongue, while she rocked herself against his enormous
erection. William growled, and his eyes shifted harshly

back into their clan form as his entire body hummed with both desire and restraint.

Layla leaned back, so she could look him in the eyes. "I want you."

He'd been with women before, plenty of them, but he'd never had a woman be quite so direct. He wanted her too. For the love of God, he wanted her more than he'd ever wanted anything in his entire existence, and based on where she was sitting, there was no denying it.

But something about this situation gave him pause.

His gut instinct told him that if he took her now, she would write him off as only doing his duty, succumbing to fate as if he didn't truly desire *her* for who she was. It would merely confirm her suspicion that their mating was a purely physical thing—and it wasn't. Because staring into those glowing orbs, he realized that somewhere along the way, he'd fallen in love with her.

He *loved* her.

William swallowed hard and held her burning gaze as the gravity of his feelings for her washed over him with the rain. He didn't know how, why, or when it happened, but it sure as hell had happened. The truth was he didn't even think he was capable of it.

He'd been prepared for the physical attraction, but not for the emotional cost, and he'd be damned if he was going to let her off the hook. Even if it took him the rest of his life, he was going to get her to open her heart.

"Did you hear what I said?" she challenged. "I want you."

Holding her gaze, William reached up, encircled her wrists, and brought her hands down to his chest. Layla's eyes shifted back to their human state, and her brow furrowed in confusion.

"We should go back to the house and get you cleaned up," he said as evenly as possible.

Layla's eyes narrowed. She shoved at his chest and scrambled off his lap to her feet. Her energy waves thumped furiously into him.

Embarrassment.

Fury.

Confusion.

Without a word, she turned her back on him, climbed over the log, and went to the horses, who were taking shelter from the rain under the canopy of leaves. She clearly had the quick healing abilities of their people, and he was incredibly grateful for it. William followed in silence, but kept his energy linked with hers, looking out for other signs of injury. He tried to help her onto the horse, but she shoved him away without looking at him.

"I don't need you or your help," she ground out.

William put his hands up in defeat and stepped back, allowing Layla to do it on her own. He pushed his wet hair off his face and let out a sigh of frustration. How could he make her understand? Dammit. He knew he was making a bigger mess of things, but he had absolutely no idea how to fix it.

He cursed softly, gathered his horse, and climbed into the saddle with ease, all the while keeping one eye on Layla. He knew she felt weaker than she let on, and he didn't want her passing out and injuring herself further. He had half a mind to throw her over his shoulder and carry her back home, but he suspected that would do nothing to help his cause.

Layla, clearly picking up on his concern, swiped at the cut on her forehead with the soaked sleeve of her sweatshirt, leaving a streak of red behind. Reins in one hand she turned Freckles back toward the house but cast William one last parting blow.

"I just thought you might like to fuck and get it over with," she snapped, her green eyes flashing wildly. "But don't think for one minute that I need you. This thing between us, whatever it is," she said, jutting her chin out defiantly. "It's chemistry, not love. This is some stupid matchmaking scheme from the universe, and obviously, the universe sucks at it. You had your chance and passed, so I'd say that this whole mate business is over."

Before William could utter a single word of protest, Layla kicked Freckles and took off down the muddy path. Undeterred, he urged his horse forward and followed closely behind. As they galloped through the sheets of rain back to the farm, he touched his mind to hers.

Don't bet on it, Firefly.

Chapter 8

LAYLA HAD NEVER BEEN SO MORTIFIED IN ALL HER LIFE. First she gets thrown off her horse, which was something that hadn't happened in close to twenty years, and then she gets thrown off William.

After their rain-and-lust-soaked ride, she needed time alone, a cold shower, and a snap back to reality. This place was real and solid—this house with the walls covered by many of the pictures she'd taken and rooms filled with love. Rosie, Raife, and Tati—they were real and true. They would never leave her or betray her, and they were the only people she could trust. She certainly couldn't count on William—not even for a quick romp in the woods. It would seem that she could depend on him to embarrass and humiliate her.

She took the clip out of her damp hair and ran her fingers through the tumble of long curls. Her face burned at the memory of his rejection. She was bewildered. It just didn't make sense that he would stop what they had both started.

He'd kissed her.

She could sense how much he wanted her, and it wasn't just from the enormous hard-on he had—it wasn't just his body's reaction to hers. Every ounce of his energy called out to hers, his eyes seemed to bore right through her, and his energy waves were ripe with lust and desire.

Layla toweled herself off and wished she could wipe away the embarrassment as easily as she could the water from her quick shower. The instant his firm, warm lips touched hers, something long dormant came to life inside of her, and she *had* to taste more of him. Screw independence and modesty, because at that moment, all she wanted was to crawl in his lap and lick every wicked inch of him.

Layla's tongue flicked out over her lips, and her heart fluttered. He tasted like newly fallen snowflakes dissolving on her tongue—wet, crisp, cool, and clean. She shivered, and her eyes shifted harshly as desire flooded her with surprising speed. Heat pooled between her legs, warmth trickled up her spine, and her breasts grew heavy with wanting him. Weak in the knees, she leaned on the counter and closed her eyes, concentrating on the cool, smooth granite of the countertop beneath her palms as she struggled to regain control over her body.

She steadied her breathing, and her eyes shifted back to their human state with a tingling snap. Staring at her mussed reflection, she couldn't help but wonder. If she was this turned on, this out of control, then he *must* be feeling the same way. After all, *he* came to find *her*, so why reject her when she'd offered her body with willingness?

She'd never been rejected by a man before—ever. Not that she went around hitting on men; in fact, it had always been quite the opposite, but the few men she'd been with had been pretty happy with her skills in the sack.

Layla rolled her eyes and started to put on her makeup. "Great," Layla muttered to her foggy reflection in the bathroom mirror. "That's just fucking great. The one guy I actually throw myself at turns me down."

She applied the mascara gingerly and inspected the cut above her eye, which was healing with remarkable speed. She, Raife, and Tati had always healed quickly, but this injury already looked two days old, not two hours old. She suspected that William had something to do with it, but she hadn't the vaguest idea as to how. Well, she'd be damned if she was going to ask for his help. No thanks. One rejection a decade was about all she could handle.

It just didn't make any goddamned sense, it confused the hell out of her, and she didn't like it one bit, but why did she even care? She barely knew him. What should it matter if he doesn't want her?

Layla brushed her teeth furiously, rinsed, and spit into the sink with far more force than necessary. How was she supposed to go to the bar with him tonight and act like nothing had happened?

When they'd gotten back to the house, Rosie had tried to look at the cut and talk her into sitting down for something to eat, but Layla wanted no part of it. She'd left William in the kitchen to do the explaining, and based on Rosie's tone of voice, he was in for one of her lectures.

Layla giggled as she wiped her mouth off with the hand towel. Good. He could stand to be knocked down a peg or two, and Rosie was just the one to do it. Nobody could deliver a dose of reality or a scolding better than Rosie.

Noise from William's bedroom caught her attention and sent her heart racing. Almost simultaneously, a light rap at the door made her jump. She clutched at the towel wrapped around her naked body and swallowed hard as her heart beat like a jackrabbit on a date.

"Layla?" His smooth baritone came through the closed door loud and clear. "Are you almost finished? I would like to clean up and shower before our plans this evening."

She struggled to find her voice. "It's all yours, counselor," she said in a far lustier tone than she'd intended.

She cringed at the sound of it. When had she become such a dirty girl? She knew that was an irrational thought, but she couldn't help it. Just those few muffled words from him made her wet and had her panting. She grasped the slick glass doorknob to her bedroom and pushed it open just two seconds too late.

William's door opened before she had time to escape into the safety of her room, and the sight of him nearly made her faint. She had planned on issuing a blistering comment for intruding on her in the bathroom and not giving her a minute to leave, but her mind went blank. Her body hummed with awareness, and her heart raced wildly as his red-hot gaze locked with hers, holding her captive. Neither moved; they just stood there with their energy waves swirling through the room, as if seeking relief from the thick surge of lust between them.

William stood before her wearing nothing but a towel, which was slung low around his hips in a dangerously loose way. He didn't just stand in the doorway—he filled it. In fact, that bathroom had never seemed so damn small. His hair hung just past his broad shoulders and framed his devastatingly handsome face to perfection.

His well-muscled chest was void of any hair, but she

noticed a long, thin scar marred the left side just below his collarbone, and she had the ridiculous urge to kiss it. Body still, her gaze wandered down his washboard abs. She lingered a bit too long on the towel and didn't dare wonder about what was underneath. He had strong legs, and as she suspected earlier, he didn't have an ounce of fat anywhere.

Good God, he looked like some kind of Viking.

William cleared his throat, and Layla's gaze snapped back up and met his. Her face heated with embarrassment for ogling him, but based on the way his towel tented in front of him, she wasn't the only one getting an eyeful. His eyes shifted briefly to their clan form before returning to normal. Her lips curved into a knowing smile.

"Apologies for intruding," he said gruffly, with a regal bow of his head. "I thought you said you were finished."

"Hardly," she said with a wink. "I'm just getting started."

His eyes darkened with the unmistakable mark of lust, and his jaw clenched. Layla left, but not before she made sure her towel rode up so that it just barely covered her ass. With a coy smile, she turned to face him, slowly closed the door, and allowed her gaze to wander over his hulking form one more time, brazenly taking in every glorious inch of him.

"Oh, and by the way, I used all the hot water." Her eyes flicked down to the protruding towel that he did nothing to hide. "But since you passed on my offer earlier, it looks like you need a cold shower anyway," she said all too sweetly. "See you downstairs."

As the door closed, the moon-glow eyes of his clan glittered brightly, and the midnight silk of his voice floated into her mind. *Count on it*.

The door may have been shut, but she couldn't get the image of William's mostly naked—and damn near perfect—body out of her mind. It was marred only by the scar below his collarbone. She frowned, wondering who or what had done that to him. Who had the nerve to damage that delectable flesh? She let out a slow breath and closed her eyes to keep them from shifting.

That man was possibly the most exquisite specimen she'd seen in her life, and that was saying something. She'd photographed some of the most beautiful people in the world, but William made them all seem homely. Judging by the erection he was sporting under that towel, he thought she wasn't too bad either. Her brow furrowed, and she let out a sound of frustration. So why did he put on the brakes earlier?

Most of the time he was so damned restrained and reserved, even in the dream realm, but in the woods today, she got a taste of his wild side, just a taste… and now she craved it. God help her, she wanted this man in the most irrational way. It really was ridiculous. For God's sake, he had rejected her a few hours ago, but here she was trying to figure out how to seduce him and find a way to make him give in to the stark need that clawed at both of them.

She wanted nothing more than to make him shed the formalities and explore the primal urges that simmered dangerously under the surface. Layla thought it would be best to remain rational about this situation. Maybe if they satisfied the physical attraction, then they could get it out of their systems and move on.

She nodded curtly at her inner dialogue, agreeing with herself for this course of action. Yes indeed, that's what they needed, just a good old-fashioned wham-bam-thank-you-ma'am. They could get the physical need, and then he would see that's all it was, and he could go on his way.

Layla rummaged through her closet in an effort to find the perfect ensemble for tonight's little outing. She pulled out her black wrap top and skinny jeans, which would be pulled together by her black stiletto boots with the zippers. Layla smiled, tossed the clothes on the bed, and took her sexiest underwear and push-up bra out of the drawer. With the help of Victoria's Secret, tonight she was pulling no punches and using every weapon in her arsenal.

She took her time putting it together and dabbed her favorite perfume at each earlobe and a bit in her cleavage for good measure, giving one last look in the large oak mirror above her dresser. Her long, curly red hair had that sexy tousled look. She used dark smoky eyeliner to bring out the green in her eyes and put just the right shade of pink gloss on her lips.

"You may keep it simple girl, but you can vamp it up when you need to," she said to her almost unrecognizable reflection. "Game on."

Layla grabbed her shoulder bag and her black leather jacket, and then headed to greet her would-be suitor. She practically skipped down the stairs, anticipating William's reaction to her body-hugging outfit.

However, all bets were off the moment she laid eyes on him.

William stood waiting for her in the front hallway with a single yellow rose in his hands. He wore the faded jeans, the pale green button-down, and the brown suede jacket that they'd purchased earlier. On anyone else these clothes would've seemed ordinary or pedestrian, but on him they screamed confidence and power. He radiated a raw, sexual energy that zeroed in on Layla mercilessly.

For the first time since she'd met him, he wore his hair loose, and it framed his handsome face, allowing his intense eyes to take center stage. Layla gripped the banister, fiddled with the bag in her other hand, and wrestled with her desire to jump his bones right there in the front hall. She stood motionless and trapped in his sights as he studied her.

Their energy signatures buzzed, and static electricity crackled in the air, causing the tiny hairs on her arms to stand on end. Her heart fluttered wildly, and she couldn't seem to make her feet move from the landing.

William bowed his head and smiled. "You are stunning," he said without taking his eyes off hers and extended the rose. "For you."

Layla took the delicate flower in her fingers and inhaled deeply from the sunny yellow bloom. The sweet scent filled her nostrils, and a slow smile cracked her face. No one had ever given her a flower before.

"How did you know that this was my favorite flower?" she asked, her lips brushing the velvety petals.

It really was her favorite flower. She wasn't being coy or trying to play the game, because with one sweet, old-fashioned gesture he'd completely disarmed her. It would seem that he was full of surprises.

Her eyes fluttered open, and to her surprise, William now stood just scant inches away. Her breath caught in her throat as heat pulsed off him and permeated every pore.

"Rosie told me," he said quietly as his gaze wandered over her features. "I suppose she took pity on me and decided to help me out." He offered her his arm and gestured to the door with the other. "Shall we?"

Layla laughed as she linked her arm through his. "You really are pulling out all the chivalrous stops, aren't you?"

His dark serious eyes flicked to hers with piercing intensity. "You deserve nothing less."

Layla searched his face for deception, for some hint that this was all a put-on or a con. However, she found nothing except sincerity, but perhaps that was the most frightening realization of all.

―◦◦◦―

When they opened the creaky wooden door to the Rustic Inn, just about every head turned to look at William, and Layla couldn't blame them. Aside from the fact that he was considerably taller than most of the people in there, he was absolutely beautiful. As a matter of fact, she had to make a concerted effort not to look at him like a lovesick teenager. She scanned the room and gratefully found that Sylvia was nowhere in sight. With any luck she'd gotten violently ill and wouldn't show up tonight.

Layla noticed that Nathan and Barbara had removed one of the pool tables to accommodate Tyler's band. They'd even taken out a few tabletops to create a small dance floor. The old brick pellet stove fireplace remained the center of the stone-lined wall, and the horseshoe-shaped bar dominated the right half of the place. It looked exactly the same as it had for as long as she could remember, and she couldn't help but smile.

Normally, the old jukebox would've been playing loudly, but Tyler's band was deep into their first set, a rousing Guns N' Roses number. The place was thick with that drunken, buzzing energy of people having a good time. Tyler spotted her and gave a quick wave, which did not go unnoticed by William.

Who is that? His sharp perturbed voice popped into her head unexpectedly, and she shot him a sideways look. *An ex-boyfriend but mostly a friend.* She noticed a shift in his energy waves, a stumble almost, and it was a moment or two before he responded. *Yes, well, I suppose the operative word in that description is ex.* Layla shook her head and made her way through the thickening crowd. *Can we not add jealous jerk to the list please?* William stayed directly behind her. *I'm not jealous. I'm merely curious.*

When Raife flagged them down from the bar, she practically ran and plowed through the people in her way. If she ever needed a drink to steady her nerves, now was the time. Raife cleared away a couple of empty glasses and gestured to the two recently vacated stools on the far left side of the bar.

He gave a cursory glance to William, but immediately turned his attentions on her. Much to her surprise, this annoyed her. She was having enough trouble figuring things out with William, and her brother causing more problems would be less than helpful.

"Hey, I was wondering if you two were going to show up here tonight," Raife said evenly.

Layla handed her purse and jacket to him. "Keep these behind the bar, will you?"

Raife shook his head, took the items, and stowed

them underneath the bar. "Why do you even bring this stuff out with you? You never use them."

However, the smile faded from his lips once he noticed the faint mark above her eye. Layla's hand instinctively went to the almost healed wound. Dammit. She should've put more makeup over it.

Raife's eyes narrowed. "What happened to your eye?" His stern gaze landed on William. "Jesus, she's with you for less than a week, and she's already gotten hurt."

William remained unfazed and sat on the stool next to Layla without taking his eyes off Raife. "She's fine," he said calmly. "Instead of getting annoyed with me, perhaps you should ask your sister directly."

Layla placed one hand on Raife's forearm. "Hey, it's okay."

Raife looked at Layla with his trademark brotherly concern. "What happened?"

"We went out for a ride today, and I got thrown off Freckles. William didn't hurt me. He helped me," she said firmly. "So, why don't you stop being an overprotective big brother and get us a drink?"

Arms folded over his chest, he let out a slow breath and looked back and forth between Layla and William. "Thrown off a horse? Off Freckles?" He shook his head and let out a short laugh. "I can't remember the last time you got thrown like that." His features softened. "You sure you're okay?"

"I'm fine," she said with a wave. "No big deal. I mean look." She pulled her curly hair back and leaned forward so he could get a better view. "It's practically gone. By tomorrow, it'll be a faint scar."

Raife nodded and pursed his lips. "We always did

heal quickly, but that's really damn fast." He looked at William warily. "Is that because of you?"

"Yes," he said with a glance to Layla. "More to the point, it's because we've found each other, and this is only the beginning. There are many other things that will... develop." Before Layla could pepper him with questions and ask him exactly what the hell that meant, Raife jumped in and changed the subject. Typical.

"What can I get you?" He was clearly not interested in hearing about this at the bar.

"I'll have raspberry Stoli and seltzer with lime," she said without taking her eyes off William.

Raife made quick work of Layla's drink, and like any good bartender, continued his conversation. "Hey, don't feel too badly about getting thrown off Freckles. You know what they say."

"If you get thrown off, you have to get right back on," William finished for him, with a knowing look to Layla.

Her face turned bright red, because she knew that William wasn't talking about Freckles. She grabbed the drink Raife put in front of her and took an enormous swig.

"So, how about you?" Raife said to William. "What'll it be? A glass of ginger ale, perhaps? Or a Shirley Temple?"

Layla watched the two of them stare at each other in silence and tried not to squirm on her stool. Their energy waves remained calm, but she wondered how long they'd be able to maintain their civility with each other. Would William take the bait, or take the high road and ignore Raife's immature attempts to insult his masculinity?

William's eyes narrowed. "Well, as tempting as those beverages sound, I'll have Grey Goose on the rocks," he said smoothly.

Okay, he earns back another point for taking the high road. Layla studied his profile as she took a sip of her drink. He sat on the stool with his hands folded in front of him on the beat up mahogany bar and looked like he owned the place.

Power.

The man radiated pure, animalistic power, and it probably frightened most people, but all it did was manage to turn her on.

Layla plucked the lime off the edge of her glass and plopped it into the drink as she examined him and took another swig. Her gaze wandered over him from head to toe, and when she finally made it back to his face, he was staring right at her with a knowing smile.

Busted. His baritone voice slipped easily into her mind and made her wet.

"Why am I not surprised?" Raife said as he grabbed the Grey Goose off the shelf and pulled a long pour from the bottle.

"What are you talking about?" she asked innocently.

"Your boy here." He nodded toward William. "Top shelf all the way," he said without looking up. To her relief, he passed the drink to William and went to the other end of the bar to tend customers, but she knew he was still keeping tabs on them.

Layla sat a bit straighter in her seat and noticed William's gaze as it flicked down to her cleavage. She smiled. *Busted*, she whispered back. His gaze meandered back to her face, and he raised his drink to her. The man had no shame, and it didn't faze him in the least to be caught staring at her boobs.

What was his deal? One minute he's putting the

brakes on a steamy make-out session, and the next he's ogling her.

"Why did you stay?" Her eyes narrowed as she leaned one arm on the bar to face him. "I mean today, after our *incident* in the woods," she said quietly, not wanting Raife to hear them. "I would've thought I made it clear that you and I are *not* going to become a *we*? You had your chance to bang me, and you passed."

The words weren't even off her lips for more than a second before she knew how untrue and hollow they sounded.

The cocky smile that had been lingering on his lips faltered, and his brow furrowed, carving a deep line between his eyes. "It bothers me that you think that's all I want with you," he said quietly. "And that is unacceptable." He placed his drink on the bar and leaned in closer, so his lips hovered tantalizingly close to her ear. "I'm not leaving before I make you understand that," he whispered.

Layla's heart fluttered in her chest as the warmth of his breath puffed past her ear. His knee brushed hers as he rose from his stool and sent a zap of electricity up her leg. Shaking and feeling like she'd just gone through a spin cycle in a dryer, Layla watched him walk toward the men's room and wondered just what on earth she'd gotten herself into.

She swiveled on her stool and braced her elbows on the bar, held the cool drink against her forehead, and focused on keeping her eyes from shifting. Playing with her body was one thing, but playing with her heart? No way. That wasn't a game that she was going to play.

"Hey there, darling!" Joyce's familiar singsong voice

pulled Layla from her thoughts. Joyce had been tending bar and waiting tables here since God was a boy, or at least that's what she always told people. "You okay? You look like you're plum wore out," she said, peering over her cat-eye glasses.

"Hey, Joyce." Layla smiled weakly. "Yeah, just a long day, I guess."

"Well, it's good to have you back." She pulled a pencil from behind her ear and grabbed a notepad from her apron. "What can I get you to eat?"

"Oh, nothing." Layla waved. "I'll just nurse this for a while."

"You got it, darlin'." She winked and smoothed her bouffant gray hair. "Say, who was that handsome fella I saw you come in with?" Joyce wiggled her eyebrows and snapped her gum loudly. "He looks like one of those fellas from the magazines." She shuddered and made a yummy noise. "All muscle and bone."

"Oh, that's William." She sipped her drink in an effort to quell the flames that sparked at the mere mention of his name. "He's just a friend."

Joyce made a tsking noise and peered at Layla over her glasses. "Honey, that man is made for more than friendship, and if I were about twenty years younger, I'd prove it." She winked. "Gotta tend to some of these tables." She shimmied out from behind the bar at the top of the horseshoe. "Tyler's band may take up a lot of space, but they sure do bring in the customers," she hollered above the music.

Layla watched Joyce as she navigated the crowd with the ease of experience. Her thoughts went back to William, and just when she thought things couldn't get any worse, an unsettling energy signature wormed its way through the bar.

Sylvia Clark had arrived.

Layla swiveled on the stool and avoided looking at the door. She concentrated on her drink in a vain attempt to avoid Sylvia and whatever crap she planned on pulling. She glanced over at Raife to see if he'd noticed her presence, but if he had, he was ignoring her and remaining focused on customers on the opposite side of the bar.

Eyes squeezed shut, Layla drained the remnants of her drink.

God, she really wanted another one. She scanned the bar, but only Raife was around, and Joyce was still attempting to manage the overflowing tables. She was about to cave in and get Raife's attention when that fingernails-on-a-chalkboard voice sliced through the din of the bar, giving her an instant headache. *Crap*.

"Well, well, well." Sylvia sighed. "Look what the cat dragged in."

Layla cursed under her breath and placed her empty glass on the bar. "Hello, Sylvia," she said with a quick sideways glance. Not a moment too soon, Raife saw what she needed before she even had to ask, and was by her side making quick work of a fresh drink, ignoring Sylvia.

"Thanks, Raife," she said with a tight smile.

"Anything for my little sister." He smiled, but his pleasant demeanor faded as soon as Sylvia slithered her way up on to William's seat at the bar.

Sylvia hitched her skirt up and crossed her long but undeniably great legs, all the while keeping her ice-cold gaze on Layla.

"Someone's sitting there," Raife said without looking up.

She shrugged off her wrap, revealing a skintight red dress that left little to the imagination. She draped the shawl carelessly over the back of her seat, while keeping her chilly blue eyes on Layla. "Are you a bartender or a census taker?" she snapped before flicking her sharp gaze back to Layla. "Always nice to see you, Layla," she said all too sweetly.

There was nothing sweet about this woman, and Layla still couldn't figure out why she was trying so hard to hang out with her. Their relationship had always hung by a thread, and once Sylvia crushed Raife's heart, and Layla had to watch him suffer—the thread snapped, and nothing but disdain remained.

So what was her endgame with this "nice to see you" crap?

"Where's that big hunk of man you were with yesterday?" She tossed her long blond hair over one shoulder and gave a casual look around the bar. "I don't see him anywhere. I was hoping he could spare me a dance tonight."

Layla's fist balled up tightly on the bar, and her jaw clenched at the very idea of Sylvia dancing with William. *Don't take the bait.* Raife's calm voice touched her mind. Layla glanced at him, but he kept his eyes on the drink he was making. *She wants you to lose your cool.*

Raife was right—Sylvia was just trying to needle her.

Layla sat up a little taller in her chair and crossed her legs while keeping her eyes on Sylvia. She knew it was ridiculous to be jealous over some guy she'd just met, and even though none of it made any damn sense, she couldn't help how she felt. She may not be ready to run off with William and make shapeshifter babies, but she also knew she wasn't prepared to give him up to the likes of Sylvia Clark.

"He's in the men's room, if you must know," Layla said evenly. "And you are sitting in his seat, so don't get too comfortable."

"See, that's the difference between you and me." She sighed. "Unlike you, I'm always comfortable, but given your unsavory childhood, it's understandable." Before Layla could respond and tell her where she could go, Sylvia threw a coquettish look over her shoulder at the band. "Tyler and his boys are really on fire tonight."

Raife placed the drink in front of Layla and shot a less than friendly look at Sylvia. "What can I get you?" he asked, as if he really didn't give a shit what she wanted, and Layla had to suppress a grin.

"I'll have a vodka stinger," she said dismissively, and then waved him off without so much as looking at him.

Raife mumbled something inaudible and likely insulting, but it seemed to have escaped Sylvia's attention. He made the drink in record time, slid it in front of her, and closed out her tab. "If you need anything, *Layla*, you just give me a shout," he said before moving to the other side of the bar.

Sylvia picked up her drink and sipped it as if she was the damn Queen of England. God, she wanted to punch her lights out. What was she up to anyway? Looking at the tight dress that stressed her big boobs, it was glaringly obvious that she came dressed to kill. With all of the divorces under her belt, she reminded Layla of a black widow spider. She may not have killed the poor bastards she'd been with, but she sure did bleed their bank accounts dry and sap their spirits.

Her eyes narrowed. It seemed that she had every intention of trying to lure William into her bed and make him her next target. As she studied the woman who sat across from her, she came to the conclusion that she was tired of wading through Sylvia's bullshit, and it was time to face it all head-on.

No more running.

Life had gotten complicated enough in the past couple of days, and she had zero desire to contend with this snake in the grass on top of everything else. Since she didn't have her camera on her, she'd just have to come out and ask.

"So, what's the deal? Or more specifically, what's *your* deal?" Layla asked the question in a calm, even tone and kept her expression neutral. "Why did you ask us to come here tonight, and why on earth are you being so nice to me? You and I haven't laid eyes on each other in years." A slow smile curved her lips as she watched the smug look on Sylvia's face fall away. "And if memory serves, that was a less than cordial exchange."

Anger flickered across her face, but she quickly squelched it, and once again wore a mask of calm detachment. "Well, forgive me for trying to put the past behind us." She smoothed out the short skirt of her dress and sipped her drink. "Is that a crime?" she asked with feigned innocence.

Layla studied her with suspicious eyes. "Not for most people."

Sylvia shrugged one slim shoulder and swirled the green drink stick in her glass. "So how is it out at the farm?" she asked, changing the subject. "It's been a long time since you've been back and all. Is everything just like it used to be?"

"It's as beautiful as it ever was, but—" She stopped midsentence and snapped her mouth shut. Telling Frank Clark's daughter her concerns would be plain old dumb. "But, it's my home, so of course, *I* think it's beautiful."

"Yes, well, I know my daddy loves that land," she said with a bit more edge in her voice. "He's been after Rosie to sell it to him for years, but she hasn't caved in to him yet." She sipped her drink, but continued to study her from over the rim of the glass. "But she will. Everyone always gives in to Daddy... eventually."

Anger flared hard and fast, and Layla struggled to keep her eyes from shifting. "Your *daddy* isn't getting our farm. Not now. Not ever," she bit out. "That land has been in Rosie's family for over two hundred years," she said in a much louder voice, "and there's no way she'd sell it. Especially not to Frank Clark!"

"Really?" A sick smile of satisfaction curled across Sylvia's face as she watched Layla get upset. "Well now, if you studied your local history, then you'd know that my family owned it before Rosie's did."

"What are you talking about?" Dread crept up her spine, and all the hairs on her neck stood on end. Raife had tuned in on their conversation and touched his mind to hers. *She's just trying to get your goat. It's all bullshit.*

"What? Rosie never told you how her great-great-something or other swindled my great-great-great somebody out of the land in some stupid bet? It was quite the scandal back in the day and… well…" She sighed. "My granddaddy made my daddy promise to get it back. In case you hadn't noticed, my daddy has bought up every other farm surrounding that one." Her smile grew bigger, and she reminded Layla of a shark. "Yours is the only one left."

"And it's going to stay that way," Layla shot back.

"We'll see." As she sipped her drink, her gaze was captured by something across the room. Her eyes grew round as saucers, and her energy signature quickened with the unmistakable pulse of lust. Layla swore silently. She knew what it was that had captured Sylvia's attention so completely and didn't even have to turn around because she sensed him there before Sylvia had seen him.

"William isn't going to dance with you, and he's not going to fuck you either." Layla practically growled, and for a split second, didn't think that was even her voice. It had been loud enough so that the people behind her even heard it.

"I beg your pardon," Sylvia sputtered while laying a hand dramatically over her cleavage. "What on earth are you talking about, and how dare you speak to me that way?"

Before she could tell Sylvia exactly where she could go and what she could do when she got there, William was standing between them, larger than life. He was staring down at Sylvia with an expression Layla couldn't quite read—and she started to feel dizzy.

One glance at Sylvia, and Layla knew there was no doubt about what was on his mind. What else could he be thinking of but sex? The woman practically screamed it. Somehow, in the five seconds Layla looked away,

Sylvia's breasts bulged out of her top even more, and the skirt had hiked up to an almost illegal point. How on earth could she compete with that?

"Well, hello there, handsome," she said as she leaned closer to him, accentuating her breasts. "How about a dance?"

William didn't flinch but kept his steady gaze fixed on Sylvia, and quite frankly, Layla couldn't blame him. The woman was sexy, had a rockin' body, and practically had a sign on her forehead that screamed "do me." The silence seemed to stretch forever as Sylvia eye-fucked Layla's supposed mate. Layla beat back the ridiculous urge to scratch her eyes out and rip that pretty blond hair right out of her empty head.

Sweat broke out on her back and the whole bar seemed smaller, louder, and upside down, all of which made her dizzy and disoriented. Did they crank the heat up in this place? An odd prickling sensation flickered over her arms and up the back of her neck. A low growl rumbled in her throat, and her eyes tingled as they came dangerously close to shifting. More new stuff? Great. Now she was growling?

Oh, no!

Panic crept in as she realized what was happening—she was starting to shift.

Sweet Jesus. The last thing she needed was to shift into her cheetah form for the first time in the middle of the bar. Layla squeezed her eyes shut and struggled for control over her haywire body. She could feel her body temperature rising as the air thickened, and an odd buzzing filled her head. Then, when she thought she was about to lose it completely, William's calm voice slipped into her mind with irritating ease. *Take some deep breaths, and keep your mind focused on your breathing. That will stop the shift.*

That took some balls. The man was hitting on another woman right in front of her, and now he's telling her what to do? Layla didn't respond—or couldn't—at that moment she wasn't sure which, but she begrudgingly took his direction.

Much to her relief, it worked.

Her skin cooled in slow ripples, and the tingling sensation in her eyes ebbed to a dull throb. She took a couple more deep breaths and happily noted that the nauseating spinning sensation had stopped too. She wanted to open her eyes, but the sight of William twirling Sylvia around the dance floor may well push her past the point of control. As she continued to filter out the swirl of sensations, William's voice cut through the bar noise and floated over the music, causing her heart to skip a beat.

"I'd love to dance," he murmured quietly. "I came over here to ask the most beautiful woman in the bar if she would do me the pleasure."

Layla's heart sank, and when she opened her eyes, Sylvia was staring back at her with a victorious smile. Then, just as she was about to tell them that they could have each other, William's strong, warm hand curled over hers. Her breath clogged in her throat, and those dark seductive eyes locked on hers as he brushed his thumb over the top of her fingers.

"May I have this dance?" His eyes twinkled as he brought her quivering hand to his warm, sinful lips. Memories of how he tasted flooded her, and she could swear that snowflakes were melting on her tongue.

Layla's mouth opened and closed a few times before she finally said, "Yes, of course… I'd love to."

After she managed to spit out the words, she hopped off the bar stool and brushed past a very pissed-off Sylvia. Normally, she'd have taken the time to make a comment, or at least throw her a look of victory, but she didn't. As William led her onto the dance floor, she didn't even give Sylvia a second thought. All she could think of, see, or feel was the man who held her hand.

As he pulled her effortlessly onto the crowded dance floor, she thought he'd release her hand, and they'd dance the way everyone else was—jumping around, clapping, and throwing in the occasional gyration. However, instead of releasing her, he pulled her up against his strong body, placed her hand on his shoulder, slipped one arm behind her back, and took her other hand in his, poised and ready to lead.

Layla just stared at him for a second, not sure of what to say. The band had just started a rousing rendition of "Shook Me All Night Long," and he was holding her as if they were going to waltz.

She didn't think anyone in the history of the planet had ever waltzed at the Rustic.

His eyes crinkled at the corners and smiled down at her, clearly amused by her confusion. "What's the matter?" he asked as his fingers dug into her back, and she instinctively clutched his muscular shoulder in response.

Her breasts pressed into his chest with every breath, and her fingers were cradled perfectly in his. Everything about them, against all odds, seemed to fit.

She moistened her lips and looked around nervously

at the sweaty, dancing crowd that was beginning to swallow them up. "I thought you wanted to dance?" she shouted above the thundering beat.

He cocked one eyebrow, and before she could say another word, he started to move—giving her no choice but to follow. Holding her close, he led her around the dance floor, spun her, twirled her, threw her around in the most controlled, and yet out of control, way.

It was akin to swing dancing but… not.

Layla couldn't catch her breath, and before she knew it, she was laughing loudly as he spun her out and pulled her back into the firm, warm shelter of his body. As the song ended, he whirled her out one last time, and she thought he might let go, sending her flying into the people who had gathered around them.

But of course, he didn't.

He grasped her hand tighter, pulled her in, slipped one arm behind her back, and cradled her neck as he dipped her low. Both of them were breathless, her body suspended just a couple of feet above the dance floor and pressed tightly to his. She barely registered the applause and hoots from the circle of people around them. They hovered there for what seemed like eons, his mouth just inches above hers, and she thought that she could get lost forever in that smoldering stare.

"I told you that I wanted to dance," he said between heavy breaths.

"That wasn't dancing."

"Oh no," he said, slowly pulling her to her feet, but not releasing her from the confines of his embrace. Eyes firmly locked on hers, his hands slid down her back and rested on her hips. "Then what would you call it?"

"Foreplay," she said in a far shakier voice than intended.

Layla tried to convince herself that she was breathless from the dancing, from the physical exertion of tearing up the dance floor, but staring into the dark depths of his eyes she couldn't lie, even to herself.

William flashed her that devastating smile. "We're just getting started."

Before she could respond, the band burst into another raucous number, and he had her twirling on the dance floor once again. As William dragged her body against his, and those thick muscles in his shoulder rippled beneath her fingers, she found herself hoping that he was right.

Chapter 9

THEY DANCED ALL NIGHT, AND THE BAND HAD EVEN stayed on for an extra set because the crowd demanded it. However, after an extra hour of performing, they finally called it quits and were packing up their equipment as the last few patrons left.

William couldn't remember the last time he had danced like that, with such complete and utter abandon, and he knew the only explanation for it was Layla. She lit something inside of him, something that he didn't think he possessed anymore.

She touched the wildest, most carefree part of his spirit, something he thought had died with his youth, but somewhere along the way, she found it and ignited it. His Firefly.

William waited patiently at the bar for Layla as she took her time using the ladies room. He wondered what on earth women did in there that took such a long time. He sipped his drink and scanned the thinning crowd for any sign of Sylvia, but she was gone. When he'd walked out of the men's room earlier that night, he'd immediately noticed a change in the atmosphere of the bar that set his teeth on edge.

A new ripple of energy snaked through the crowd, and it wasn't good; in fact, it felt downright hostile, and it didn't take long for him to find the source. It was coming from Sylvia Clark, and she was sitting at the bar next to Layla. Her hostility was most definitely directed at his mate, which was not at all acceptable.

Her energy signature was remarkably strong for a human, and when he attempted to scan her mind, he couldn't get a solid read on her. She hadn't been blocking him, at least not intentionally, but she was without a doubt, definitely *not* a typical human. Most humans were transparent, and their energy signatures were wispy, akin to tissue paper, practically nonexistent compared to the Amoveo.

The only humans he had ever encountered with dense energy signatures like Sylvia's were psychic. In most cases, he'd be thrilled to encounter a woman like that, because she could potentially be a mate for one of his people. However, this woman's energy also contained an extra layer of darkness, an ugliness that he couldn't quite decipher, and that darkness had been aimed at Layla.

"Looks like you're playing your cards right." Raife's voice pulled him from his thoughts. William turned to face Layla's brother, who regarded him carefully from behind the bar. "I can't remember the last time I saw her have that much fun."

He spoke calmly as he wiped glasses dry before placing them on the rack. "I have to admit that she seems more comfortable with you than she does with most other people." William opened his mouth to respond, but Raife held his hand up. "I'm not saying I like you," he said abruptly. "But if you can make her happy, then that's all I really care about."

William nodded slowly. "Thank you... I think."

The energy waves coming from Raife were thick with

love and protection for his sister. He knew that Layla's brother would do anything to keep her safe, and that was more than enough. William couldn't help but like him.

Raife leaned both hands on the bar and brought himself eye to eye with William. "But if you hurt her," he said in a quiet, deadly tone and with a smile that promised retribution. "I'll tear off your feathered head."

William held up his drink in a toast. "I would expect nothing less," he said before taking a sip. Raife's most admirable quality was his obvious devotion to his family, and that was something William could easily relate to. He hoped that Raife would come around where the rest of the Amoveo were concerned, because he could be an excellent ally against the Purists, and he had a sinking suspicion they were going to need all the help they could get.

"You would expect nothing less about what?" Layla asked as she hopped into the seat next to William. She narrowed her eyes and looked back and forth between the two men. "What are you two talking about? If I didn't know better, I'd think you were actually getting along."

"With this guy," Raife smirked and tossed a crumpled napkin into the trash. "I'm just being nice to the customers. All that dancing must've left you a little light-headed."

"Mmm-hmm," Layla murmured through a laugh that belied her doubt.

Their energy waves had shifted considerably over the course of the evening. They were actually starting to get along, and William could tell she wasn't sure if that was a good thing or not.

"Well," she said, answering Raife but turning her attentions to William, "you're right about the dancing. It's left me a little dizzy."

"Let's just say that we have one thing in common," William said evenly as his gaze slid over her slowly. A smile played at his lips when their eyes met. "And it would seem that just one thing is quite enough."

"Oh really?" Layla cocked her head and pursed her lips. "You know something? You are… unexpected."

William's eyebrows flew up in surprise. "I thought you've spent your entire adult life avoiding me, so how on earth could I be unexpected?"

"Hey, Layla," Tyler shouted from across the bar and interrupted before she could answer him.

William attempted to hide his annoyance, especially from her ex-boyfriend. He assessed Tyler as he approached them: messy hair, along with disheveled clothing and black nail polish. All came together to create a typical indie-rock band lead singer.

Men like this had groupies, didn't they? They banged women two at a time, and based on the girls lingering around the band, he imagined that Tyler was no different.

William's jaw clenched at the idea of this person laying a finger on his mate. *Don't be a dick*. Her perturbed voice sliced into his mind. *He's just a friend*.

William flicked his gaze back to Layla as she hopped out of her chair to greet her friend. He didn't know what to say, because she was right. He was overreacting. He'd never been jealous of another man, and he didn't like the way it felt one bit.

When Layla hugged Tyler with familiar ease, the most irrational flash of anger flared through William like a tsunami, and it took every ounce of self-control to keep his eyes from shifting. He wanted to pummel Tyler into the ground, and for a fleeting moment, he was afraid he'd actually do it. Steeling himself against the unfamiliar onslaught of emotions, William barely noticed Raife smirking at him.

"You know," he said, hardly covering his amusement, "she never loved him. They were just kids when they dated." William glanced at him as he continued to clean up behind the bar. "To be honest, I don't think she's ever been in love—at least not yet." He sighed and shook his head. "So why don't you quit fuming at the guy, and go over and introduce yourself? I thought you were a badass?"

A slow smile crept over William's face. "I have my moments," he said quietly.

As much as he loathed admitting it to himself, he knew Raife was right. It was evident that Layla didn't love Tyler and wasn't even attracted to him, since her energy waves pulsed with the warmth of nothing more than friendship. Accepting his stupidity, he did all he *could* do and walked over to be introduced to the man embracing his mate.

To his great relief, the two stopped hugging before he reached them.

William slipped his left arm around Layla's waist and glowered at Tyler. "I don't think we've had the pleasure of being introduced."

Tyler's eyes widened as he looked William up and down. "Damn, man." He laughed. "I'd definitely remember meeting you." He offered a big smile and extended his hand. "I'm Tyler. Layla and I go way back."

He grimaced as William shook his hand with a bit more firmness than necessary.

Be nice. Layla elbowed him. *You're twice his size.*

"It's nice to meet you." William released Tyler's hand and did his best not to smile. He was considerably bigger and could literally crush this human like a bug, so for now, just knowing that was more than enough satisfaction. "Your band is quite good. I haven't danced like that in many years." He looked at Layla and stroked her waist with his fingers. "It would seem I just needed the right dance partner."

"Yeah, man." He rubbed at his sore hand absentmindedly. "You two were tearing up the dance floor." He looked back and forth between them. "So how long have you two been... dancing?" he asked with a knowing smirk.

"Oh... you know." Layla laughed nervously. "Say," she said swiftly, changing the subject, "I heard you guys are cutting an album. That's really exciting."

Chicken. William teased.

"Yeah, actually, that's why I wanted to talk to you. We need some shots for the website and the album cover. And since you're the best photographer I know, and you just happen to be in town, I was hoping you would be willing to do it." When she didn't respond right away, he put his hands together as if in prayer. "Please?"

"Sure," Layla said with some hesitation as she leaned into William and wrapped her arm around his waist.

William would've been completely ecstatic about her attentions, if it weren't for the fact that she seemed to have done it out of the need for support. He sensed her nervousness and imagined that it had to do with what she might see in the pictures she would be taking. What worried him was how her abilities might be intensified by their growing connection, and there was no telling how her gift would amplify once they were actually mated.

"That's freakin' awesome," Tyler shouted and pumped his fist in the air dramatically. "Sweet. She's gonna do it, guys," he shouted to his bandmates and then quickly turned back to Layla. "How much is it gonna run us?"

"Don't insult me, Ty," she said in a voice edged with humor. "Your money is no good with me, but when you get rich and famous, I get front row seats and backstage passes for the rest of my life."

"Done!" He pointed at her and smiled, but his smile faded when he caught William looking at him. "I'd hug you, but I'm afraid your boyfriend will kick my ass." He laughed and backed away dramatically as he looked from William to Layla. "We're playing here again in a couple days. Can you come and take performance shots on Saturday night?"

Layla nodded and chuckled. "You got it, Ty. What time?" she shouted after him as his attentions were being demanded by the gaggle of ladies waiting.

"We set up at seven." A young blonde draped herself over him and nuzzled his neck. "I'll see you then." He waved, and within moments, he was swallowed up by the group of girls buzzing around him. William fleetingly wondered if that's why they called them *groupies*.

Layla glanced at her watch and whistled. "Holy Moses! It's after two in the morning," she said with more than a little amusement. "We better get home."

Her green eyes peered at him from under dark red lashes, and she smiled. "I may be almost thirty years old, but Rosie will still give me the stink-eye tomorrow for coming home so late."

Layla slipped out of his embrace and headed back to collect her jacket and purse that she'd asked Raife to stow behind the bar. William looked for Tyler only to find that he was nowhere to be seen and neither were the girls. It didn't take a mind reader to figure out where they'd gone, and what they'd gone to do. He knew several men, human and unmated Amoveo, who were constantly in the relentless pursuit of female companionship, and in his youth, William had done the same.

However, looking at Layla, he could no longer comprehend the desire to be with anyone else. She walked toward him, smiling, and tossing a wave to her brother. His throat tightened as the gravity of his feelings for her settled over him. He really did love her. There was no doubt about that, but one thought gnawed at him, and it was the one thing that threatened his very existence.

Would she ever love him?

On the drive back to the farm along the dark, tree-lined streets, Layla blasted the radio and sang lustily to the music at the top of her lungs. William hoped that the people in Upper Falls were heavy sleepers. Her energy waves were lighter. She was the happiest he'd ever seen her, and William couldn't help but feel partially responsible for it. At least, he hoped like hell it was because of him. Or better yet, because they'd found each other.

Layla's positive mood was contagious, and he even

found himself tapping his fingers to the beat of the music as the crisp fall wind blew through the open-air Jeep. Perhaps things were actually starting to come together, and for just a moment, he allowed himself to believe that everything would work itself out.

It seemed a moment was all the universe would allow.

The dark surge of energy swamped him the instant Layla whipped the Jeep into the gravel driveway of the farm. The sudden wave of evil stole the breath from his lungs and had him struggling for control. *Pull over, Layla. Stop the car now.* He shouted it into her mind with all the force he could muster as his eyes snapped to their clan form.

Another Amoveo had been at the house.

The Jeep shuddered to a halt at the bottom of the driveway, but not before running over one too many rocks and popping a tire with a deafening sound that shattered the evening. With the engine idling, the two sat for a minute, breathless and shaking, as the air from the tire hissed like a snake beneath them.

Layla, sensing the same sinister energy, white-knuckled the steering wheel, and her eyes glowed brightly in the moonless night. Her small body shook with thready, uneven gasps, and her lips quivered with fear and anger.

"What-the-fuck-is-that," she seethed through heavy breaths. She turned to him, her glowing eyes pleading with him for answers. "What the hell is that I'm feeling? I feel like I'm either going to puke or beat the shit out of someone."

William steadied his breathing and wove his energy signature with hers, hoping to give and receive comfort.

"I'm not sure," he said, prying one of her hands off the steering wheel and cradling it in his. To his relief, she didn't pull away, but linked her fingers with his. "Give me a minute to get my bearings."

"Okay," she said through a deep breath. Her glowing gold and green eyes flicked to him nervously, before fixating on the house at the top of the driveway.

Her skin had paled considerably, and she was still shaking, which did nothing to calm his nerves. How could he collect himself when he was worried about her? If she didn't calm down soon, it was going to drive him mad.

How did Malcolm and Dante do it? How on earth did they manage to keep their composure when their women had been in such danger?

"Focus on your breathing, just like you did tonight in the bar," he said quietly, keeping his eyes on her.

Layla's energy flickered with the unmistakable flare of anger, her back straightened defensively, and she removed her hand from his. "I got it," she bit out with her gaze still fixated on the house. "Now can you please tell me what is going on?"

Disappointed that Layla was pulling away from him again, but satisfied that she had a handle on her own situation, William turned his attentions back to the dark energy that still surrounded them. He closed his eyes and searched for the source, only to find that whoever was responsible was no longer there.

The tendril of evil that slithered around them was a phantom, a ghost left behind, and it was definitely coming from the farmhouse. The energy was layered with something else he couldn't identify, but he was certain that at least one Amoveo he didn't recognize had been here.

His thoughts instantly went to Rosie.

"Rosie," Layla whispered. "Oh my God."

William's eyes flew open just as Layla let out a small cry and scrambled out of the Jeep. With genuine awe, he watched her run up the hill at a breakout pace. Whether or not she realized it, she was channeling the speed of her cheetah, and it was evidence that their connection was developing with far greater speed than he expected.

He didn't have to tell her Rosie was in trouble. She'd sensed it when he did. Her life force was firmly linked with his, and she'd felt everything he did when he scanned the area.

William cursed loudly and took off after Layla, who was propelling herself straight into danger. Running up the hill, he uttered the ancient language, *Verto*, and within moments the familiar warmth of the shift pulsated over his skin. The jarring sensation of his feet pounding against the gravel was swiftly replaced with air currents rippling through his feathers as he pumped his wings, flying low and fast in pursuit of his mate. In his gyrfalcon form, it didn't take him long to catch up and ultimately pass her. He soared down like a bullet, landed in the open doorway of the house, and shifted back to his human form.

His heart sank at the sight before him. The house was completely ransacked. Pictures were smashed and strewn around the parlor, lamps and furniture were overturned, and Rosie lay dying in the middle of it all.

Before William could reach her, Layla tore up the steps and pushed past him. "*No*," Layla screamed as she stumbled blindly into the room and knelt next to Rosie. "Oh my God! Who did this?" Layla turned her over gently, cradled her bloodied head in her lap, and brushed the hair from her face. She placed a kiss on her forehead. "Rosie, I'm here. It's going to be okay."

William knelt down next to her and linked his life force with Rosie's to study her injuries. "She's in grave condition, Layla."

"William," she pleaded. "Who did this?" She looked at him through tear-filled eyes, and his heart squeezed painfully in his chest at the sight of her grief. "Oh my God, Rosie." She brushed the woman's cheek with her fingers. "We have to get her to the hospital."

William gently pushed Layla aside, and keeping Rosie's injuries in mind, he scooped her up with as much care as he could muster. He held the wounded woman's limp body close and looked at Layla over her broken and bleeding form.

"It will take an ambulance too much time to get all the way out here, and the Jeep's tire is flat." He kept his voice calm. "Even if it weren't, it would take far too long to drive her there."

"Use that blinky thing you did before," she said urgently, scrambling to her feet. "You can get her there, right?"

"I have never been to the hospital here, but I'm sure you have," he said, keeping his serious gaze locked with hers.

"Yes." Layla sniffled and looked at him through confused eyes. "But I don't understand what that has to do with anything." The frantic, panicked tone of her voice tore at his heart and threatened his sanity.

"We can use visualization for travel if we have imprinted on the location or on a person already there." His mouth set in a firm line. "*You* have to get us there, Layla."

Layla shook her head adamantly. "No, I can't—"

"Layla," he barked. "Yes, you can." He softened his tone and glanced at Rosie, still cradled against his chest. "Rosie needs you to do this, and we are running out of time. It's very late, and we can likely arrive there without being seen. I don't have time to argue with you about this," he said with gentle authority. "And Rosie definitely doesn't."

She looked back and forth between his face and Rosie's, as if weighing her options. "Okay." She wiped at her eyes. "What do I do?" William watched with pride as she steeled herself against her fears and doubts. "Tell me."

"Put one hand on Rosie and one on me," he said quickly. "Close your eyes and visualize the hospital parking lot, preferably a spot that would be relatively secluded. Keep your breathing steady, and hold the picture of where you want to go in your mind—the feel of the place, the sounds, the smells. Call up anything you can remember about it. But whatever you do," he added firmly, "don't let go of me until I tell you to."

"Got it," she whispered. Layla did as William instructed, and she placed one hand on Rosie and the other on William's shoulder. She closed her eyes, and deep red lashes fanned fair skin as her concentration deepened. "I see it," she murmured, her body relaxing into the memory.

He watched her eyes move behind her lids, as if she was dreaming, and relief washed over him. She found the sweet spot, exactly where she needed to be to utilize her visualization abilities. He had a newfound respect for Layla. She put her own fears and doubts aside—concern for her own feelings took a backseat to helping Rosie.

Hybrid or not, she had the steely strength of his people and an indomitable will, and she was his.

William closed his eyes, linked his energy signature with Layla, knowing that their combined strength would be enough to take them where they needed to go. As his life force joined hers, everything that Layla felt and saw in her mind's eye flooded him with vivid intensity.

The high-pitched sound of an ambulance wailed in the distance. The smell of wet asphalt in the cool evening filled his nostrils, and the glow of street lamps washed lightly over the emergency room entrance in the distance. As the emergency room sign came into focus, he knew the connection was complete, and uttered the ancient language, *Verto*.

The crackling rush of static electricity and warmth surrounded them, accompanied by the momentary sense of displacement. Seconds later, William opened his eyes to find they were standing in the poorly lit parking lot of the hospital with Layla still latched onto them both.

Layla's eyes flew open, and the look on her face was one of genuine awe. "We did it," she said in a rush. The smile that had begun to form on her lips faded the second she looked at Rosie. "She looks worse, William. Come on, we have to get her inside."

He nodded grimly. "I'll follow you."

"She has to be alright, William," she said urgently. "Who on earth would have done this to her?"

William carried Rosie into the hospital, looked down at her bloodstained face, and made a silent promise to find out who it was and make them pay.

Chapter 10

"I JUST DON'T KNOW WHO WOULD'VE DONE THIS TO Rosie," Layla said through quiet sobs against his chest. "All she ever did was take care of other people."

William cradled her in his arms and fought against the urge to smash every piece of furniture in the waiting area of the hospital. He stroked her back and sent her soothing waves of energy, which he hoped would help them both, because with every sob, with the drop of each tear, it was like acid poured into his heart.

Before meeting Layla, he wasn't even sure if he had one.

"I'm sorry to ask you questions like this, Layla." The officer looked at her through pale, sympathetic eyes, and periodically jotted in his spiral notebook. The pie-faced boy didn't look like he was old enough to drive a car, let alone run a police investigation. "But could Rosie have been involved in anything that you didn't know about?"

Layla squeezed William tighter and shot the kid a look that could kill.

"Barney Stevens," she bit out. "How could you even *imply* that Rosie was involved with something shady or that she somehow brought this on herself?" She glared at him through red, teary eyes. "You've known Rosie your entire life. She took care of you when your Mama was too drunk to see straight, so don't you dare act like this is somehow her fault."

"Now, Layla," he said calmly. "I'm just covering every angle. The boys are back at the farm now collecting evidence and talking to Raife. You know that I love Rosie too, and I want to find out who did this."

He immediately turned his attention to William.

"How long have you known each other?" He hitched his belt up and eyed William warily. "I don't recall seeing you in town before this, and I don't believe Rosie ever mentioned knowing some fancy New York City lawyer."

Before William had time to be insulted by what Barney said, the doctor emerged, looking weary and grim.

"Oh my God," Layla whimpered and clung tighter to William. "Is she…" Her voice trailed off, clearly unwilling to utter their worst fear.

"She's stable at the moment. We have her in a medically induced coma due to the swelling on her brain. The injury to her shoulder is less severe than we first thought and luckily won't require surgery." He glanced from Layla to William. "It's going to be touch and go for the next few hours with that head injury. It's a good thing you got her here so quickly."

"Oh, thank God." She leaned into William, her body and spirit weak with relief. "Can we see her?"

"Yes." He nodded and gave a wave of acknowledgment to the nurse vying for his attention. "We'll run more tests in a few hours and see where we stand."

Layla thanked the doctor profusely before rushing off to see Rosie. William watched her disappear through the swinging door, but the sadness he felt turned into fury as Barney looked at him with suspicion.

He glared down at the man with obvious irritation.

"Like I was saying," Barney said firmly. "I don't recall seeing you around here before Rosie got hurt. So I'm wondering if you have any information that might be helpful to our investigation?"

William wrestled with his burgeoning frustration. Of course he had an idea of who could be involved, but it was of little use to the police. He couldn't tell them that he suspected Purist Amoveo came to the farm looking for his hybrid mate, and poor Rosie just got in the way. He highly doubted that his explanation would satisfy this human.

He mustered up the nicest smile he could.

"Officer Stevens, isn't it?"

"Yes." He stood up to his full five-foot-seven inches. "That's right."

"I can assure you that if I had any information I thought would be of value to you… I would give it to you immediately."

He rocked on his heels and made more notes on his trusty pad. "Well, you just be sure that you don't leave town quite yet. We may have more questions for you."

"Of course." William bowed his head in deference. "You have my word that I will not be leaving Layla's side until this matter is resolved."

He watched Barney make his way out of the hospital, and William knew that as well-meaning as the police may be, they would be of little use against the Purists. William knew what he had to do. It was time to call on Malcolm and Dante, because he doubted Barney would be much of a wingman.

"How is she?" Raife shouted as he burst into Rosie's room. "What in the hell happened?"

Fists clenched at his sides, he practically charged Layla, but William stepped between them before he could reach her. For a split second, she thought the two were going to start brawling in the middle of the hospital like the first time they met.

God, was that only a few days ago? Somehow, time seemed to have ground to a halt since she met William. Either that, or suddenly, she could barely recall a time in her life without him.

Either way it freaked her out.

"She has been put in a medically induced coma," William said in a calm voice. "There is some swelling on the brain. She dislocated her shoulder and had several stitches, but the doctors are monitoring her condition. They are keeping her under for her own well-being, to give her body time to heal." Layla watched as he attempted to calm Raife down, which was really no different than running in front of a charging bull. However, William did it with his usual cool and detached attitude. "We are all upset about what happened to Rosie."

"*We?*" he said incredulously.

Layla insinuated herself between the two men and placed one hand on each of their shoulders, but they continued their alpha-male-chicken-who'll-blink-first game. This was ridiculous. She had zero patience for male posturing on a good day, and this was anything but a good day.

"If you two are done having your pissing contest," she hissed. "Can we please sit down and talk about this quietly? In case you hadn't noticed, Rosie's right here.

A little respect, gentlemen," she said with an exaggerated whisper and a nod toward Rosie's hospital bed.

Raife's expression softened the moment he laid eyes on Rosie. He pushed his way past Layla and went directly to her side. Taking her limp hand in his, carefully avoiding the IV tubes, he sat in the chair at her bedside that Layla had occupied until a moment ago.

Layla went to the other side of the bed and sat on the radiator, but William stayed standing at the foot of the bed with his sharp gaze fixed on her. Since they got to the hospital, William had barely taken his eyes off her, and he hadn't said much. It probably should've been unsettling, but the truth was that she found it comforting. He was not a man who was a natural at expressing his emotions, but based on his actions, the subtle way he tracked her every move, she could tell he was worried about her.

"She looks so fragile," Raife said softly. His eyes shifted to the bright blue of his clan. "They better find out who did this, so that I can kill him." Layla's heart broke for her brother. Even though they all loved Rosie, he was particularly close to her. "I told Tati what happened, and she was going to get on the first plane back home, but I told her to stay put."

He turned his anger-filled eyes on William. "It's not safe here."

"What? Why? What did the police say to you?" she asked, looking from William and back to Raife again. "Did they find anything at the house that would help them figure out who did this? Barney Stevens was here earlier and took our statements, but unfortunately, we didn't have much to tell him. I don't understand why you think that Tati wouldn't be safe."

"Oh, it's not just Tati I'm worried about." His brow furrowed, and the crease between his eyes deepened. "The cops don't have a clue."

He lowered his voice and glanced at Rosie, clearly not wanting their conversation to disturb her or float into the hallway.

"After you reached out and told me what happened, I called the cops and got over there as fast as I could. They were taking pictures and putting shit in little baggies, but they don't have the foggiest idea who would've done this or why. They think it was personal, that someone had it in for Rosie, because nothing was taken." He leveled his stern gaze at William. "But something tells me that they would never guess who was responsible for this," he said tightly. "Would they, William?"

Layla swallowed the lump in her throat. She knew exactly what Raife was alluding to. She'd felt it the moment they'd pulled that Jeep into the driveway, and the mere memory made her want to vomit.

Another Amoveo had been there, and based on the calm, unsurprised look on William's face, he suspected it as well.

"No, Raife." William crossed his arms over his broad chest. "I don't suppose they will figure it out because they're not looking for an Amoveo."

No one moved. The tension was thick in the air, and Layla thought she might choke on it as he verbalized what she'd been afraid of.

"Layla and I both sensed an Amoveo energy signature at the house last night, so it would make sense that a Purist was there looking for Layla or possibly for you. I didn't recognize the individual's energy, and given the situation, the only thing that makes sense is that this Amoveo was a Purist. I agree with you that it's safer for your sister Tatiana to stay where she is and away from this situation. However, I do not appreciate your accusatory tone."

Layla narrowed her eyes and studied William's unflappable expression. "No one is accusing you of anything, but if you know something, or have any idea who did this, you have to tell us." Anger flashed, and heat flared up her cheeks. "Don't protect them."

"The only people I have any desire to protect are in this room," he said.

William's energy waves pulsed violently in the air, causing the floor plant nearby to shake and quiver as if in fear. The hard angles of his face sharpened, and that biting gaze of his pierced her in a split second.

He was furious.

"Do you really think that I would protect the person who did this to Rosie?" he said in a deadly tone. "You believe that I would shelter someone who invaded your home and came dangerously close to harming you?" The words came out in a barely audible rush, and his glowing ebony eyes narrowed, but his gaze didn't move from her face. "No," he bit out. "I don't know which one of our people did this, but you can bet that I'm going to find out."

He glanced out the window and took a deep breath as his eyes shifted back to their human form. "If you'll excuse me," he said without sparing a look to either of them. "I am going to get a cup of coffee and step outside for a few minutes before I say something I'll regret." He opened the door to the hall and threw a pointed glance to Layla. "Do not leave this room until I return."

The swarm of emotions that battered Layla ran the gamut from heartbreaking regret to spitting-nails mad. She'd never encountered anyone who could send her through such a broad range of emotions in such a short time. One minute she felt like a complete shit for implying that he had any knowledge of who'd attacked Rosie, and the next she was ready to kill him for having the nerve to tell her what to do.

However, her anger was swiftly set aside as she remembered the look on his face when she'd accused him of knowing who'd done this. The hurt in his eyes… that look would haunt her. Even as the words came out of her mouth, she knew it couldn't possibly be true.

What. A. Bitch.

She swore softly and turned to look out the window. William had been nothing but kind, chivalrous, loving, and attentive since he'd arrived, and she knew that he would never in a million years hurt Rosie. He was overbearing, bossy, and ridiculously uptight, but he wasn't cruel.

Layla let out a slow breath and pushed her hair off her face. Nope. She seemed to be the one who had cornered the market on cruelty.

After everything he'd done and all the things he'd shown her, she repaid him with a thinly veiled accusation. For Christ's sake, he taught her how to use her visualization skills to help Rosie, and he did it without any comment or remarks about the fact that she'd never used them before. William's primary concern had always been for her feelings, and she returned his kindness with betrayal.

"Dammit." Layla pulled a hair elastic out of her pocket and tied back her unruly curls.

"Oh calm down, he'll be back." Raife kissed Rosie's hand, gently laid it on her blanket-covered belly, and sat back in his chair. "Unfortunately."

Layla spun to face him. "William doesn't know who did this to Rosie," she said vehemently. Her eyes snapped to their clan form as she glowered at her brother. "You've been hard on him since the second he got here, and he's been nothing but gracious."

"Feeling protective, are we?" Raife's eyebrows flew up. "It looks like he's growing on you, Red, but let's not forget a couple important facts," he said with no humor. "Number one, he says that you sensed there was another Amoveo at the house last night, and number two, they just *happen* to show up after William appears." He leaned his elbows on his knees and kept his eyes locked with hers. "Do you really think that's a coincidence?"

Layla's eyes tingled and shifted back to their human form as she struggled with the reality of what Raife said. "No, I don't." She looked at Rosie who still lay unconscious, covered in tubes and bandages, and tears pricked at the back of her eyes. She rubbed at them furiously before they could spill over. "But I am telling you, there is no way that William is involved in this." She sniffled and locked her serious gaze with Raife's. "He cares for Rosie and for me. But at the moment, I'm not sure why, since I've done nothing but hurt him."

Feeling every bit as guilty as she sounded, Layla sat on the edge of the radiator and studied her brother's face. "Do you know how we got her to the hospital last night?"

"No." He shrugged and sat back in his chair. "I figured an ambulance, why?"

"Remember that incident I told you about the other day?"

"You mean the one where he just appeared in your Jeep?" he asked the question tentatively, but his body visibly tensed as he waited for her answer.

"Yes." She nodded. "Well… we did that." Layla folded her arms over her breasts in a vain effort to steady herself. "More to the point," she said softly, "*I* did that."

"You? I don't understand. Why wouldn't bird boy do it?"

"He'd never been here before. Apparently, we have to imprint on the location or on a person at the place we want to go. That day in the Jeep, he tapped into my energy signature and was able to use visualization skills to get to me. Anyway…" she said with a sigh. "Last night he showed me, or helped me, to use that ability to get us here."

She looked at Rosie, and her throat clogged with emotion. "If he hadn't showed me how to do that, I don't think we would've gotten her here in time. She was pretty banged up and had lost a lot of blood."

She watched Raife absorb what she'd told him. He rubbed his mouth and made a sound of understanding.

"He knows," she said softly.

"Knows what?" Raife asked as his face twisted in confusion.

Layla straightened her back, instinctively feeling defensive. "He knows that I've never been able to shift."

"Are you sure?" His lips set in a tight line. "What did he say?"

"Well, that's just it. He didn't *say* anything. He just knew. Last night at the bar, when Sylvia was there being… Sylvia… she got under my skin." Her lips curved at the irony of the statement. "So to speak."

Raife's eyes twinkled with excitement for his sister. "You started to shift." He knew how much it bothered her that she'd never been able to shift like him and Tati. "You know, I thought I sensed something last night, another ripple in your energy signature, but I wasn't sure exactly what it was."

"Well, if it hadn't been for William, I probably would've shifted into my cheetah right at the damn bar, and most likely ripped Sylvia's head off."

Warmth washed over her at the memory, but she suppressed the smile that was brewing, unsure if her brother would share her enthusiasm. She suspected that no matter how much he said that he hated Sylvia, there was a part of him that still loved her and probably always would.

"William sensed the shift coming on, knew that it was happening beyond my control, and talked me off the ledge. He showed me how to get a hold of it before it got a hold of me. And you know what? He never once acknowledged that I'd never done it before or called attention to my inadequacy… he just helped me. The same thing happened last night when he showed me how to get Rosie here. He knew what we needed to do and got it done. There was no shame, no mention of me being a hybrid, or being behind the curve somehow." She let out a soft laugh. "It was the most thoughtful thing anyone has ever done for me."

"Maybe," he said quietly. "But that doesn't change the fact that there are other Amoveo who have found us, and they're the ones who did this to Rosie." His eyes flickered, but he kept them from shifting. "Since lover boy has been so helpful, maybe he can use some of his awesomeness to find the animal." His hands balled into tight fists, and his body tensed as he looked like he was choosing his words carefully. "You should probably show him my mother's diary."

Layla couldn't have stopped from looking surprised if she wanted too. That diary was his prized, sacred possession.

"Are you sure?" she asked gently.

She knew how special that diary was to Raife and Tati; she'd never asked them if she could read it. He'd offered, but somehow, it felt like a major invasion of privacy. Besides, it wasn't her mother's story. However, given the latest developments, privacy would have to take a backseat to their safety.

"You want us to read it?" Layla lowered her voice. "Are you sure?"

"*Want* wouldn't be exactly accurate." Raife leaned one elbow on the arm of the chair and rubbed his mouth against his fist. "I'm not letting him read it to bond with the guy, and I'm not psyched about it," his voice softened. "There might be something in there he can use."

Layla walked around the bed to her brother and wrapped her arms around him. "Thank you," she whispered and placed a kiss on his unshaven cheek. "I love you, Raife."

"Yeah." He patted her arm and gave her a quick squeeze before releasing her. "I love you too, Red."

The door to Rosie's room swung open, and William walked in bearing a tray with three cups of coffee and a brown bag that looked suspiciously like a bag of doughnuts. He stood there for a moment watching them, clearly uncomfortable that he'd walked in on an emotional moment for the siblings.

He cleared his throat and awkwardly held out the tray and the bag. "It's been a long night, and I thought you could both use coffee and something to eat."

"Unbelievable," she said softly.

Once again, he showed consideration for her and her comfort, even after she'd been so horrible to him. A huge smile cracked Layla's face, and before he could put anything down, she rushed over and wrapped her arms around him. She rested her face against his warm, firm chest, and tears stung at her eyes.

"Thank you," she mumbled against his shirt. He smelled like the woods in wintertime.

"You're welcome," William said evenly. His arms still outstretched and his hands full, he remained stone still, but she could feel his heart beating rapidly beneath her cheek. "I'll have to bring you coffee and doughnuts more often."

"You look ridiculous," Raife said as he took the items from William's hands. "You better hug her back before she starts bawling," he grumbled and brought the items to the nightstand on the other side of Rosie's bed.

"I don't bawl." Layla sniffled into his shirt. William's strong arms wrapped around her, and he kissed the top of her head. She squeezed him tighter, as if he might slip from her grasp and vanish. "Thank you," she whispered.

"You are most welcome," he said as he brushed his hands down her sides. He leaned back and tilted her chin up with the tip of one strong finger, forcing her to look him in the eye. His dark, moon-glow eyes glimmered down at her intensely. "I swear we'll find out who did this, and when we do," he said with deadly intent, "I will make them pay."

The stern tone of his voice was matched by the fierce look in his eye, and Layla knew he was telling the truth. She wanted to tell him how sorry she was, that she knew he wasn't behind any of this, and to kiss those firm, warm lips of his senseless, until he forgave her. However, the sound of Raife loudly clearing his throat broke the spell and set her cheeks aflame with embarrassment.

William's lips curved, and his eyes shifted back to their human state as she slipped out of his embrace.

"Here," Raife said as he handed a cup of coffee to her and one to William. "Do me a favor and drink the coffee, so I don't have to watch you two grope each other." He took doughnuts out of the bag and handed one of the sugar-coated concoctions to each of them. "There, now both hands are full of something other than each other," he said with a satisfied smile as he took a massive bite out of his pastry.

He chewed and quickly swallowed his mouthful without taking his eyes off William. Layla blew on her coffee and watched Raife study him with his usual bold demeanor. She could tell he was deciding exactly what to say, and based on William's calm, controlled stance, he was aware of it and didn't seem bothered by it in the least. To his credit, he said nothing, but simply sipped his coffee with the same regality one might drink a fine glass of champagne.

No one was saying anything, and the only sound in the room was the steady beep of Rosie's heart monitor.

Layla half expected Rosie to sit up and tell them all to stop being so childish, but she continued to lie silently amid the tension of the room.

After what felt like an eternity, Raife finally broke the thickening silence.

"I may not trust you entirely," he said, wiping his mouth with the back of his hand. "But my sister does, and that's good enough for me, because I don't know if you've picked up on this yet, but she doesn't trust many people." He crumpled the now empty brown bag and tossed it into the small garbage can in the corner. "So here's the way I see it," he continued calmly, with his hands on his hips. "An Amoveo was at our house tonight, and that's probably who did this to Rosie."

"Most likely," William said quietly. "However, if it was a Purist, based on their previous actions, I find it strange that they left her alive." His massive body didn't flinch, but Layla could see he was primed and ready to leap into action if necessary. "No one else will be harmed. That much I can promise you. If it's alright with the two of you, I would like to ask my friends Dante and Malcolm for their assistance. Their mates are hybrids. They have had some run-ins with the Purist sect, and their experience would be quite valuable." His dark eyes flicked to Layla briefly before going directly back to Raife. "They could also provide us with additional security at the farm and here at the hospital."

Raife crossed his arms over his chest as he looked from Layla to William. "You trust them?" he asked pointedly. "You would trust them with Layla's life?"

"Yes," he said firmly. "But you don't have to worry

about Layla, because I won't let her out of my sight until the situation is settled."

As the words escaped his lips, William's energy signature buzzed loudly in her head and merged with Layla, as if tethering her to him. The suddenly increased connection caught her off guard, and she sucked in a sharp breath in an effort to acclimate to the new sensation.

William didn't take his eyes off Raife and seemed unaware of the newly sharpened connection between them. As the buzzing subsided, and her body adjusted to their amplified bond, her mind raced with the possibilities of what it all meant.

"Fine," he said quietly. "Call in your friends." His serious blue eyes studied William intently, and the lines in his forehead deepened. "I have one more question for you. Do you have anything against killing one of your own?" Raife asked, pulling Layla from her thoughts.

Killing people? Raife was talking about killing the Amoveo who did this? What the hell? She looked at the two men as if they'd lost their minds. Maybe they had, and perhaps she had too.

"I have no problem with it." William's eyes flickered and shifted brightly. "Whoever did this *is not* one of my own." His voice, barely above a whisper, filled every inch of the room as his glowing eyes latched firmly onto hers. "I will protect what is mine at all costs."

A shiver ran up Layla's spine at the possessive tone in his voice, and her heart leapt into her throat. He meant her. As if the bizarre bonding of their energy signatures wasn't enough, he felt the need to verbally claim her in front of her brother? If they weren't standing in the middle of Rosie's hospital room, she would've decked him square in the jaw.

"Good." Raife gave a curt nod, and without a glance back, he sat in the chair next to Rosie. Her brother was obviously unfazed by William's caveman professions and actually seemed comforted by them.

Now she wanted to punch them both in the face.

"Excuse me," she said in the most serene voice she could muster. "I am not some helpless damsel in distress, and I don't need either of you to protect me."

Having suddenly lost her appetite, she threw the rest of her doughnut in the garbage can and brushed the sugar from her hands briskly.

"Aside from the fact that I am an independent woman who has traveled to some of the most dangerous parts of the world on assignment, I also happen to be half cheetah and could kick both of your asses sideways if I wanted to."

Hands on her hips, she glared at them, daring them to challenge her.

Raife let out a short laugh. "Oh, I know you could, but you also tend to act before you think and would probably run off half-cocked and get yourself killed. So if bird boy here can help keep an eye on you, then I'm all for it." Raife glanced over his shoulder at William. "I'm not leaving Rosie's side until you find the sack of shit that did this. I'm sure your friends are just freaking peachy, but I'm not leaving Rosie alone."

"Understood." He gave a sharp nod and turned his dark eyes on Layla. "I am well aware of how capable you are," he said quietly. "I didn't mean to belittle you or make you feel as if I don't respect you or have every confidence in your abilities." He moved his massive frame closer and linked his fingers with hers. Her heart skipped a beat as their flesh connected, and every nerve ending in her palm came alive. "Forgive my overprotective nature, but I couldn't bear it if you were harmed."

Layla couldn't find her voice amid the rush of his skin against hers and the hum of their mingled energy waves. Looking into those dark brown eyes, she knew he was being truthful, and the childish flare of anger subsided. Wanting to protect her, to keep her safe—that was something she could understand—but binding herself to him for eternity wasn't as easy a concept to grasp.

How could she possibly tell him that was never going to happen?

"There will be justice," William murmured and turned his attention to Rosie. "There will be justice for Rosie. I promise."

Layla could feel and see the anguish that tore at William from the inside out in a more profound way than ever before. It was as if she had a direct line to his emotions. Although his eyes were in their human state, she felt the barely contained fury that rushed beneath the surface. Under that calm, cool-looking exterior, Layla detected a turbulent sea of rage and a stark need for vengeance that sent a ripple of dread up her back.

Was it only yesterday that she'd wanted to see him reveal the primal side of himself? As she watched the tiny muscle in his jaw flicker, and his powerful stare remained locked on Rosie, she thought of that old saying: *Be careful what you wish for… you just may get it.*

Chapter 11

WHEN THEY SET FOOT IN THE HOUSE, WILLIAM HAD been prepared for Layla's reaction but not his own. The first floor of the house had been ransacked, and the sight of Layla's photographs smashed and strewn around the floor was almost more than he could handle. The dark energy signature from the night before was almost gone, and even though that should've been a comfort, it wasn't. Pure-blooded Amoveo energy didn't usually dissipate this quickly. There was something off kilter about the phantom of energy left behind, but he couldn't quite nail down what it was.

Who in the hell had been here?

William slammed the door behind them, and his eyes shifted to his clan as he surveyed the wreckage left behind by the attack and the subsequent investigation.

Layla stood silently next to him, but her energy signature whipped around like a whirling dervish.

"I feel violated." She hugged herself, which prompted William to pull her into his embrace.

He didn't even think about it. It was instinctive and a sign that their comfort level with each other was moving in the right direction. Perhaps something positive would come of this horrific situation after all.

"It was always safe here, William. Woodbine was the one place in the world that I felt safe, and now some sick bastard has taken that away."

"Don't do that." William lifted her chin so she was looking him in the face. "Don't give up your power like that."

She stilled. "What did you say?"

"Don't let the Purists or anyone else take that iron-clad strength you have inside. It's one of your most beautiful qualities. I realize Rosie isn't a blood relation, but it seems to me it's something you've learned from her." He ran his hands down her arms and linked her fingers with his. "Don't give anyone that kind of hold over you. People are only powerless when they *believe* they have no power."

Layla smiled and hugged him tightly. "You're right," she said. "You've only been here for a couple of days, and you already sound like Rosie."

"Well, something tells me that when she gets home, it would put her back in the hospital to see things like this," he said, looking around at the mess. "What do you say we take back the house and wipe away any evidence of the incident?"

"I say, absolutely," she whispered as one large tear rolled down her cheek.

She pulled away, but he held onto her hand.

"Until we find the person that did this, you are not going anywhere without me." His eyes glittered like black diamonds, and the lines in his forehead deepened. "Do you understand me? You will go nowhere unattended."

She tugged on her hand, attempting to free herself from his grip, but said nothing. He could see the wheels turning and knew her instinct was to fight him on the subject, but to his relief, she simply nodded and said, "Okay."

He suspected there was a good chance she was placating him, but he'd take it. For now.

As the sun set, William put the last of the garbage bags outside in the shed and took a quick survey of the property. He uttered the ancient language and shifted into his gyrfalcon. Everything on the farm looked normal, but while soaring above the property, he sensed something else. He closed his eyes and tuned into the phantom energy signature that had been left behind from their intruder.

It hummed, almost imperceptibly around the farm, as William strained to connect with the wispy trail. Eyes closed, he rode the air currents silently, and then he found it—a subtle stumble within the larger energy wave. There were two different patterns within the ghostly stream, one darker than the other.

There had been two individuals here the night Rosie was attacked.

William's eyes snapped open, and fear gripped his heart. Why hadn't he sensed it before? Had they returned? Panic swamped him as he searched for Layla's sweet, bright signature.

He shot down to the house like a bullet, shifted midair, and his feet barely hit the ground before he was running up the steps and into the house. The rational side of his brain knew that it was highly unlikely they'd come back. As irrational as it was, William had to see her, to know she was still safe. He barreled through the front door, and Layla looked at him like he'd lost his mind.

"You're alright?" he said through heavy breaths.

William looked around the first floor and scanned the area. Much to his relief, the second signature was indeed only another ghost left behind. William stood in the front hall, a tad dumbfounded, and realized that for the first time in his life—he had overreacted.

"What the hell happened out there?" she asked as she hung the last picture back on the wall. "You look like you're ready to kill someone."

"Nothing." William shut the front door securely and gave one last glance outside. Although the second signature was only a phantom, he was now absolutely certain there had been two people here the night Rosie was attacked. But he didn't know who they were dealing with and wanted to get Malcolm and Dante's opinion before he said anything to Layla.

"I'm just eager to find out who did this. It's easier to defeat your enemy once you know them."

"Okay." She looked at him through weary eyes. "I'm not sure you're being completely forthcoming with me, but I'm so freaking exhausted, I don't have the energy to argue with you. I suspect you're keeping something close to the vest until your friends get here." She cocked her head and analyzed him with frightening accuracy. "Maybe you want to get their opinion on things before you share it with me?"

William's face heated with embarrassment. No one had ever seen through him, or read him so easily before now. He cleared his throat and avoided her gaze.

"We've been working for hours, and I don't think you've eaten anything since that horrid doughnut at the hospital." He took her hand in his and led her into the family room. "Come with me."

She didn't argue or press him for information, but she didn't take her eyes off him. He picked up the large plaid blanket draped over the back of the sofa and gestured for her to sit. Layla smirked and flopped onto the couch with a contented sigh as he placed the blanket over her lap.

"This is all very nice, but we can't just sit here while Rosie is in the hospital."

"I beg to differ," he said smoothly. "If Rosie were here, the first thing she would do is try to get you to eat something, probably a piece of her pie, and if I didn't do it, she'd smack me in the back of my head."

"You're right," she said through a weak smile. "But I—"

William placed one finger over her lips, silencing her.

"Not another word. You are going to sit here and enjoy the fire while I gather something to eat."

Layla arched one eyebrow and glanced past him to the cold, empty fireplace. "What fire?"

"This one," he said.

He uttered the ancient language, waved his hand, and within seconds a roaring fire blazed brightly in the stone hearth.

"Not bad," Layla said. She made a face of approval. "You're a regular boy scout."

The look on his face must've been amusing, because she burst out laughing.

"I am many things, but I was never a boy scout," he said firmly.

Layla rolled her eyes and chuckled. "I don't doubt it."

William smiled in spite of himself. "Well, while you're having a laugh at my expense, I'll be getting us something to eat."

His stomach rumbled as he went into the kitchen

and whipped up some food. After a little rifling around in the unfamiliar pantry, he put together a nice tray of cheese, crackers, and grapes, and even rustled up a good bottle of Shiraz. He grabbed a couple of wineglasses and carried their makeshift dinner into the family room, but when he turned the corner, he stopped dead in his tracks.

Layla sat curled up on the couch and the flickering firelight that emanated from the hearth bathed her in an ethereal glow. She reminded him of fairies from the stories of his childhood, or what the fairies would have looked like, if he could've brought them to life.

Beautiful.

Elusive.

Vibrant.

Magical.

She was the most spectacular creature he'd ever laid eyes on.

The sun had all but gone down, and since she hadn't turned on any lights in the room, the only light was coming from the fire—or maybe... it was coming from her. At the moment, he couldn't separate one from the other. She looked peaceful and cozy, but he, better than anyone, knew that turmoil swirled beneath the surface. Her energy waves had been thick with grief, confusion, and anger all day, and things hadn't improved now that she was reading Raife's mother's diary.

In fact, it had only gotten worse.

Steeling himself against the power of her emotions, William circled the couch, placed everything on the knotted pine coffee table, and sat next to his mate. He poured a glass of wine for each of them and held hers out, but lost in her thoughts and the hypnotic dancing light of the fire, she didn't even notice.

"Layla," he said gently as he held the glass out. "I poured you some wine and got us something to eat."

"No, thank you," she said softly.

The sadness in her voice just about ripped his heart out and made him feel completely powerless. Put him in the heat of battle, in a courtroom, or in the sights of the Caedo, and no one could shake him, but put his brokenhearted mate in front of him, and he turned into a fumbling oaf without the slightest clue how to help her.

"Any word from Raife about how Rosie's doing?"

"Yes," she said without looking at him. "She's still unconscious, but the doctors are a bit more optimistic. I wish she'd wake up," she said in a quivering voice. "She can't die, William. She just can't."

Emotions. He really, really sucked at dealing with emotions—especially the sensitive kind. Anger, hatred, revenge—those were easy. Cold and calculated, that was his comfort zone, but love, loss, and sadness were not things he knew how to remedy. There was no case law to cite or Caedo to defeat. There was simply the heart of his mate to cradle, and he hadn't the foggiest notion how to do it.

Layla looked down at the worn brown leather diary in her hands, and William watched helplessly as one large teardrop rolled down her cheek. She sniffled and brushed it away, as if it was more annoying to her than anything else, and William could tell it bothered her to lose control of herself that way. She seemed almost as uncomfortable with it as he did—perhaps they had more in common than he previously thought.

"I don't think there's much in here that will help us," she said tightly. "Raife's mother doesn't even divulge his father's name or where he was from. She says he was part of the Timber Wolf Clan and that his own people killed him." She glanced at him. "Amoveo may be hard to kill, but apparently, decapitation works just fine." Layla shook her head as if trying to erase what she'd just read from her memories. "Most of it is just very sad."

She handed the timeworn diary to him before picking up the wineglass he had put out for her. William took it in his hands and hesitated to open it. Although Raife had given them permission, his gut told him that it was really only for Layla.

"She was desperately in love with him… whoever he was." She sipped the wine but kept her eyes focused on the fire. "The saddest entries are the ones she wrote after he was killed."

"Well, that makes sense, don't you agree?" William meant it. He couldn't imagine the grief he would feel if he lost Layla, and they weren't officially mated yet. "She'd lost the love of her life."

"No." Layla shook her head and shifted her body so she faced him. "It's more than that. It was as if she died when he did. After his death, her words were hollow, and she became a ghost of herself without him." Layla's eyes were filled with fear. "Is that what happens?" The words came out in a rush, and her voice rose. "When people are mated, do the women completely lose themselves and become a mere extension of the men and just disappear?"

"No," William said quietly. He placed the diary on the table, leaned his elbow on the back of the couch, and took her face gently in his hand. "*We* do not absorb *you*... don't you see?" he whispered.

He brushed away the tear track on her cheek with the pad of his thumb, and she shivered under his touch. His eyes remained locked on hers as her energy waves fluttered faster through the room. His throat clogged with unfamiliar emotions, and he struggled to find the right words, worried that if he didn't, she would slip away. He tangled her soft curls between his fingers and chose his words carefully.

"You and I will become a part of each other in every way—physically, mentally, emotionally. We will complement and enhance one another. When Amoveo are mated, we become true life partners, and there is a give and take on both sides," he assured her. "I'm sure you've noticed that since we've found one another, certain changes have occurred, but neither is dominant over the other."

"Is it because she was human?" She nibbled on her lip, and her large green eyes searched his for answers. "Is that why Raife and Tati's mother got sick and died? Was she too weak to handle it?" Layla tore her gaze from his and looked down at the glass in her hand. "Like my mother," she said in a barely audible whisper.

"Is that what you believe?" he asked, his heart breaking for her. "You think that your mothers got sick and died because they were humans who had mated with Amoveo?"

Layla nodded, pushed his hand away, shoved the blanket off her legs, and rose from the couch. As difficult as it was, William didn't resist, but let her take the space that he knew she needed and watched her as she walked to the fireplace.

"She was crazy, you know, and a drug addict." Layla picked up another log and added it to the fire but kept her back to William as she spoke. "She didn't find out what my father was until after they had been together for a while, and she was already pregnant with me. It sent her over the edge. Although I suspect she'd spent most of her life flirting with the edge of sanity."

She told her story as she looked into the dancing flames, too ashamed to look him in the face, while she divulged pieces of her past. William wanted nothing more than to scoop her up in his arms and tell her that none of that mattered, but he stayed where he was and allowed her to tell her story on her terms.

"I didn't spend an enormous amount of time with my mother. Child Services removed me from the home when I was just two or three. She tried to get herself clean now and then, and I would go back into her custody briefly, but it never lasted long," she said with a shrug. "The drugs had a bigger hold on her than anything. She knew things too. She could tell me things about the different families that I'd been staying with, but I'm not exactly sure what her psychic ability was, or how she received her information. I don't think it was through pictures like it is for me, but the sad truth is that I just don't know."

She glanced at him briefly over her shoulder. "I was only eight when she died from a drug overdose, and the only thing I'm certain of is that she was too weak to handle everything that had been thrust upon her, and my *father*, whoever he is, wasn't around to pick up the pieces," she said in a voice edged in bitterness.

Unable to keep his distance, William rose from the

couch and moved around the other side of the coffee table to stand beside her. They stood there for a moment, side by side in front of the roaring fire, neither saying a word.

There was so much he wanted to say, but he didn't even know where to begin, and since he thought that nothing he could possibly say would be right, he simply reached over, linked his arm around her waist, and pulled her into the shelter of his body. To his great delight, she buried her face in his shirt with a sigh and wrapped her arms around his waist.

"I'm sorry, Layla," he whispered against her hair as he rocked her slowly. "It sounds like your mother struggled with her own psychic ability long before she met your father. As for Raife and Tati's mother, I can't imagine the grief she suffered after losing her mate so violently." He leaned back so she could look him in the eye, and the pained expression on her face made his throat tighten. "I am Amoveo," he said gruffly. "But if I lost you, there would be no measure of time long enough to heal, and death would be a welcome relief."

"What if I can't handle it?" Layla's large green eyes searched his as they flickered and shifted to the glittering eyes of her clan. "I'm only a hybrid."

"Layla." William took her face in his hands as his eyes shifted to their clan form. "You are exactly what you are supposed to be," he murmured. "You… are perfect."

The heat in the room thickened as their energy waves mingled, and William fleetingly wondered if the roaring fire had anything to do with it.

Not likely.

Looking down at that flawlessly beautiful face, he

was held captive by the assault of his own emotions. Terrified for her safety, saddened by her lost childhood, incensed that someone was intent on hurting her, and most terrifying of all… he was irrevocably in love with her.

Cradling her face in his hands, lost in the seemingly limitless depths of her eyes, he wrestled with his desire to claim her, but when she wiggled that tight little body up against him, and those delicious pink lips curled into a wickedly inviting smile… the last shred of William's restraint shattered.

He captured her mouth with his on a curse or a prayer—he wasn't sure which. Pleasure flooded him as Layla opened her soft lips and stroked her tongue seductively along his. He angled her head and delved deeper, savoring the wild, sweet taste, and doubted he would ever get enough of her.

Layla responded eagerly and moaned as she wrapped her arms tighter around him, untucked his shirt, and slipped her delicate hands beneath the waistband of his jeans. When those devilish little fingers slid along the skin at the top of his ass, sizzling streaks of pleasure shot straight to his crotch. A growl rumbled deep in his throat amid the explosion of lust, and he knew he couldn't wait another minute to have more of that ivory skin pressed against his.

He grabbed the hem of her sweatshirt, and in one swift movement, whipped it over her head, revealing the most immaculate bare breasts he'd laid eyes on. No bra. He couldn't have stopped the look of surprise on his face if he'd wanted to. His startled gaze met her smile—her desired effect had been achieved.

When they got back to the house, she'd changed into her favorite, ratty old sweatshirt and jeans... but apparently, nothing else. *Minx*.

She looked at him seductively through heavy-lidded eyes as she unsnapped the fly of her jeans and wiggled those slim hips. The jeans gratefully fell to the floor, revealing the sexiest legs he'd ever seen. William swallowed hard and let his heated gaze travel back up her gorgeous form.

The fading light of the fire flickered over her naked body, and it was all he could do to keep from licking his lips. Their connected energy signatures thrummed through the room in thick, pulsing waves. His fingers itched to touch her again, but he knew she wanted to retain control, and for the first time in his life, he was happy to let someone else take the wheel.

Layla inched her gloriously nude body closer to his and released the buttons on his shirt one at a time. "Like what you see?" she asked through heavy breaths without taking her gaze from his. "I know I do."

Layla undid the last button, pushed the shirt off his shoulders, and he barely noticed when it fell to the floor. She ran her hands tantalizingly over the muscles of his chest and flicked his nipple with her tongue as her pert breasts scraped along his hypersensitive skin. His fingers clenched and unclenched at his side, and a low growl rumbled in the back of his throat as she stood on her tiptoes and rasped her tongue along the scar on his chest. "You taste like snow," she whispered against his heated flesh.

William's eyes fluttered closed as he allowed himself to experience the exquisite effect of her touch. He shuddered with pleasure as her nimble fingers wandered along his rib cage, and she ran her nails down his sides. He was hard as a rock—everywhere—and if she kept this up, he might just lose control, and this whole thing would be over before it even got going.

Not yet, counselor. That sexy voice floated into his mind with the same seductive caress that her fingers gave to his flesh. *We're just getting started.*

William opened his eyes to find Layla smiling at him—she looked like the cat that ate the canary. He arched one eyebrow and reached for her, but she stepped back, shook her head, and wagged her finger at him. "Ah-ah-ah," she scolded like a teacher from his dirtiest fantasies.

Layla placed both hands on his chest, pushed gently, and urged him backward. Like any man who didn't have enough blood pumping into his brain, he did the only thing he could do—exactly what she wanted.

His gaze slid over every visible inch of that fair freckled skin as he backed up, taking in the sight of those tight breasts, the tantalizing dip of her waist, the subtle curve of her hips, but she kept her glowing eyes fixed on his face. Layla urged him back until his legs hit the edge of the oversized chair, and her lithe, supple body brushed against him, a teasing whisper of what was to come.

Gazes locked, her tongued darted out and moistened her lower lip. Layla released the buckle of his belt, pulled it like a whip from the loops of his jeans, and tossed it across the room. William's pulse thrummed rapidly, and sweat broke out on his brow as he struggled for restraint. All he wanted to do was throw her on the floor and bury himself deep inside her.

Not yet.

She unzipped the fly of his jeans, reached inside, and slipped her warm hand around to cup his ass. William groaned loudly as she used the other to curl her nimble fingers around the hot length of his engorged cock and started to stroke. He threw his head back and cursed as she ran her hand up and down in slow, tormenting caresses, and brushed her thumb over the swollen tip. She squeezed his ass, grazed his nipple with her teeth, and then soothed the tiny hurt with her wicked tongue.

Just as William thought he was going to lose control and come, Layla released him from her grasp, and those talented hands wandered back up to the unyielding planes of his chest. Lust clawed at him insistently as he grappled with the animal need to claim her, and just when he thought he couldn't bear it for one more second, Layla whispered two words that severed his resolve.

"Fuck me."

———∾∾———

Carnal desire was all that Layla could feel as the blinding pull of lust fogged her brain. The touch of William's flesh against hers was mouthwateringly erotic, and stroking the weight of him in the palm of her hand made her wet and wanting. Yet any control she thought she had faltered when the moon-glow eyes of his clan zeroed in on her as soon as she uttered those two tiny words. *Fuck me.*

Fire flashed hard and fast up her spine. The juncture between her legs tingled and pulsed. She shoved at the rock hard muscles of his shoulders, pushing him into the oversized chair as he grasped her hips and pulled her down with him. Frantic to have him inside her, needing him to satisfy the throbbing ache between her legs, she straddled him, positioned the head of his enormous erection against her slick folds, and threaded her fingers through the long strands of his hair.

Eyes locked, she hovered there for a moment as his fingers dug into the soft flesh of her hips, and she savored the delicious torture of waiting just one... more... second.

Painstakingly slowly, Layla captured his warm, firm mouth with hers. She sank onto his rock hard shaft inch by agonizing inch until she had him buried deep inside of her tight, wet channel. The breath rushed from their lungs in unison as he filled her and stretched her farther than she thought possible. They stayed there for a moment, locked together in the most intimate way, as her body adjusted to the sheer size of him.

Firefly. He whispered into her mind, which heightened the physical sensation in an enticing, erotic way.

Now this part of being Amoveo was something she could get used to.

William sat up, still buried in her, and feasted on one rosy nipple, sending searing and purely hedonistic pleasure—*everywhere*. Layla tangled her fingers in his hair, held his head to her bosom, and arched back as he suckled and nipped at her eagerly.

Then she began to move.

Knees braced against the sides of the chair, Layla rose and fell time and again, sliding her tight sheath up and down in agonizingly slow strokes. White hot friction sparked and raced through her sweat-covered body.

As her pace increased, he filled her more completely than any man ever had.

Other men? Had there ever been any others? All she could remember was him. That fierce look in his eyes, the ones that reminded her of a moonlit sky, the hair that slipped through her fingers like silk, and the flawlessly formed body that would make the Viking Gods proud.

How could she ever think of another?

Damn him.

William rained kisses over her collarbone and along the hollow of her throat as she continued to writhe and buck against him. He ran his hands up her back and down again. His eager mouth found hers and kissed her like he would never get enough. It was a frenzy, both of them tasting and touching as if this moment could disappear in a blink.

Passion edged with desperation created a potent combination. Savage desire built and coiled tightly inside, as the pleasure rushed through her veins at a brutal pace. Her breathing came in quick, panting gasps. She rode him furiously, chasing the rush of orgasmic gratification that was so frustratingly close. It was the orgasm she'd been chasing since the day he found her and started haunting her dreams.

William's strong hands held onto her hips, anchoring her to him as he pumped into her, matching her frenzied rhythm. With one final stroke they cried out in unison and tumbled together over the precipice and into oblivion.

Layla collapsed, breathless and limp, on top of William's equally spent body, but he was still locked tightly inside of her as the tiny aftershocks rocked and quivered their exhausted forms. She rested her head on his shoulder, and her eyes fluttered closed while his fingers brushed an achingly tender trail up and down her back. With their slick bodies nestled together in the most intimate of positions in the large, soft chair, she couldn't help but notice every inch of exposed flesh where their bodies met.

She noticed something else as well.

Their energy signatures were more than just connected—the buzzing that had accompanied it before was no longer there. The connection was there to be sure, but somehow, it seemed smoother... almost seamless... as if she could no longer tell where his ended and hers began.

Panic bubbled up as Layla realized the consequences of what they'd just done. It was happening—the mating process, or whatever the hell they called it—it was happening. Without a word, she scrambled off William and pulled her sweatshirt and pants onto her quickly cooling body with record speed.

She knew William was watching her. He'd obviously sensed her panic and need to escape, but he didn't have to have a bonded energy signature for that. A blind monkey could've picked up on her sudden desire to bolt.

Layla not only felt his eyes on her, but she sensed the change in *his* demeanor as well. That cold, calculated, arrogant bastard switch had been flipped again, and he was studying her like she was some defendant in one of his court cases.

"You can relax. We're not officially mated yet," he said in that irritatingly calm voice. The one that made her want to throttle him. She hated being told to *relax*, and it only served to piss her off. "We didn't say the ceremonial bonding rites," he continued nonchalantly.

William stood from the chair that she'd never be able to look at again without getting wet, adjusted himself, and zipped his fly as if they hadn't just been fucking like a couple of horny teenagers. She'd barely registered that he never took off his pants entirely—not that it had slowed them down. She tried not to admire that smooth, beautiful skin, but the memories of lapping and nipping at his flesh would be emblazoned into her memory in living color.

Layla stoked the fire that had just about gone out in an effort to keep from drooling over him—again—but she couldn't help it. She glanced over as he scooped up his shirt and shrugged it on and blushed when he caught her ogling him.

"So you don't have to worry." His brown eyes narrowed and latched onto hers as he slipped the buttons back into place. "All we did was fuck."

Layla's heart skipped a beat, and her throat tightened. Even though she managed to keep her face a calm mask of detachment, it didn't matter. He knew what he'd said had hurt her—she couldn't hide it from him.

For the first time in her life, she was exposed to another living being, and it terrified her.

His hands dropped to his side, and he kept his intense stare locked on her face. "That is what you wanted, isn't it?" His voice dropped to barely above a whisper, and the lines in his face deepened as he moved slowly toward her. "Just a fuck, right?"

Layla couldn't move as he closed the distance between them. Her feet seemed to be nailed to the floor, and even though her brain told her to get the hell away from him, her body wouldn't cooperate.

She was going to get hurt.

Her head kept telling her that. Hell. History told her that. Getting mixed up with an Amoveo mate was a one-way ticket to pain and suffering—that was what she'd always been told. However, looking into his warm eyes the cracks of doubt widened. Maybe he was different.

Maybe wasn't a good enough answer to risk her heart.

"Yes," she whispered. Layla cleared her throat and stuck her chin out defiantly. "Yes, you gave me exactly what I asked for—a great fuck." She tore her gaze from his and fixed the fireplace grate, even though it didn't need fixing.

William took Layla's hands in his, interrupting her busy work, and turned her to face him. He cradled her small hands in his significantly larger ones, pulled her close, and held her hands over his heart, which thrummed strong and steady.

"It *was* great," he said gently. "In fact, I think referring to it as great, or trying to describe it as anything less than mind-blowing, would be insulting to us both." He lifted her chin with their joined hands and fixed his serious gaze on hers. "But you and I both know it was more than just some random fuck."

She knew he was right, and that's what grabbed her by the soul and wouldn't let go. The onslaught of emotions was almost more than she could handle, and her energy waves zipped through the room like out of control firecrackers.

"So the question is what do we do now?" he asked,

brushing butterfly strokes along her hands with his thumbs.

Lost in the shelter of his embrace and trapped in that laser-sharp gaze, several possibilities raced through her mind. Running away or pushing him away—those were her knee-jerk reactions—but along the edges of her mind was the tiny voice of hope that whispered... *try*.

She wanted to try and tell him, intellectually verbalize what she was thinking. She knew William could read her emotions, and he could hear her telepathically when she allowed him to, but how could she explain it to him? Maybe the Amoveo didn't need to put their feelings into words, but she wasn't entirely Amoveo, and at the moment, her human half was analyzing the shit out of her feelings.

Before she could gather the nerve to tell him what she was thinking, a log popped loudly in the fireplace, and sent sparks flying. Trance broken, they both jumped, startled by the sudden noise, and a smile crept across Layla's face as she stamped at the spark that had escaped onto the braided rug.

"I guess that answers that question." She laughed as she smothered the pesky ember. "We keep Rosie's house from burning down."

Layla leaned over and adjusted the fireplace screen to be sure no more embers escaped. As she stood and brushed her hands off on her jeans, something caught her eye above the mantle. It looked like an envelope sticking out from behind her photograph of the cottage.

"What's this?" She reached up and pulled the

mysterious missive from behind the portrait, and her blood went cold when she saw her name scrawled in bright red letters.

"Holy shit," she whispered, holding the white envelope in shaking hands. "It's for me."

Chapter 12

WILLIAM'S SENSES INSTANTLY WENT ON HIGH ALERT AT the sight of Layla's name written across the front of the envelope. Maybe Rosie left it? Raife? As the various possibilities raced through his mind, everything came to a shuddering halt when Layla flipped it over, and he saw what held it closed.

It was the wax seal of the Council.

"Wait," he shouted and took the envelope from Layla, before she could open it. "It can't be."

"Hey!" She tried to take the letter back, but he rushed over to the side table and turned on the lamp. "What is going on, William? Why are *you* so freaked out?" Layla asked as she followed him. "I don't think anyone is going to jump out of the envelope and kill me."

William barely heard her above the pounding of his heart and the blood that rushed through his veins. He leaned in closely to inspect the red wax seal with the scrolled letter *A* stamped in the middle, hoping and praying that he was wrong, and that the light was playing tricks on him. However, no matter how much he squinted, it wasn't going to change.

The letter was from a member of the Council.

William let out a slow breath and hoped that he didn't come off as unhinged as he felt, but one glance at Layla's worried expression told him he hadn't managed to hide a thing. He held the envelope out and struggled to keep his voice as calm as possible.

"Have you ever seen this seal?" he asked as she took it from him.

"No." Layla frowned as she looked from William back to the seal. "But I'm assuming, based on your reaction, that you have."

"Yes." He nodded and gestured to the couch. "I think we should sit down."

"Don't treat me like a child." Layla held her ground. "What is it?"

William glowered at Layla and cursed under his breath, but she didn't move. Damn this woman. Why did she fight him on everything?

"That letter is from someone on the Council," he said bluntly. "And the energy signature on it…"

Layla rubbed the envelope between her fingers. Her eyes shifted, and her nostrils flared as she made the connection. "It's the same person who was here the night Rosie was attacked."

Layla's jaw fell open, and her large eyes flicked back to the envelope. "Okay, if this is from the person who was here, then they hurt Rosie. So why the hell would I want anything from them?" she said furiously.

"Because there was more than one person here that night."

"What?" Her eyes burned brightly.

"When I was surveying the property earlier, I discovered two energy signatures tangled together. One stronger than the other, so much so that it masked the weaker one." He glanced at the envelope. "Whoever left this note for you was here that night, and if they used that seal, then they're on the Council. That's the only thing we know for sure."

"I think I'll sit down now." She backed up and sank into their oversized chair without taking her eyes off the seal. "I'm freaked out." She looked at William through confused eyes. "This should freak me out, right? I'm not overreacting."

"No." He shook his head and kept his sights on her. "You are not overreacting at all. That seal is from a ring that is worn only by our Council members. Obviously, your existence has not been kept a secret as we thought."

Her energy waves whipped through the room, reflecting the same apprehension that he was feeling. She stared at the envelope and let out a slow breath. William couldn't stand the space between them, and the urge to comfort her had become too strong to ignore. He took a seat on the arm of the large chair next to Layla and rubbed her back reassuringly.

"Here goes nothing," she murmured.

Layla straightened in her seat and gathered her resolve as she peeled open the envelope and broke the seal with a thin snapping sound. She pulled the folded card out and opened it with care as William leaned over her shoulder and read the flowery script along with her.

> *Dear Layla,*
>
> *I am sorry that I must write this letter with such secrecy, but it remains uncertain who can be trusted. I know you must feel abandoned, but I wanted you to know that I have been watching you grow and thrive over the years. It's clear that we chose the perfect safe house for you to*

grow up in, and someday, I hope we can thank Rosie for all the things that she has done for you—for all of us. Before his mating with your mother, your father was a high-ranking member of our clan, and his efforts to keep you safe cost him his life.

I do not tell you this to punish you or to hurt you, but to be sure that you understand the danger that you are in. I want nothing more than to fulfill my brother's wishes and bring you into the fold of our clan, but I fear it isn't safe—at least not until you bond with your mate. I know that William has found you and that you are reluctant to give in to what the universe intends, but I beg you to keep your mind and heart open. The Purists have become increasingly aggressive, and it is imperative that you have all of your wits about you.

Embrace Your Fate.
—xo Bianca

They both sat for a few minutes reading and rereading the note, but it wasn't long before William broke the silence.

"Bianca Wayland," he said evenly. "She sits on the Council as the female representative for the Cheetah Clan. I can't believe Bianca would hurt Rosie after all the lengths she went to keeping you hidden safely here," he said tightly as apprehension crept up his back. "There was someone else here besides her that night, and that has to be the person who attacked Rosie. Bianca would never hurt the woman who protected you."

"Bullshit," Layla shouted. She crumpled the note in her hands as her energy waves increased in tempo and temperature, and her body shook with fury. She whipped her head up, and her glowing, gold and green eyes zeroed in on William. "This is such bullshit!"

William watched with genuine confusion as she stood, threw the note across the room, and tore her fingers through her wild red curls. She paced back and forth in front of the fireplace with her hands curled into tight fists, and the air in the room thickened in response to her emotions.

William stood slowly and kept his gaze fixed on Layla, waiting for what she would do next. Had they read the same note? He was saddened by it, and perhaps expected her to cry, as much as he dreaded the idea of it, but anger? Now that was unexpected. Would he ever figure this woman out?

"Layla," he said gently. "I understand that you're upset, but—"

"So this chick is my aunt, I guess," she spat. "It looks like she was here but probably didn't hurt Rosie. However, there's still someone out there who did. By the way, if she was here, why didn't she help Rosie?"

"I don't know." William's jaw clenched. "We'll find out who else was here, but at least you have some kind of answers from this letter."

"Are you kidding me? All I have are more questions." She put her hands on her hips and looked at him as if he'd just sprouted an extra head. "How would you like to be tricked and cheated out of your choices? These people—your people." She pointed at him accusingly, and her eyes flashed with anger as she stalked toward him. "They moved me around like a pawn on a chessboard and played with my life, as if it didn't make a damn bit of difference, as if I had no feelings about anything.

"She tells me my father is dead in a freaking letter? She lets me go on all these years thinking that he abandoned me and that I wasn't wanted." Her voice cracked with emotion. "Do you have any idea how that feels, to think that I was tossed away like defective trash?"

Her body shook with fury, and her energy waves pummeled him harshly, causing the glasses to skitter nervously along the weathered surface of the coffee table. The room pulsed with years of pent-up anger and frustration; the storm of her emotions filled the house and tore at his heart.

"No one asked me what I wanted," she shouted with tear-filled eyes. "No one thought that it would be hell on earth to grow up a freak, like some half-breed mess who doesn't belong in either world. I'm not exactly human, but I'm definitely not Amoveo," she let out a harsh laugh, and her jaw clenched with determination. "I-I can't even shift."

William's face softened, and his heart broke at the wounded tone of her voice as she admitted what she'd been trying so desperately to hide. She stood her ground, eyes blazing, daring him to say something and looking for a fight.

However, William wasn't taking the bait.

"I never could, and maybe I never will. Is that what you want?" Her shaky voice dipped to just above a whisper. "To be tied down to some weakling for eternity?"

The suffering written across her face grabbed him

by the throat. How could she think that? How could he make her understand that she was everything?

"Layla," he whispered. William reached out to take her in his arms, but she shoved him away and pushed past him toward the front door. "Please wait."

"Don't." She whipped around to face him and held her hand out to stop him from coming closer. Her eyes glowed brightly in the dimly lit hallway and reflected the swirling turmoil within. "Rosie is hurt because of me, because whoever hurt her was probably here looking for me." She swiped at her eyes. "I'm nothing more than a mistake that needs to be corrected."

As she ran out the front door and into the pitch black night, William reached out and whispered into her mind.

You are not a mistake. You are the answer.

———ᴡᴡ———

Tears blurred her vision as she bolted blindly out the door into the chilly damp night and ran as fast as she could toward the woods. Her bare feet pounded through the wet grass up the hill, but she hardly felt it. The only thing she could feel was the all-consuming rage of being what she was and having no control. She barely noticed the biting cold of the wind whipping over her tear-stained face, and only one word thundered through her mind as she bolted through the moonlit woods.

Why?

Her legs pumped faster as questions raced through her mind. Why did they hurt Rosie? Why did people she never met want to kill her simply because of what she was? Why didn't they tell her sooner that her father didn't abandon her? Why couldn't she shift like Raife and Tati? Why couldn't she give William her heart? Why was she such a freaking mess?

She raced along the leaf-strewn path as twigs and pine needles spit up from her heels. The trees went by in a distorted blur, and the image of her cheetah filled her mind. She saw everything that she was able to become in the dream realm—the golden coat spotted with black, sharp claws, and a mouth full of razor-sharp teeth that could tear through tender flesh like butter.

Her cheetah likeness blazed brightly and held firm in her mind's eye as she sprinted through the darkness at inhuman speed. Fury flooded her mind and flashed fiercely through her small human body as static electricity rippled over her skin with dazzling, vivid intensity, and white lights danced behind her eyes.

Everything shimmered, and for the first time in her life, the world came into perfect focus as her body undulated, swelled, and stretched into the unrestrained form of her clan.

In one giant leap—she was free.

An unfamiliar strength coursed through her veins as she ran on four legs instead of two. Her claws dug deliciously into the soft earth, giving her the traction she needed to shoot like a bullet through the dark forest. Her furred body pulsated brilliantly with power, and her muscles worked, stretched, and strained in the most refreshing way.

She'd never felt more alive or more in control of her body, her life, or her mind. For the first time, everything made sense. She no longer felt out of step or behind the curve—this body, this form… it was always there, lurking, and waiting to be discovered.

Layla snarled and bolted around the bend of the familiar path, and within seconds the old cottage from her photograph came into view. Like her sprinting cheetah counterparts in nature, her burst of speed was not for distance.

Heart hammering her in her chest, she slowed to a trot and padded over to the entrance of the rundown cottage, which had been her playhouse as a child. When the kids teased her at school for her freckles and red hair, or when Raife and Tati would shift and run in the forest together, this is where she would come to lick her proverbial wounds.

She sensed William's arrival before she saw him. His energy signature, tied firmly to hers, signaled to Layla as he flew closer. Breathing heavily, her long tail switching slowly behind her, Layla arched her neck and looked to the sky in search of William. She was surprisingly eager to have him see her in her clan form, and she wasn't sure if her heart was racing from apprehension or exhaustion. Perhaps it was a bit of both.

When she saw his graceful form silhouetted against the full moon as he circled above, the world around her fell away. He shrieked loudly, announcing his presence to the rest of the night creatures—or warning them— she wasn't sure which. Layla sat on her haunches and watched as he soared down to her, his wings pumped with unmistakable strength as his moon-glow eyes shone brilliantly in the night. His deep baritone voice floated in her mind. *Verto.*

Layla watched with genuine awe as he shimmered, shifted in midair, and implemented a sure-footed landing on two feet directly in front of her. Radiating raw power, he towered over her in his human form. The stern look carved into his face and the thick turmoil of his energy waves left little to the imagination.

"Why would you run out here alone?"

I can take care of myself. Layla stood and circled slowly around William, while the two inspected one another. *I did that for a long time before you showed up.*

He made a small sound of understanding but clearly not in agreement. "Looks like you can shift after all." He kept his sharp gaze fixed on her as she stalked around him. "You didn't have to use the ancient language like most of our people do. Samantha and Kerry can shift without it as well, so it seems hybrids have some unique advantages over pure-blooded Amoveo."

A growl rumbled low in the back of her throat. *That must really chap some pure-blooded Amoveo ass.* Layla turned her back on William and entered the open doorway of the old cottage with her lover close behind. *I have to admit this was definitely worth the wait. My whole body is buzzing, and I feel like I could kick some major butt.* She threw a glance over one shoulder and snarled. *So you better watch out, or I just might start with you.* Her teasing voice touched his mind with an unsettling familiarity.

The interior of the tiny, one-room cottage was practically empty. The wood floors had all but rotted away with weeds and dirt poking through the broken planks. The fireplace overflowed with a mass of leaves and a nest from some kind of animal. The yellow floral curtains Layla had put in when a young girl were tattered and faded from years of exposure. Even the table and chairs she used to inspect her photographs was faded and warped, but the old place still felt like a second home.

Familiar white moonlight filtered through the cracks in the roof, giving the entire place an ethereal glow. The funny hint of energy she always sensed was there, embedded in the property... or maybe it was only in her memory. Whatever it was, it made her feel safe.

Layla took a deep breath, closed her glowing eyes, visualized her human form, and within seconds, she stood on two feet instead of four.

Light-headed, but no longer fur-covered, Layla smiled at her newly mastered ability and stretched her arms over her head. Her muscles felt more alive and energized than ever before.

"I could definitely get used to this," she said as she reached over and touched her fingers to the floor. Bent over, back to the doorway, Layla loosened the muscles in her legs.

"Me too," William said with his eyes fixed firmly on her ass.

Her heart skipped a beat at the sight of William standing there watching her. He filled the doorway of the cottage the same way he filled every other space he entered—completely. His sharp, glowing eyes tracked every move she made, but he said nothing as she straightened and walked around the cottage, absently touching the fluttering curtains in the open window. Standing on the opposite side of the room, he gave her what she knew was a false sense of security.

She'd allowed him into her body, and now into her hideaway.

What was next... her heart?

Layla turned her back on William and looked out the open window at the moon-dappled forest. All the memories of her childhood and feelings of inadequacy came flooding back in vivid color, and she let out a gentle laugh. *No more*. She'd shifted, after all these years... she'd done it... and she knew that William was partially responsible.

Layla nibbled on her lip and folded her arms over her chest, wishing this big sweatshirt really could swallow her up. "I used to come out here all the time as a kid. Whenever I felt like a freak, when Sylvia and her flunkies gave me grief, or when I got lonely, I would come to this place, and somehow, everything felt okay," she said without turning around.

Layla swallowed the lump forming in her throat and kept her gaze fixed on the woods. She didn't have the nerve to look at William. At every turn he'd been there to help, and she'd done nothing but run or hide. *Coward*.

"You knew, didn't you?" she asked quietly. "You knew I'd never shifted before."

"Yes." Layla glanced over her shoulder to find he'd stepped into the cabin and was looking around the small space. "I suspected it when we were in the dream realm, but the other night at the bar"—he gazed at her—"when you started to shift involuntarily, that was when I knew."

Layla made a small sound of understanding and looked at the curtain she was worrying between her fingers. "It didn't bother you?" She leaned against the rotting window sill and looked him in the face again. "It didn't upset you to know that I was so... inept?"

"You are not inept," he said as he slowly closed the distance between them. "You shifted tonight, as I knew you eventually would, and I agree with you." He smiled and took her face in his hands. "It was definitely worth the wait, Firefly."

Layla's brow wrinkled with confusion as she tried to ignore the pull of desire that thrummed strong and steady between them—so much for thinking that a quick tumble would satisfy the crazy attraction she felt. She couldn't have been more wrong, because it had only grown in its intensity.

When he brushed his thumb along her cheek, she heard him whisper that odd nickname along the edges of her mind, *Firefly*. A delicious tingling fluttered over her breasts, and heat flared between her legs.

"Why do you call me that?" she asked in that shamefully lusty voice that didn't sound like her. She covered his hand with hers and searched his eyes for answers. "Why do you call me Firefly?"

Every cell in Layla's body flamed to life, and her heart hammered in her chest in perfect time with the pounding pulse of their mingled energy signatures. William loomed over her, his long blond hair fell across his forehead, and she couldn't help but brush it back and tangle one hand in those soft locks.

His lips curved into a smile as he strummed featherlight strokes along her cheek. "You are my firefly, Layla," he whispered without taking his eyes off hers. "You are the beautiful and elusive pinpoint of radiance that lit up the darkness and called me home."

Her throat clogged with emotion, and the cabin swirled with the intense pulse of their combined energies, sending visible ripples like a heat wave through the confined space.

"I love you, Layla." His mouth set in a firm line, and his jaw clenched. "Fate or imprinting, or whatever the hell my people want to call it—*none* of that can *make* me love you." His voice dropped to a harsh whisper. "I love *you*, Layla. I love your stubborn streak, the way you love Rosie, Raife, and Tati. I admire your desire for independence, and Lord knows, I love your moxie." He bent down, brushed his lips against hers, and murmured, "Fate didn't make me love you... *you* did."

His name rushed from her lips on a sigh, and tears pricked her eyes as she greedily captured his mouth with hers. Layla deepened their kiss as William cupped her bottom and lifted her easily off the ground. She wrapped her legs around his waist and clung to him as he pinned her up against the wall. Desperate to get closer, to show him how much he meant to her, she ripped his shirt open, sending buttons flying across the room.

Still too afraid to say what she wanted... all she could do was show him.

Lips suckling, tongues tangling, she drank greedily from his perfect mouth and stroked his bare chest. *I need you inside of me. Now.* When she touched her mind to his, he moaned and trailed kisses down her throat as he reached up under her shirt and palmed her sensitive breast. He rolled her nipple between his talented fingers and sent her an image of their naked intertwined bodies. "Verto," he murmured against her neck.

Static flickered around them, and within seconds their clothes were gone, and they were naked. A wicked smile curled across William's flushed face before he captured her lips with his, reached down, and slipped himself inside her.

She hooked her ankles behind his back, anchoring to him, as he held her ass and pumped into her with slow, deliberate strokes. Her bare breasts crushed against his chest as his mouth devoured hers time and again.

White-hot pleasure blazed over her skin as he thrust his hips and filled her over and over. Layla reached up with one hand and grabbed the edge of the open window for support as he picked up pace and drove into her, harder and faster. Then just when she thought she'd reached the peak, he stopped and carried her to the small table while still buried deep in her tight channel.

"I have to taste you," William said gruffly.

He set her down on the table and disengaged from the warmth of her body, but before she could say a word, he dropped to his knees, spread her legs wide, and put his mouth on her. Layla cried out as his tongue found her most sensitive spot. She lay back and basked in the pleasure that flared through her body in lightning-fast streaks.

She threaded her fingers through his hair, while he feasted on her and worked that sensitive nub with his devilish tongue. His arms, like two bands of steel, held her to the table as she writhed and bucked her hips furiously beneath his unrelenting assault.

"Please," she said between panting breaths. "I want you inside me."

William trailed kisses along her thigh, and his eyes smiled at her over the edge of her leg. "My pleasure."

Layla scooted off the table and stood in front of William, but before he could pick her up, she spun around, leaned over the tabletop, spread her legs, and offered herself to him. That was all the invitation William needed.

With one sure stroke, he drove deep. He held her hips as he thrust into her again and again. Every time he filled and stretched her, it sent wicked licks of fire through her body, and the coil of lust tightened with every breathtaking pass, until finally, he surged into her one last time as the orgasm crested and carried them over the edge.

Sweating, panting, and spent, William collapsed over Layla but was careful not to crush her. He leaned on one elbow and whispered into her ear, "This table is not the most comfortable place to rest."

"I know." Layla laughed as he placed a kiss on her hair. "I think I have about fifty splinters in my ass from this table."

"I believe I can remedy that and find us a more comfortable spot."

Just as she was going to ask him what he was planning on doing, the image of his bedroom at the farm floated into her mind. The eyelet curtains, the wrought iron bed frame, and the warm glow from the antique lamps on the nightstand, all shone brightly in her mind as William whispered, "Verto."

Static electricity. Displacement. A subtle breeze.

Moments later, they were lying on a downy mattress and covered by the familiar quilt of the guest room. A huge smile cracked Layla's face as she lay in bed naked and wrapped in William's arms. Propped on one elbow, he had a look of satisfaction as he coiled one of her long curls around his finger and smiled at her.

She narrowed her eyes. "You think you're pretty

slick don't you, counselor?" Layla held the covers over her naked breasts as he played with her hair.

"I have my moments," he said quietly. "You should get some sleep. We still have a lot of unanswered questions. Malcolm and Dante will arrive with their mates in the morning, and something tells me things are going to get worse before they get better." His serious brown eyes latched onto hers. "We still don't know who attacked Rosie, and until we know who that is, I'm not letting you go anywhere without me. Agreed?"

Layla studied his face and nodded silently. She knew there was little point in arguing. She'd do whatever she had to for Rosie, and if it made William feel better to think she'd follow his orders, then so be it. She gave him a quick kiss and turned onto her side as he snuggled up behind and spooned her body against his. As they lay with their bodies nestled together, she listened to the steady pattern of William's breathing as he fell asleep, and she struggled to shield her emotions.

She tried not to think about the fact that he didn't say the ceremonial mating rites when they'd made love in the cabin. She thought for sure that since he'd pledged his love, he would've bound them together forever. She'd been with him again, knowing that it was likely he would do it… but he didn't.

Layla expected to feel relieved, but she felt something far more surprising… disappointment.

Chapter 13

THE SMELL OF BACON FRYING FILLED THE BRIGHT country kitchen and sent William's stomach rumbling. He padded around silently on bare feet as he cooked breakfast for Layla and their guests. Dante, Kerry, Samantha, and Malcolm were due to arrive. He tuned in on Layla's energy signature and found that she was finally awake and in the shower. She'd looked so serene this morning that he couldn't bear to wake her up, and hopefully, she wouldn't mind that he was making himself at home in Rosie's kitchen.

He smiled at the memory of Layla sleeping peacefully. He'd never get tired of seeing her red curls splayed over snow-white sheets, or the graceful curve of her bare shoulder that peeked out from under the covers. He warmed as he recalled everything they'd shared last night—she was beginning to trust him, but she still had doubts.

He'd wanted nothing more than to say the ceremonial mating rites and bind her to him for eternity, but no matter how much he desired it, he couldn't do it—*wouldn't* do it—until she was ready. He wanted her to be certain of what she was doing and understand that there was no going back. She had to be willing to bind her life to his—it had to be *her* choice. As William set the table for breakfast, he couldn't shut out the nagging question. *What if she never did?*

The sound of tires crunching up the gravel driveway captured his attention, and he sensed the familiar energy signatures of his friends. Within seconds, Layla's panicked voice whipped into his mind. *Who's here? Jesus Christ! William, how many are there?*

He smiled. As difficult as it was to hear her that alarmed, it was also a blessing. She picked up on their energy signatures as swiftly as he did, and that was one sense she would need to master for her own safety.

Yes, it's Malcolm and Dante. He touched his mind to her, sending her soothing energy as he looked out the window at the approaching car. *And as I suspected they would, they brought their mates with them as well.*

They came in a car? Isn't that slumming it for the Amoveo? Her jab sliced into his mind with all the sass she'd intended.

William sighed audibly and shook his head at her clear annoyance. *First of all, they've never imprinted on this location. Secondly, we can't just materialize in and out of places all the time. We have managed to stay hidden for hundreds of years, and that wouldn't have happened if we were constantly appearing out of nowhere.* He softened his tone and sent her subtle waves of reassurance. *Come downstairs, so you can meet them.*

She shut her mind to him on a curse, which only served to broaden his smile. He didn't know exactly why her mild irritation was amusing, but it was. Perhaps it was due to a new comfort level they had with each other, or perhaps it was because he enjoyed needling her. Maybe it was both.

William tossed the dish towel over his shoulder and opened the front door to greet his friends who were already walking up the steps. However, instead of the warm embraces he expected, and was mildly uncomfortable with, he was greeted by four shocked individuals who stared at him as if he'd shapeshifted into a squirrel.

Dante and Malcolm, overnight bags in hand, looked him up and down and shook their heads in disbelief as both women gave each other a knowing glance.

"Looks like someone finally figured out how to loosen you up," Samantha said with a wink as she tucked her long blond hair behind her ear.

William pushed his hair off his reddening face and snatched the dish towel off his shoulder in a vain attempt to straighten his rumpled appearance. His button-down shirt wasn't tucked into his jeans and looked like he'd slept in it—even though there'd been little sleeping last night. His lips curved at the memories.

Dante let out a slow whistle. "Oh man." He laughed. "I never thought I'd live to see the day that William Fleury wears anything but a three-piece suit." He pointed at his feet. "Holy shit! He's barefoot too."

"If you must know—" William sniffed and wiped his hands with the towel. "I've been busy making you ingrates breakfast, but I have half a mind to feed it to the horses."

"Barefoot *and* in the kitchen?" Malcolm chimed in. "You're not pregnant, are you?"

William cast him his signature glare, but it did little to snuff out their amusement at his expense, but the truth was that he couldn't blame them. They were right. He looked and felt nothing like the man he'd been a few days ago. He was no longer weighed down by the worry of never finding his mate, and it showed in more ways than one. He was lighter, less encumbered, and it was reflected in everything from the way he dressed to the way he wore his hair—and it was all because of Layla.

"Leave him alone, boys," Kerry added. The statuesque beauty with the raven hair linked her arm with Dante's.

"Kerry's right," Samantha added. "Something tells me he's got his hands full enough without you two giving him a hard time."

"Your mates are very perceptive women." He bowed his head and stepped back to allow them entry into the house. "Welcome to Layla's home, *ladies*."

William filled them in on the latest developments over a hearty breakfast, and he was relieved to find they were as surprised by several of the revelations as he was.

"Interesting," Dante mused before sipping his coffee. "Raife and Tatiana are the first hybrids that we've encountered who were able to shift before finding their mates. Maybe it's because they're twins, and their combined energies helped bolster each other?"

"I'm more curious about the chick who left the note—Bianca," Kerry added. She turned her large brown eyes to William. "I understand why Layla is so pissed. People have been playing with her life and taking away her choices." She let out a slow breath. "I can totally relate."

William watched Dante take her hand in his as she smiled lovingly back. The unfamiliar feeling of jealousy crawled up his back. Would Layla ever be that comfortable with him?

"Speaking as the other hybrid in the room, I agree with Kerry on both counts. I have a question," Samantha said as her big blue eyes flicked around the table at them. "Is anyone else a little unsettled by the fact that we have a Council member hiding three hybrids, and obviously keeping it from Richard and the rest of the Council?"

They all looked at her and then at each other.

"Hello," she sang. "If Bianca knows about Layla being here, then she *must* know about Raife and Tatiana, right?" She retrieved the pot of coffee from the counter. "William, didn't you say that in her note she referred to this house as a 'safe house'?"

William furrowed his brow and frowned. "Well, yes, she did."

"Hmm," she murmured as she poured more coffee for herself and Malcolm. "I wonder how many other 'safe houses' there are?" Samantha sat back down, and Malcolm rubbed her back reassuringly. "What really bothers me is that Richard told the Council members about the Purist movement and their crimes. So why would Bianca continue to keep these safe houses, and the hybrids living in them, a secret? Why wouldn't she have told Richard and the rest of the Council?"

She looked around the room at each. William nodded in agreement as understanding washed over him, and the cold hand of dread ran up his belly.

"It could only mean that what we've feared the most is true." William looked from Malcolm to Dante, while the gravity of the situation settled. "There are Purists on the Council."

"I thought the Council members wanted to protect us?" All eyes turned to Layla.

She stood in the doorway of the kitchen with her arms folded tightly over her chest, regarding them through serious green eyes. She had never met another Amoveo or hybrid other than William, Raife, and Tati, and she had no idea what to expect.

She'd met Dante and Kerry on the photo shoot in New Orleans, but somehow, they seemed different now, more at ease with one another. Kerry was almost as tall as her auburn-haired mate, who looked like he could model alongside her any day of the week. She gave them a tight smile and nod.

Layla's gaze instantly went to the other two she hadn't met and could only assume were Samantha and Malcolm. The curvy, stunning blonde had smiling, blue eyes and an open, welcoming energy signature. Her mate, Malcolm, was as gorgeous as she would expect any Amoveo man to be.

Shit. Did the Amoveo even make unattractive people? They were all good-looking, and even though she should feel at home—after all it was her house—she still felt like a freak. *Raggedy Ann doesn't belong in this dollhouse.*

She knew William would sense her apprehension as her energy signature rolled and tumbled through his. She flicked her eyes to his as he rose to greet her. Layla tugged at her plaid flannel shirt, wishing she'd put on something nicer than this old shirt and her jeans. These two women looked absolutely stunning, and she looked like a hayseed.

"Good morning." Taking her hand, he pulled her into the shelter of his embrace and placed a gentle kiss on her head.

As she studied each of their guests carefully, her body trembled in spite of her best efforts to keep her nervousness under control. *They're here to help, Firefly. You can trust them. I promise.* She didn't answer but glanced at him briefly before introducing herself.

"Hello again," she said with a quick wave to Kerry and Dante. "Weird, huh?" She shrugged, which only made William squeeze her tighter. *Awkward.*

"Hey." Kerry winked. "Good to see you again. It's a small world, isn't it? Last month you're shooting my layout, and this month we're practically related." She raised her coffee mug and smiled broadly. "Welcome to the family, girl."

"We haven't been properly introduced." Samantha hopped out of her chair, skirted the table, walked over, elbowed William out of the way, and proceeded to wrap Layla up in a hug. "It's so great to meet you."

"I should've warned you," Kerry said with a smile at Layla's shocked expression as she received the unexpected embrace. "She's a hugger."

"Good to meet you too." Layla looked at them through surprised eyes as she hugged her back.

"I feel like I just gained a long lost sister." Samantha released her from the embrace, wiped at her eyes, and sat down next to Malcolm.

"Oh yeah." Kerry laughed. "She's a crier too."

"Hey—" Samantha giggled and swatted her friend playfully. "I can't help it if I get emotional, and now that I'm pregnant, it's about a million times worse."

"Oh please." Kerry rolled her eyes and turned to Layla. "Don't let the pregnancy excuse fool you for a second. She's always been a crier, no matter what she tells you."

"Pregnant?" William shook Malcolm's hand, who was grinning from ear to ear. "That didn't take long—you two have only been mated for a couple of months."

Samantha turned beet red, but Malcolm gave them a bigger smile and draped his arm around Sam's shoulders. Layla observed the stunning couple and wondered how on earth they could be so happy, considering all the dangers that lurked around every corner.

After all, their child wouldn't be considered a pureblood, and that meant it would be fair game for the Purists. How they could intentionally bring a child into this crazy world?

"Congratulations," Layla said. She sat in the chair that William held out for her and snagged a piece of toast. Bland bread was about all her nervous stomach could handle.

"Have you heard from Raife this morning?" William asked.

"Yes," Layla said as she swallowed a bite of her toast. "Rosie is still sedated, and he's *still* refusing to leave her side. I told him we'd bring a change of clothes at some point today." She glanced around the room at the others, before looking back to William. "Besides, I'll need to introduce him to whoever is going to help cover the hospital. I'll feel much better when we get the person who hurt her." *And have fewer shifters in the house*.

"Well, let's take a look at the evidence so far," William said, ignoring her comment.

He poured some coffee and sat next to her at the unusually crowded table. Layla cast him a sidelong glance as she sipped her coffee. He'd obviously put his bossy boots back on and was in lawyer mode.

"The letter was written by Bianca Wayland, who claims to be your aunt, and we know she's a member of the Council. It doesn't make sense that she would harm Rosie." He looked pointedly at each of them. "What we *don't* know is who else was here that night and why they hurt Rosie, which is why I've asked you all for help."

"You've got it," Malcolm said firmly. "We're here until we've got more answers, and we know that Layla and her family are safe."

Layla's eyes flicked to Malcolm in surprise. *Her family*. He'd acknowledged her adoptive human and hybrid family with genuine respect; there was nothing coming from him that suggested anything else. She watched the way he doted on Samantha, and it was evident that he loved her, and she was clearly gaga for him. Maybe fate knew what it was doing.

William stood and cleared his dishes into the sink. "After I clean up, I'd like to take Dante and Malcolm around the property so they can develop some familiarity and imprint on the farm. I was hoping you could show Samantha and Kerry where they'll be staying, and then we can go to the hospital to see Raife and check on Rosie."

He turned to face her, and his penetrating brown eyes scrutinized hers with an intensity that had become oddly comfortable. When did that happen? Her throat suddenly dry, she sipped her coffee and nodded agreement.

After a record-fast clean up, William took the men out to survey the farm, which left Layla with two strangers in the kitchen. She rinsed her cup and set it in the overflowing dishwasher, before turning it on.

She discovered Samantha and Kerry waiting for her

in the front hall. She didn't make friends easily, and these two were already friends. It was never easy to be the third wheel, and it made her feel like an interloper in her own home.

Sam and Kerry were admiring her photographs.

"They're gorgeous," Samantha breathed, snapping Layla from the dismal thoughts. She stood and gave Layla a huge smile. "You are so talented. I can't wait to see the shots you took of Kerry on the bayou."

"William said that you get psychic impressions from photographs," Kerry said bluntly.

Layla's startled eyes flew to Kerry's face. No one other than her family knew about her gift, so it wasn't exactly something she was used to talking about.

"Don't bug out." She laughed. "I have second sight when I touch people, and Sam's artwork carries her energy signature." She shrugged and threw her hands up in mock defeat. "We're a bunch of freaks. What can I tell ya?"

"Yeah." Layla relaxed her shoulders, and a faint smile cracked her face. "I think that's why I'm beginning to like you."

She did like Kerry and appreciated her direct nature, because she needed more guessing games like a hole in the head. Both women were stunning, which was expected since Kerry was a model, but Sam was lovely in her own way. Samantha's positive energy was inescapable, and she had an infectious smile. Against all odds, Layla felt surprisingly comfortable around them, and hope flickered at the edges of her mind.

"So, what do you see?" Sam asked with genuine curiosity. "You took Kerry's pictures out in the bayou. Did you see anything different with her than you would see from a typical human?"

"Yeah." Layla sighed and shoved her hands in the pockets of her jeans. "With most people, I get images, pictures, and emotions." She scrunched up her face, searching for the right words. "It's kind of like a silent movie that only I can see." She glanced at Kerry, who was leaning against the banister and hanging on every word. "But when I took your picture, I saw your clan animal. The panther, right?"

"Yeah, girl." Kerry nodded slowly and grinned. "Why didn't you freak out and split?"

Layla shrugged. "I figured you were a hybrid like me, Raife, and Tati because your clan image was mixed with your human image. I saw both just like I always have with us." She let out a slow breath and looked from Sam to Kerry. "I was afraid to say anything. I didn't know if you even knew what you were, and I thought that if you *did* know, you might be linked up with other Amoveo. I didn't want to rock the boat." She cleared her throat. "But then William found me, and well… you know the rest. Come on." She headed to the stairs, desperate to change the subject. "I'll show you to your rooms."

As they headed upstairs, Layla made a mental list of the sleeping arrangements. Dante and Kerry could have Tatiana's old room, and Samantha and Malcolm could use her room. She knew that William would simply expect her to stay with him in his room, and given what they'd shared, she couldn't blame him for assuming that. However, she needed some space and some time to get her bearings.

"Hey, everything okay?" Samantha asked, concern

in her blue eyes. "You look like you're going to puke." She put one hand on her belly and grimaced. "Jeez. Your energy waves might make *me* puke but don't take that personally," she added quickly and put her palm against Layla's arm reassuringly. "I think it's the pregnancy. I'd gotten a pretty good handle on tuning out other people's emotions, but ever since I got pregnant—all bets are off." She made a face. "Is it us? I mean, having us here in your home? We did kind of invade your space."

"No." Layla gave her a friendly smile. "Well, I'm getting used to it." Sam came right out and acknowledged that their presence might be uncomfortable for her. She liked them more by the second. "You're here to help us, and I understand—about the energy waves—I mean," Layla said as she opened the door to Tatiana's room. "I noticed that my abilities are heightened since William found me."

"Yeah," Kerry snorted and took her bag into the room. "Just wait until you're fully mated." She wiggled her eyebrows. "Everything is heightened."

"So what is it?" Sam asked with genuine interest. "What's up? I mean aside from the obvious shit storm."

"Well," Layla began, "it's just that Kerry and Dante will be staying in here." She gestured around the room. "And I'm going to put you and Malcolm in my room." She nibbled on her lip and shoved one hand through her curls. "So that means…"

"Oh," Sam breathed as a look of realization washed over her face. She smiled and exchanged a knowing look with Kerry. "So you two haven't… y'know."

"We have… I mean… yes…" Layla's face heated with embarrassment as she stumbled over her words.

"We've had sex already." Layla cringed. How could she have just blurted it out?

She couldn't believe she was telling these women such personal things about herself and William. She shouldn't be this comfortable with them so quickly, but she was. Maybe it's because they were hybrids like her or because she'd missed having her sister around, but whatever the reason, she was grateful to have them to talk to. She was ready to go out of her mind, navigating the waters of her new life, and here were two women who had traveled the same bumpy seas. Who better to talk to?

"Hmm," Kerry mused. "Do tell." She elbowed Sam and winked. "I think we may have to whip up a pitcher of margaritas for this conversation." She made a tsking noise and feigned annoyance at her friend. "Too bad you're knocked up. Damn, girl, you're spoiling all the fun."

Smiling at their friendly banter, Layla walked out into the hallway and led them down to her bedroom. She swung the door open and was really glad that she'd taken the time to remake the bed and straighten out the room. She smiled. It would make Rosie proud.

She placed Sam's bag on the bed and spun to face them. "Actually, scratch that previous answer." Layla put her hands on her hips and sucked in a deep breath. "We didn't just have sex, ladies. We had hot, sweaty sexplosions," she said with more giddy excitement than she intended. To her relief, they didn't look at her like a sex-craved, horny hellcat, but like they knew exactly what she was talking about. "Somehow, the thought that we'll be sleeping in the same bed, sharing that space night after night… now… that is more intimacy than I'm used to," she said through a fading smile.

"It's a wild ride, and I'm *still* trying to figure it all out," Samantha said through a smile. "Kerry and I didn't even find out what we were, or who we were, until a couple months ago." She sat on the edge of the bed and tucked one leg under her. "Malcolm tells me that you, Raife, and Tati have known since you were kids."

"You mean you two *just* found out?" Layla fiddled with the bedpost. "Didn't you notice you were different?"

"I did," Kerry said, raising a hand as she flopped onto the bed and leaned on one elbow. "Before Dante and I found each other, I couldn't touch another human being without blinding pain. Good times." She gave two sarcastic thumbs up. "But once we connected, that all changed." She shrugged. "A missing piece to my puzzle was finally found, and everything just slipped into place."

"Your germ phobia, the one I read about in the papers, was a smoke screen." Layla nodded slowly and smiled. "Good cover story." She sat on the other side of the bed. "What about you, Sam?"

"I walked in the dream realm lots of times, but I didn't really understand it until Malcolm and I connected. I'm impressed that Raife and Tati have been able to shift. Kerry and I didn't shapeshift until after we were mated, so you really shouldn't feel weird about this." She reached out and took Layla's hand. "It gets easier. Honest."

Layla did feel better, and emotion tightened in her throat. "It already is." She looked at the women in front of her. "I thought I was a freak because I couldn't shapeshift, but Raife and Tati could. I have to admit, it makes me feel better to know that neither of you shifted until the guys found you." She grimaced. "I hope that doesn't sound horrible."

"Actually." Kerry narrowed her eyes. "I think we should tell Raife and Tatiana that they're the freaks," she said playfully. "What's with them being able to shift before they've found their mates? They're hybrids too." She stuck out her lower lip in a dramatic pout. "Where's a hybrid handbook when you need one?"

"But don't you think this whole mate thing is some bizarre prearranged marriage?" She looked from Sam to Kerry. "Where's our choice in all of this?"

Kerry raised her eyebrows. "Did William force himself on you?"

"No!" Layla insisted. "Not at all. It was most definitely mutual," she said with a grin, but her brow furrowed as she tried to explain. "I'm not talking about the physical stuff. It's the whole binding-to-each-other-for-life-thing. Didn't you take issue with that?"

Both women nodded.

"It *was* unsettling," Samantha said. "I think I was mostly freaked out by the overwhelming attraction I felt for Malcolm and the sudden onset of everything. My feelings for him were harder to wrap my brain around than the telepathy or shifting." She turned her serious blue eyes to Layla. "Putting my heart on the line was the hardest choice to make, but at the end of the day it was *my* choice." She rubbed her slightly rounded belly and smiled. "Best choice I ever made and I can't imagine my life without him."

"Ditto," Kerry said. "Ditto to everything she said."

She pushed herself off the bed and latched her big brown eyes on Layla. "But, it's *not* just about changes or sacrifices for *you* though." Kerry got off the bed and wandered to the window as she surveyed the space casually. "It impacts William, too," she said as she pushed the white curtain aside. "It already has."

"I know," Layla said, hoping she didn't sound as defensive as she felt. Maybe this whole girlfriend thing was overrated. Layla shifted her position on the bed and looked from Samantha to Kerry.

"He's in love with you," she said without turning around. "In fact, I keep expecting one of the pigs from your barn to fly by."

"What's that supposed to mean?" Layla asked. Apprehension mixed with a touch of annoyance crawled up her back.

Kerry turned to face her, leaned back against the wall, and eyed her carefully. "It means that *he's* already put his heart on the line, and we all know he's damn well ready to put his life on the line for you." Kerry waved one hand dismissively. "The life on the line thing—that's not a big deal for these guys. They'd lay down their lives for each other and for us any day of the week... but William's heart?" She scoffed. "I didn't even think he had one, until I saw him on the porch this morning."

"It's true." Sam nodded in agreement. "I barely recognized the man. The first time I met him he scared the shit out of me." She giggled. "Kerry calls him 'Iceman,' but it would seem that you've melted good old Mr. Freeze."

"I can't be held responsible for his feelings," Layla

said quickly. "I'm having enough trouble with my own emotions. Besides, all I'm worried about right now is Rosie and finding out who in the hell put her in the hospital. Then once that's settled, I want to go to the Council, so good old Bianca and I can have a chat. She has to answer for all of this, and I want her to answer for it in front of the Council—including the prince."

"I don't know," Kerry said hesitantly. "The guys are pretty convinced that if Bianca kept you a secret all these years, it was because there are Purists on the Council. I don't know how smart it is to stir up trouble like that."

"You're right. There probably are Purists on the Council." A smile crept over her face. "I imagine if three hybrids came to a Council meeting… it would be mighty difficult for the Purists to keep their mouths shut. I don't know about you ladies, but I'm tired of running."

"Oh my God," Samantha gasped. "That is brilliant. We force a situation where they have to reveal themselves?"

"Yup." Layla looked back and forth between the two women. "The devil you know is better than the devil you don't."

"Good point," Kerry agreed. "It would be a lot easier to defend ourselves if we actually knew who wanted us dead." She narrowed her eyes. "Have you suggested this to William yet? I can tell you right now, he's going to give you a hard time about picking a fight. Like I said… he loves you, and since you two haven't completed the mating rite yet, your powers aren't at full strength."

"No. It's not up to him." Layla shook her head adamantly. "This isn't about me. It's about all hybrids, and if he doesn't like it… well, that's too damn bad. I make my own choices."

Struggling to keep her conflicting emotions hidden from her new friends, Layla rose from the bed and opened the bathroom door.

"There are towels in here, but there are more in the closet at the end of the hallway. I'll let you get settled," she said abruptly. "I have to pack a bag to bring to Raife at the hospital. I'll see you downstairs."

Without another word, she left and shut the door behind her. She needed room to breathe, and Raife's bedroom was the only one, other than Rosie's, that wasn't taken. She flung herself face first onto the bed and pulled a pillow over her head, but no matter how much she wanted to, she couldn't block out what Kerry said.

William *was* in love with her. Hell—he had laid it all out on the table, and he'd already proven that she could trust him, even with her heart. Locked in the quiet solitude of her brother's bedroom, she wondered why on earth he trusted her with his.

Chapter 14

WILLIAM DIDN'T WANT TO COME BACK TO THE RUSTIC Inn, but Layla had her tunnel vision set on taking those damned pictures for Tyler and his band. For the past few days, Raife refused to leave Rosie's side but had at least agreed to additional help. Malcolm and Samantha had been spending much of their time at the hospital, keeping an eye out for anyone suspicious. Kerry and Dante patrolled the farm, but the attackers still hadn't revealed themselves, and they weren't likely to get any answers soon. When Rosie woke up, they hoped she'd tell them who it was.

The only thing that had gone well over the past few days was that everyone seemed to be getting along. Although Layla remained guarded, she was making an effort to get to know the others. Raife, Malcolm, and Dante had bonded over football, which was fine with William, as long as they didn't make him discuss it too.

William watched Layla as she rifled through her camera bag and chatted with Tyler while the rest of the band set up for their performance. They had made so much progress, but since the others arrived, she seemed distant. He'd hoped she would come to him and share his bed, but she didn't. She'd stayed in Raife's bedroom and hadn't come to him even in the dream realm. Although their energy signatures were still linked, she'd been shielding her mind from him, and had kept their telepathic communication to a minimum.

At first he was confused—but now he was just pissed.

"You know, you're starting to resemble that miserable, cold bastard you used to be." Kerry's teasing voice interrupted his thoughts as she sidled up to him at the bar. "Margarita on the rocks, with salt," she said to the bartender before turning her inspecting gaze back on William.

"What on earth are you talking about?" he said without taking his eyes off Layla.

"Really?" Kerry arched one dark eyebrow and made herself comfortable on the open bar stool next to him. "Are we going to play this game? I don't have the time, patience, or inclination to wade through your alpha-male crap." She nodded toward Dante, making his way through the thickening crowd. "I have Tarzan to deal with, so gimme a break," she added playfully.

"She is infuriating." William flicked his eyes to her briefly. "The woman is impossible to figure out, and I don't know what I have to do to make her understand. She insisted on coming here tonight to take these damn pictures." His mouth set in a firm line as he wrestled to keep his explosive feelings at bay. "The combination of intoxicated energy that will inevitably develop and the sound waves from the music are going to make it challenging to read the room, which will in turn, will make it difficult for me to keep her safe. She's a stubborn, defiant, and hard-headed woman who baffles me at every turn."

He cursed and threw back the rest of the vodka in his glass before slamming it down on the bar. He looked up to find Dante and Kerry smirking, clearly amused by his obvious frustration with his mate. William sat up straighter in his seat, pushed up the sleeves of his shirt, and loosened his collar as they continued to study him through amused expressions.

"Man, oh man, have you got it bad," Dante said, smiling. "Your foul mood wouldn't have anything to do with the fact that she's been staying in a separate bedroom from you, would it?"

"Piss off," William said as he kept his gaze fixed on Layla.

Dante was right on both counts. He did have it bad, *and* he was positively irked that she chose to sleep away from him. It wasn't the lack of sex—although that admittedly sucked—it was the lack of her presence, and that was most unsettling of all. He missed having her next to him and feeling her heart beat in time with his, the steady pattern of her breathing as she slept… all of it… absent.

When she wasn't with him, there was an empty space that only she could fill, and that was a new challenge. The only thing harder to accept was the fact that Layla didn't seem to suffer from the same affliction.

"Yes," he bit out. He glanced briefly at Dante and Kerry as he struggled to admit the truth. "I do have it bad, but *she* apparently *doesn't*."

"It's funny." Kerry laughed. "I never pegged you for a moron."

"Excuse me?" William's dark eyes flew to hers. "What did you say?"

"You can't be so dumb and blind to think that she doesn't love you?" Her eyes narrowed. "Can you?"

Kerry picked up her margarita and took a sip as she eyed him over the glass. William struggled with his growing annoyance, and if it had been anyone other than his friend's mate, he would've told her to piss off too, but out of respect for his friend, he gave her a chance to finish.

"I guess you can." Kerry made a sound of disgust. "She told me about how her mother went crazy and got all drugged up, *and* we heard about Raife and Tatiana's mother too." Kerry licked some salt off the rim of her glass. "You should've seen the look on her face when she heard what happened to my biological mother and Sam's mother. I thought she was going to shift into her cheetah, run away, and join the circus." She leaned one arm on the bar and put her drink down but kept her eyes fixed firmly on William's. "Can you really blame her?" Her voice dropped to just above a whisper. "How can you fault her for being afraid?"

William watched Layla as she took test shots of the band, and he couldn't help but notice the growing crowd. Her energy signature flowed thick with confidence and comfort as she worked in her wheelhouse and snapped pictures furiously. Every now and then, there would be a blip in her energy waves, and he knew it was from whatever psychic impressions she was getting through the digital shots.

It was the first time since Rosie's attack that she seemed completely comfortable.

"No," he said quietly. "I suppose I can't."

"She'll come around." Kerry stood up from her stool and gave William's arm a squeeze. "But it has to be on her terms, William. If you push her, she's just going to bolt."

Dante stepped aside so Kerry could get by but gave her a quick kiss on the cheek as she escaped his grasp. William watched her walk over to Layla and whisper something in her ear before heading to the ladies room. She was right. Intellectually, he knew she was right, but his brain was overrun by his heart… and other parts of his anatomy.

"I spoke to Malcolm," Dante said between sips of beer. "He and Samantha are headed back to the farm, but Raife is staying at the hospital again." He glanced at Layla. "Malcolm said Rosie has made some progress, and they're easing back on the sedation. She may be out of it by tomorrow."

"Good," William murmured. "Perhaps she'll be able to tell us who attacked her."

William could feel Dante's eyes on him, studying him, while he in turn tracked Layla. "What's on your mind, Dante?"

"You sure do have your hands full with Layla."

William's eyes flickered briefly to their clan form before latching onto Dante's. "What does that mean exactly?" he asked in a low, deadly tone.

Much to his surprise, Dante burst out laughing and slapped the bar twice between guffaws. William looked at him as though he'd lost his mind. Red-faced with tears streaming down his cheeks, Dante wiped at his eyes as the laughter subsided, but William looked no less confused.

"I'm sorry," he chuckled as he swiped at his eyes. "I just never thought I'd see the day that you'd be undone by a woman." He let out a long sigh and took a pull of his beer. "I meant what I said. She's a handful, man. And believe me, I know what I'm talking about because Kerry is the most spirited woman I've ever met, and my life will certainly never be dull with her." He wiggled his eyebrows, but his smile faded when William remained unamused.

"Layla, Kerry, and Samantha want to confront Bianca in front of the rest of the Council. Their theory is that if the three of them call Bianca out for hiding hybrids, then it will rile up any Purists that might be on the Council."

"Interesting," William murmured. "What are your thoughts on this?"

"I think they're absolutely right." Dante took another swig of his beer. "If we go there with our hybrid mates and tell everyone what Bianca's been up to… I can't imagine that the Purists in the room will remain silent. We kill two birds with one stone. Layla gets to take Bianca to task, and we get our enemies to show themselves."

The band broke into their first number with ear-shattering volume, and William instantly sought out Layla. She was down in front of the band, shooting from every angle she could get amid the swiftly growing dance mob and groupies. The bass beat thrummed through the small bar, and the wispy energy waves of the humans buzzed around the room like annoying flies that he couldn't shake. In the middle of it all was Layla—as beautiful, elusive, and wild as ever.

As lead attorney for the Amoveo Corporation, he had direct ties to the Council and the prince. Attending the meeting wouldn't be an issue, but he knew that the subject matter was likely to generate nothing but trouble. However, if it would give Layla peace of mind and resolution to speak with the Council, then he would do it.

"I'll set it up."

Dante stilled and kept his sharp amber gaze on William. "You'll set what up?" he asked warily.

"The meeting." William's dark eyes locked with Dante's. "We will take our mates to the Council and see if it gives us the results we're looking for."

"My sister, Mariana, took my father's place, and she's expressed concern about certain members on the Council. I don't think she knows what to make of it, and since she's new, she doesn't say much in or out of the meetings."

William watched as Dante struggled with the unpleasant memories and steeled himself against his rumbling energy waves. He still blanched at the fact that his own father had been a Purist and had tried to kill Samantha. William couldn't imagine dealing with that kind of betrayal.

"I can't believe she's on the Council." Dante shook his head and let out a short laugh. "She's always fighting against the grain, y'know. The party girl who never wanted to grow up." He sighed. "And now, she's seated on the Council representing the Bear Clan." He shook his head. "It's bizarre."

"Does she know?" William asked above the music. "Does she know about what Brendan—your father—did?"

"No," he bit out. Dante's jaw clenched, and he took a swig of his beer. "She thinks he died trying to protect Samantha, not kill her."

William made a small sound of understanding but silently wondered if that impacted Marianna's overall feeling about the hybrids. If she thought her father died in an effort to protect one, would she embrace their existence at all?

"I do have one lingering concern," William confided. "Since Layla and I haven't completed the mating rite, our powers aren't as strong as I would like them to be."

"You don't even have to ask." Dante cut him off before he could say another word. "We'll have your back, just like you've always had ours."

"Thank you." William shook his hand firmly. "I'll confirm the meeting time tomorrow."

"What meeting?" Kerry asked as she draped one arm over Dante's shoulders. Her dark eyes widened as she realized exactly what he meant. "Holy crap! We're gonna do it. We're going to the Council." She threw her head back and let out a lusty laugh. "I freaking love it."

"Good God, woman." William's brow knitted together in confusion as he watched Kerry's reaction. "Can you please tell me what on earth is so funny?"

"*You*, that's what." She leaned over, snagged her drink off the bar, and took a sip. "A few weeks ago, the idea of stepping outside the box of your three-piece suit would've been totally unheard of. You were so uptight, if I shoved a lump of coal up your butt, I would've gotten a diamond in return." She raised her glass in his direction and looked him up and down. "Now here you are, in a pair of jeans, no tie, hanging out in the middle of a loud hometown bar, planning on taking three hybrids into a Council meeting so your mate can confront the woman who's been meddling with her life, *and* provoke any Purists to reveal themselves for the prejudiced bastards they are." She let out a hoot, planted a kiss on Dante's cheek, and grinned at William. "You, my friend, are finally likable, and you owe it to that spunky chick with the camera."

"She's right." Dante stifled a laugh. "But I always liked you… most of the time."

"Ah, bullshit." Kerry bumped him with her hip. "You tolerated him, but *now* you like him." She winked at William. "Just kidding, tough guy." She grabbed Dante's hands, pulled him out of the seat and up against her long form. "Come on, lover. It's time to dance."

William watched them hit the tiny dance floor, and memories of his dance with Layla came flooding back in living color. He reached to her with his mind, an instinctive reflex, but found that same mental barrier solidly in place. He cursed under his breath and flagged down Joyce for another drink. He had to do something to put out the combustible force of desire and frustration.

Joyce complied with a wink and made quick work of his drink, but before he could take another sip, a vaguely familiar tendril of dark energy slithered into the bar. William's entire body tensed, and he instantly sought out Layla.

She stood in the midst of the crowd, but instead of shooting pictures of the band, her camera was aimed at the front door. She remained frozen in the throng of dancing bodies, the camera glued to her hands, her eye placed firmly at the lens, and her finger on the trigger. Her energy waves pulsed like rapid machine gunfire and hammered at William with vicious intensity as she kept her sights fixed firmly on her subject.

In a blur of inhuman speed, he cut through the crowd, and seconds later was standing at her side, along with Dante and Kerry. With one hand placed gently on her lower back, he sent her subtle waves of reassurance as he looked up to see what had her so transfixed.

Anger flared as his suspicions were confirmed. Sylvia Clark was back.

The shadowy tentacle of unpleasant energy had skittered over Layla and grabbed her by the throat with record speed. She knew it was Sylvia, but it was stronger, denser than it had ever been, and she'd picked up on it faster than ever. Layla had instinctively turned with her camera, poised and ready to shoot, but nothing could've prepared her for what she saw, and for the first time, *heard* through that lens.

Frank Clark. Red-faced. Screaming. Menacing. Physically restraining his weeping, pleading daughter by the shoulders. *You'll do as I say, or we both end up in prison*. Backhand smack across the face. Blond hair whipping through the air. Screams… and then… nothing.

The deep bass of the band pumped through the bar, and the sweating bodies writhed around them, blissfully unaware of the private feature Layla had just witnessed. She lowered the camera with shaking hands. Her breath came in short, thready gasps, and the only reason she wasn't passed out on the floor was because William had somehow gotten to her side. He was holding her up, physically and mentally.

What did you see? William's soothing baritone floated into her mind, but she couldn't answer him because she was too fixated on Sylvia, who was staring right back.

Layla struggled to fight through the lingering violence

of the vision and leaned against William's strong body as she watched Sylvia walk directly toward them. His arm linked around her waist easily and held her against him. *Layla, what did you see?* He asked again, pushing her to answer him.

Layla glanced up and sucked in a shaky breath as she opened her mind to him again. *Her father smacked her around pretty good, and she's terrified.* She turned to Dante and Kerry, who had sidled up to her right, and looked primed and ready for a fight. Their energy signatures hummed and pulsed around her in a protective manner. *She's a bitch, but she's harmless.*

Kerry hooked her arm around Dante's waist. *I doubt it. She's psychic. I can tell by her energy signature.* She arched one eyebrow and threw a quick look in Layla's direction. *And don't even try to tell me you haven't suspected it.*

"I agree with what Kerry said." Dante exchanged a look with William. *Her energy signature is definitely not normal for a human. She's not a hybrid, but she's got something beyond a typical human.*

Layla heard them loud and clear, and based on William's energy signature, he'd heard them as well. As Sylvia got closer, Layla saw faint red marks and what looked like a bruise on her left cheek, obviously left over from where her father smacked her. Her large blue eyes, usually filled with disdain, were round with fear as they flicked around the room nervously.

She stood in front of them, looking and acting nothing like the cold-as-ice woman she'd always been. Huddled up in an oversized sweatshirt, she wore no makeup, and she'd definitely been crying. Her blond hair, usually coiffed to perfection, was thrown up in a hair clip and looked as if it hadn't been brushed in days. Quite frankly, she looked like a hot mess.

"I have to talk to you, Layla." She sniffled and hugged her arms tighter over her breasts. *Please*. Her tear-stained eyes flicked over all four of them, and she nibbled on her lip. *There's something I need to tell you.*

When Sylvia reached out to them with her mind, Layla's jaw dropped, William's body tensed, and Dante and Kerry cursed out loud. Sylvia was telepathic? What the hell? Before Layla could formulate any coherent response, telepathic or otherwise, Sylvia was making a beeline for the door at the back of the bar that led to the enclosed courtyard.

God, I love being right, Kerry teased as they followed Sylvia through the white-paneled door and out into the crisp, fall evening. In the warmer months, the courtyard would be buzzing with customers and the occasional DJ, but since it was so chilly out and a band was playing, it was empty, except for the two smokers hanging by the door.

Sylvia brushed past them, pulled the hood of her sweatshirt on, and headed for one of the leaf-strewn picnic tables to the far right of the courtyard. She slid onto the bench and squished herself far into the corner. Back to the weathered picket privacy fence, she eyed them intently as they sat down. Layla sat next to her, leaving as much space as possible between them. Dante and Kerry slipped into the other side, and William grabbed a lone folding chair and positioned himself at the head of the table.

Their amped-up energy signatures mingled with

the brisk wind as it whipped around them and blew
leaves onto the table. The only sound was the muffled
music coming from inside the bar. They stared blatantly at Sylvia, and it was a moment before anyone
said anything. William, seated ramrod straight with
his hands folded serenely on the table, was the first to
break the silence.

"You're full of surprises, Ms. Clark." His voice
seemed unusually loud now that they were no longer
amid the music and din of people. "I suspected that there
was more to you than met the eye, but I must admit—I
wasn't expecting telepathy."

Her eyes grew rounder. "You heard me too?" She
looked from William to Layla. "I only thought you'd
be able to hear me, like Raife can." She shrugged and
shook her head quickly. "Or could anyway." Her gaze
lowered to her hands, and her voice dropped to just
above a whisper. "I haven't spoken to him that way for
a long time."

"What?" Layla shouted and looked wildly around
the table at her equally surprised friends. "What the hell
are you talking about? What is going on?" Her heart
thumped in her chest, and her hands curled into fists,
ready to pummel her into the ground, if she didn't come
up with answers pretty damn quick. "Start talking."

"My father," she said through a shuddering breath.
"My father is responsible for Rosie's attack." Her blue
eyes, rimmed with tears, latched onto Layla. "He's to
blame. He's to blame for *everything*."

Layla's head was spinning. Frank Clark attacked
Rosie, and Sylvia was throwing him under the bus for it?

"Wait. I don't get it," Layla said. "Why would your

father beat up Rosie? It doesn't make sense. If he really did this, *why on earth* would you give up Daddy dearest?" She looked at her with blatant suspicion. "You don't do anything that he wouldn't approve of. I mean, you broke Raife's heart and ditched him at the altar to please your father, so why tell us something that you know will land him in jail?"

"My father has run my life and controlled everything I've done from the minute I was born," she said through a sniffle as she swiped at red-rimmed eyes and turned a stony gaze on Layla. "Who I dated. Who I married *and* divorced. *Everything*. My money, where I live—he has controlled it all. Every time I found happiness, my father found a way to ruin it, and every time I ended up alone." She crossed her arms over her breasts and leaned against the fence. "When I heard about what happened to Rosie, I confronted him. I knew he'd been planning to speak to her about the farm, and when I asked him about it, he went crazy."

"I know," Layla said quietly. "I saw what he did to you." Sylvia's hand went to the red mark by her eye, and shame washed over her face. "It's not the first time he's hit you, is it?"

"No." Sylvia shook her head, and the tears fell freely. "He's known about my telepathic ability since I was a child. He told me that I wasn't normal and that if people ever found out, I would be hounded and dissected like a freak. He had me convinced that he was the only thing keeping me out of the loony bin." Her tear-filled eyes looked pleadingly at Layla. "But hurting Rosie? That was the last straw."

"Why on earth would you stay under his roof?" Kerry

asked. She placed both elbows on the picnic table, rested her chin on her folded hands, and leveled her bold gaze on Sylvia. "Seriously. Haven't you been married as many times as Elizabeth Taylor? What the hell? Why didn't you just ride one of those guys out of town?

"Oh I tried," she let out a bitter laugh, before turning a dead-serious gaze at them. "But Daddy has a way of getting what he wants, especially from me. My husbands were all lured into big money jobs in Daddy's company, but soon enough… Daddy would get bored with them, or they'd say something he didn't like, and they'd be on the chopping block." Her eyes darted from Kerry to Samantha. "I know how pathetic I must seem to you," she said shakily. "I should've stood up to him years ago when he told those lies to Raife, but I couldn't, and by then Raife was so mad at me… he wouldn't let me explain. He told me to stay the hell away from him," she said, her voice edged with bitterness. "So I have."

"The wedding," Layla mused. "You didn't want to call it off, did you?"

"No." She shook her head adamantly. "Daddy did. He told him that lie about me going away for the weekend to get rid of him. I was in love with Raife, and I wanted to marry him more than anything in the world." Her gaze landed on Layla. "He's the only man I've ever loved," she whispered and lowered her eyes. "The only reason I flirted with William was to try and make Raife jealous." She made a sound of disgust. "If he disliked me before, he's really going to hate me when he finds out that Daddy is the one who put Rosie in the hospital."

With the numerous revelations, Layla had almost forgotten about this particular part of the web of deceit.

"What exactly did your father do?" Layla thought maybe he'd hired some thugs to toss the house or threaten her. She couldn't imagine that Frank had done it himself. "Who did he send over there?"

"No one," Sylvia insisted and let out a long breath. "He went over himself to talk some sense into her because she'd told him that she had decided not to sell him the farm. Daddy was desperate to get the land. It had nothing to do with my granddaddy and that stupid bet from years ago." Her eyes narrowed, and her features sharpened with unmistakable anger. "It was all about the money. Daddy doesn't have any left." She laughed through her tears. "It's all gone. *Everything*. In addition to gambling in the stock market, he's taken to hitting the casinos as well. He's lost almost everything."

She flicked her gaze to Dante and Kerry, who were listening with rapt attention.

"Rosie's farm is smack dab in the middle of Daddy's other properties, and if Rosie didn't sell, then the developers couldn't do what they wanted to do." She clapped her hands together sharply. "No deal equals no money, and Daddy would be up shit's creek without a paddle."

"Oh my God," Layla said. "He did it. He actually did it."

"He says he didn't mean to, of course, that he shoved her. She fell and hit her head." The tears came again, faster this time, and her words rushed more frantic as the memory of what he told her came barreling back. "He panicked and tried to make it look like a robbery or something." She turned her pleading gaze to Layla and grabbed her hands. "I would never want anything bad to happen to Rosie. I swear it. Daddy has been home since it happened, and I couldn't get away until he left tonight for some stupid card game." She squeezed her hands. "Please, Layla. You have to believe me. I'll go with you to the police and turn Daddy in," she said quickly. "I'll tell them everything. I know how much Rosie means to Raife, and I would never want anything bad to happen to her."

Layla studied her intently, but found no sign of deception. *I believe her.* William's deep baritone touched her mind like a fresh winter breeze. Even though he hadn't said a word, his presence was much appreciated, and his energy bolstered hers. Layla glanced at him. *I can't believe I'm saying this, but I do too.* She reached out to Kerry. *Kerry, are you buying this?*

Kerry extended her arm onto the table. "Gimme your hand." She snapped her fingers at a teary Sylvia. "Let's go. Fork it over, blondie. I'll find out whether you're telling the truth."

Sylvia didn't move but looked at Kerry with genuine confusion until Kerry's voice cut into her mind. *Right now.* Sylvia's eyes widened as she looked around the table.

"You guys aren't the only freaks at the table." She sighed loudly and wiggled her fingers impatiently. "We'll explain it all later. Let's go. Hold my hand so I can see if you're being straight with us."

Layla gave her a reassuring nod, and with a deep breath, Sylvia placed one shaking hand in Kerry's open palm. Kerry closed her eyes, curled her long fingers over Sylvia's, and her body jolted as the connection was made. Dante rubbed her back in soothing circles as Kerry's eyes flickered furiously behind her eyelids.

After several minutes, Kerry released her hand and let out a long whistle as she opened those huge dark eyes and zeroed in on Layla. "Your old man is one cold-hearted bastard," she bit out through a shaky breath. Kerry looked at William and then Layla. "After what I saw, I'm surprised she's still alive, let alone has found the nerve to turn him in."

Sylvia closed her eyes and let out the breath she'd been holding. "Thank you."

"We need to go directly to the police station so you can tell them what you just told us," William interrupted. Sylvia looked at him with that same panicked expression she'd had earlier, but William wasn't backing down. He turned that penetrating gaze onto Sylvia. "Right now." It came out as a command, not a request.

Sylvia nodded, tucked a stray lock of hair behind her ear, and rose from the bench obediently. Layla shuddered at how quickly Sylvia followed William's command. She'd been controlled and manipulated for so many years that it seemed like all she knew how to do was follow orders. Sylvia had always presented an image of being in control, but it was clear that she had been anything but that.

Now Layla really felt sorry for her. As much as her own life had been manipulated, Layla had never suffered the kind of abuse and domineering control that Sylvia had.

William took Layla's hand in his and linked his fingers with hers. He said nothing, but he didn't have to. The simple gesture of holding her hand spoke volumes. Layla swallowed the lump in her throat and rose to meet him. She popped up on her toes and placed a quick kiss on his warm lips. *Thank you*. Her words whispered along the edges of his mind as a smile softened the sharp edges of that handsome face.

"What did it?" Kerry asked. She leaned into Dante's comforting embrace as they crossed the courtyard. "What made you decide to end this?"

"Raife," Sylvia said softly. She looked over her shoulder at them briefly. "It would drive him crazy to never know who did this, and feeling the pain he's been suffering over the past few days has been driving *me* crazy."

They exchanged curious looks with one another as they walked back into the bar and out toward the gravel parking lot. Layla could sense Raife's emotions? Sylvia definitely wasn't a hybrid. Her clan image would've come through in the pictures, but she was one hell of a strong psychic.

She thought back on the different pictures she'd taken over the years, and all were blurred. At the time, she'd thought it was because Sylvia was so nasty, but now, in hindsight, she realized it was from her efforts to keep people from seeing the ugliness and violence that she lived with.

She's his mate. William's matter of fact tone cut into Layla's mind with cold precision, but as much as Layla hated to admit it, she knew deep in her gut that he was right.

Sylvia was Raife's mate.

Chapter 15

AFTER SPENDING MUCH OF THE EVENING AT THE POLICE station with Sylvia while she made her statements, William wanted to take Layla straight home, but she wouldn't hear it. As he suspected she would, she insisted on going to the hospital to check on Rosie and speak with Raife. William pictured himself throwing her over his shoulder and dragging her home. However, one look at that ferocious glint in her eye, and he quickly dismissed the thought. He doubted it would help his cause.

Kerry and Dante had gone back to the farm hours ago to get some sleep and fill in Malcolm and Samantha. Based on the evidence they already had and Sylvia's statement, the police had arrested Frank Clark at his house when he returned from his card game. Since he was such a flight risk, he'd been denied bail and would likely be spending quite a long time in jail.

The others had offered to come by the hospital, but since Rosie's attacker was in custody, and there didn't appear to be a looming Purist threat, things were under control at the moment. William adjusted the blanket on the hospital bed.

There was justice for Rosie after all.

"You better stop hoverin' over me, boy," Rosie rasped weakly. "Or folks are gonna start talkin'."

William poured a cup of cold water for her. She'd come out of the sedation early that morning as spunky as ever. She'd calmed down once they'd told her what had transpired, and the only person more surprised than *she* was by Sylvia's confession was Raife.

William glanced to the door of the room, waiting for Layla to return. She'd left with Raife a while ago, and not having her near him was causing a ridiculous amount of anxiety.

"She'll be back soon." Rosie laughed softly, but it quickly turned into a cough. "Damn. That hurts." She winced as her hand went to the bandage on her head. "That son of a bitch is lucky he knocked me cold 'cause I was about ready to whip his ass."

"I don't doubt it." William chuckled as he helped Rosie sit up and sip her water. "Looks like you'll have to keep from whipping any ass for a while. That shoulder of yours is going to take some time to heal."

William kept his sharp eyes fixed on her as he sat down in the chair next to her bed. His brow furrowed, and he lowered his voice to a conspiratorial whisper. "I could reach out to one of our Amoveo healers... Bianca must have told you about them."

Rosie stilled, and her smiling eyes latched onto his as a grin spread over her face. Her gray eyes studied his brown ones, and in that moment, William knew that Rosie was privy to more than she'd let on.

"I guess Layla found the note?" She made a grunt of approval. "Good. Bianca asked me to let her know when her mate came to find her and promised me that she'd tell Layla everything then." She huffed. "Some horseshit about mate-bonding and full strength—blah, blah, blah."

"I'll be damned." William leaned back in his chair

and folded his hands in his lap. "You do know Bianca. All this time, you've known who Layla's family is?"

"Hold on there, just one damn minute." Her heart monitor beeped faster as her heart rate picked up, and she wagged a finger at him. "I knew something was up when a woman from *social services*," she said, making air quotes with her fingers, "shows up on my doorstep with a scared little girl."

William made a face that reflected his confusion.

"Oh, for Christ's sake." She sighed. "I was never registered as a foster parent. I adopted Raife and Tati. Why in the hell would a social worker show up on my doorstep out of the blue with some kid? Get it?" She waved a wrinkled hand at him and lay back on her pillows wearily. "Besides, I could tell that Layla was a hybrid right away."

"What?" Layla's shaking voice cut through the air as she barreled through the hospital room door. "Rosie, what are you talking about?" Layla came directly to the other side of Rosie's bed with an equally confused Raife right behind her. "What do you mean, you knew?"

Layla's confused and stressed-out energy waves filled the room along with Raife's as they stared down at Rosie. "Answer me, Rosie. You said you didn't believe any of it until puberty hit the house."

"Well, I may have fudged things a little bit." She pursed her lips. "I *did* realize you were different like Raife and Tati. I may not have the second sight like my sister did," she huffed. "But I do tend to pick up on things that other people overlook. I knew you were a hybrid as soon as I laid eyes on you." She looked at Raife. "Just like I've always known that Sylvia was hiding something, aside from the fact that she's crazy in love with you, Raife."

She let out a tired laugh as Raife shifted his weight and stuffed his hands in the pockets of his jeans, visibly uncomfortable at the mention of Sylvia. Rosie turned her attention back to Layla, who stared down at her intently.

"And that Bianca broad was no regular person— no way. I knew she was full-blooded Amoveo like Raife and Tati's daddy, and she wasn't some damn social worker."

"Why wouldn't you tell us this?"

"Layla, honey," Rosie said weakly. "You didn't know anything about the Amoveo, and I sure as hell didn't want to scare you more than you already were." She smoothed the sheets over her lap. "I decided to let nature take its course and see how things played out, and sure enough, when you hit puberty, the floodgates opened."

William touched Layla's mind. *Are you alright?* To his great relief she responded immediately and kept her mind open to him for the first time in days. *Can anyone be honest with me about anything?*

Before he could respond, Rosie continued her explanations and reclaimed Layla's full attention.

"I've spoken with Bianca only twice. Once, the day she brought you to live with me, and then just a few days ago when William showed up." Her mouth set in a firm line. "Listen, girl." She sighed. "All I know is that when she showed up with you, she knew about Raife and Tati, and don't ask me *how*, because I haven't the foggiest notion."

Rosie lowered her voice. "I do know that Bianca

believed you'd be safe with us, and you needed a loving home." Her gray eyes wrinkled at the corners as she reached out, took Layla's hand in hers, and gave it a squeeze. "She told me your parents were gone and that you shouldn't find your clan until you had bonded with your mate." Rosie nodded toward William. "She gave me an address with a post office box and said that when your mate found you, to let her know, and then she'd handle the rest."

Layla, wide-eyed, looked from Rosie to William as she wrapped her brain around yet another revelation. He could practically see the wheels turning in that sharp mind of hers, and he knew exactly what she was thinking about—the Council meeting.

"Bianca came by to see me the night Frank showed up." Rosie's face darkened at the memory.

"So, Bianca's energy signature *was* the only Amoveo we sensed at the farm," William surmised. "And it was mixed with Frank's signature." His brow furrowed. "All this time, we were looking for another Amoveo—a Purist—and it was a human." He made a sound of disgust at his obvious error.

"Man," Raife mused with a sidelong glance at William. "Malcolm and Dante were right about you." He delivered a crooked grin. "You *hate* being wrong."

"*We* weren't entirely wrong." William sat up straighter in the chair, and his jaw clenched. "There was an Amoveo at the farm that night, just not a Purist." He flicked some lint off his jeans. "The possibility that a human attacked Rosie was admittedly overlooked." He locked eyes with Raife. "But you can rest assured that won't happen again."

Raife chuckled and folded his arms over his chest. "Slice it any way you want, brother. Wrong is wrong."

"Whatever," Layla said through an exasperated sigh at their childish sparring match. "Can we please get back to Bianca and why she was at the farm?"

"Happily." Rosie gave Raife a scolding glance before continuing. "I told Bianca to leave the letter for you and said that you would get in touch with her, if that was what *you* wanted," Rosie said, pointing an IV-draped hand at Layla.

Layla's shoulders relaxed at the mention of it being her choice, and her energy waves softened. She sighed with relief. In that moment, William realized how important having a choice was to her, and he knew that their bond could only be completed if she specifically requested it.

The voice of doubt crawled into his heart. *What if she didn't?*

"Bianca pulled her disappearing act when she heard the car in the driveway." Rosie shrugged her uninjured shoulder. "She's kind of flighty around humans, I guess, and maybe she didn't want to be exposed to more people than she already was. Now, I don't know much about her, but I do know she's extremely protective of you, even of Raife and Tati."

"Protective and manipulative," Layla huffed. She ran her hands over her face and turned her tired, but determined, eyes to William. "I've had enough of this secrecy bullshit. I can't wait to face this woman and the rest of the Council." Before William could even respond, she looked at Rosie, and her features softened. "What happened next?"

Rosie frowned. "Don't remember too much after that, but I do remember enough to want to stick a cattle prod up Frank Clark's ass."

Layla covered her mouth and tried to smother the chuckle that bubbled up at the idea of Rosie using her cattle prod on Frank, but she failed miserably. It was a matter of seconds before all four were giggling like children at the thought.

As they shared a good belly laugh, William watched Layla swipe at the tears that fell down her cheeks. Warmth washed over him. He didn't think anything could make him happier than finally being mated with her, but he was wrong. Seeing her smile and sharing her laughter was the most exquisite bliss of all.

Layla dragged herself out of the Jeep with all the speed of molasses in winter and just stood in the gravel driveway. She couldn't recall a time when she'd been this tired, and she was so exhausted, she hadn't argued when William insisted that *he* drive. He'd even said it in that bossy-boots tone she'd come to know so well—the one that made her want to deck him... or kiss him.

Her lips curved with satisfaction. She closed her eyes and lifted her face to the sun.

Rosie was going to be okay, Frank had been arrested, and as far as they could tell, no Purists were hunting her down. All in all, it had turned out to be a surprisingly good day, and now, all she wanted to do was sleep for about a week.

Her body wavered from exhaustion, and she thought fleetingly that she might just pass out in the driveway.

William, once again sensing her needs, scooped her up in his steel embrace before she could tumble to the ground. Layla let out a girly squeal as he lifted her into the air, and she instinctively hooked her arms around his neck.

"What are you doing?" she asked with a yawn. Her head rested against his shoulder, despite her best efforts to keep it upright. "I can walk up there on my own," she said sleepily as her eyes closed.

Verto.

A soft breeze, a momentary sense of displacement, and the oddly comforting sensation of static electricity sizzled in the air around them. Within seconds, Layla was nestled in William's arms in the soft bed they'd shared a few nights ago.

She lifted her heavy eyelids and found him staring at her intently with those intense chocolate brown eyes. Layla stroked her fingertips along his unshaven cheek. His energy waves shifted subtly, and his strong body hardened as it lay against hers.

"Go to sleep," he murmured tenderly and placed a gentle kiss on her forehead. "I promise I'll behave myself."

"Yeah, right," Layla mumbled sleepily and nuzzled her check against the warmth of his muscular chest. "You can't resist my feminine wiles."

William chuckled. The deep sound rumbled through his chest and vibrated along her cheek as she snuggled herself deeper into his embrace. Wavering at the edges of sleep, she noted how perfectly her body fit with his and the way the curve of his arm cradled her at exactly the right angle. A smile played at her lips as she slipped into the soft, welcoming cloud of sleep. William's silky voice wafted into her mind. *Sweet dreams, Layla.*

~m~

Layla woke up and stretched languidly as she looked around the empty room. She squinted against the waning light of the sunset as the last shreds streamed through the bedroom and wondered how long she'd been asleep. Shoving her unruly curls out of her face, Layla noted that William was nowhere in sight and that she was fully clothed. *Damn.* Her lips curved. *He had been a gentleman.*

Layla got dressed with minimal fuss, feeling awkward that she slept the day away, and her guests were left to fend for themselves. Layla knew the circumstances were extreme, but she still heard Rosie's voice in her head, reminding her that she was the hostess. It wasn't a telepathic voice, but it was just as profound. It was that whisper of conscience, the voice of the only mother she'd ever really known. The voice that taught her right from wrong, that sang her to sleep, and comforted her when the nightmares came.

She pulled on a black cardigan and headed downstairs to find the house empty. The entire first floor was dark, lit only by the swiftly fading light outside. The low hum of the dishwasher could be heard from the kitchen, but there was no sign of William or the others.

Had they left?

Her heart gave a funny little tug at the idea of not saying good-bye to her newfound friends, but when the soulful howl of a wolf called from the surrounding woods, she knew she wasn't alone. A smile cracked her face. She knew that had to be Samantha.

Layla stuck her feet into the duck boots she kept by

the front door and pulled her sweater tighter against the cold November wind. She stepped onto the porch but didn't have to look far to find them, and the sight in front of her made her heart skip a beat.

It was recognition, a primal connection, and an innate sense of belonging.

Trotting out of the woods by the edge of the horse's corral was an enormous gray wolf with glowing blue eyes of the Amoveo that reminded her of Raife and Tati's, a sleek black panther with eyes that burned yellow, and a gigantic red fox that looked more like a wolf. Circling high above them, and screeching into the darkening sky, were two enormous birds of prey, one of whom she knew was William, and the other she could only assume was Malcolm.

Samantha, Kerry, and Dante stopped at the ridge of the hill as Samantha tossed her head back and let out a lonesome howl to the purple and indigo twilight sky. Her singsong voice touched Layla's mind with a familial warmth. *We thought you were never gonna wake up, Layla.*

Kerry snarled and roared in response as her long dark tail switched behind her. *Whaddya say you trade those freckles for some bigger badass spots?*

Her skin tingled with the animal instinct to shift, and her eyes snapped brightly to their clan form as she gazed upon her peers, and for the first time in her life, felt the unique sensation of truly belonging. It wasn't just to these particular individuals but to the Amoveo as a whole, and that was more unexpected than anything else.

William's vibrant energy signature grew stronger as he soared down to meet her, shimmered, and shifted just before making a sure-footed landing at the foot of the porch steps. Layla's heart skittered, and her breath caught in her throat at the sight of him shifting from gyrfalcon to the strikingly handsome man she'd come to know.

Dear God, the man was spectacular.

He cut a hulking figure in the early evening light. His blond hair blew free in the wind, and his moon-glow eyes gleamed brightly in the darkening night. Every cell in her body lit up brilliantly as his gaze slid over her, while he stalked up the steps, until he was just inches away.

Layla didn't move. She was locked in the limitless depths of his eyes as everyone else seemed to fade away. Her feet felt like they were glued to the wooden planks of the porch as she heard Dante chuckle at the edges of her mind. *Looks like we're running on our own tonight. Something tells me these two have other plans.*

She sensed the waning energy signatures of the others as they ventured back into the woods along the edge of the farm, leaving her and William utterly alone.

"Sleep well?" His deep baritone voice wafted over her deliciously as he brushed a stray curl off her forehead.

"Yes," she whispered as she held his gaze.

His tall male body radiated heat, and memories of his warm flesh sliding against hers came roaring back. She licked her lips and watched the muscles in his jaw clench. Layla ached to touch him, but she sensed resistance behind the pulse of desire that thrummed strong and steady in his energy signature.

"Good," he said firmly as his eyes shifted back to their human form, "because tomorrow we're going to meet with the Council."

William turned on his heels and trotted back down the steps to the driveway. It was like getting doused with a bucket of cold water. He did what she wanted. William got her a meeting with Bianca and the Council, but why in the hell did he change gears so easily?

How could he just cut it off like that? One minute he was practically giving her an eyegasm, and the next he was acting like she was some clerk in his law office. Layla stared after him, and if looks could kill, he'd be six feet under, but it was herself she was furious with.

How could she blame him? She'd been the one to withdraw from him over the past few days, but hadn't he kept telling her he'd give her time? Apparently, time had run out, and he was tired of waiting for her to make up her mind. Layla swallowed the lump that had formed in her dry throat.

William seemed unfazed by her current annoyance and stared right back with that calculated, unaffected demeanor he'd had the day he arrived.

"You should shapeshift tonight and run with us." His face and voice were void of emotion. "The practice will do you good, and since we're not formally mated, you'll need to have a solid handle on your abilities before the Council meeting. I am less than enthused about taking you before the Council without the full power of your abilities, but I know enough about you to know that trying to talk you out of going would be an exercise in futility. If there are Purists hiding on the Council, they may reveal themselves with violence, and although our friends will be there to assist us, we have to be prepared. Once you get the answers you're looking for from Bianca, you and I can go our separate ways, and your life will be yours to do with as you please."

Layla hugged herself against the cold—but it was more from William's words than the wind.

"That is what you want?" His nostrils flared, and a cloud passed over his features. "Isn't it?"

"Yes." Layla stuck out her chin defiantly. She'd be damned if she was going to tell him how much it would hurt to lose him. "My life, my choices."

William's face remained stone cold. Not even a flicker of emotion rippled to disrupt his collected self. "As you wish."

Layla watched as he whispered the ancient language, shimmered, and soared into the sky like a white and brown spotted bullet. *That cold son of a bitch.* She slammed her mind shut to him and instinctively reached for the energy signatures of Samantha and Kerry, which she found with surprising ease.

Blinking back tears, Layla ran down the steps and raced up the hill toward the moonlit woods. In a blinding blur of speed and with newfound expertise, Layla shifted into her cheetah form and ran like the wind through the tall grasses. As the cold air whipped over her spotted coat, and her claws tore up the tender flesh of the earth, Layla tried not to think of how much it hurt to have William pull away.

She rounded the corner by the fallen tree where they'd shared their first kiss, and the memories battered her viciously. Breathless, heart pounding against her ribs, Layla wondered when exactly had she fallen in love with William?

Damn.

Chapter 16

A FLASH OF BRILLIANT WHITE LIGHT AND THE SIZZLING snap of static electricity accompanied their arrival at Richard's ranch in Montana, but the second she felt the hard ground beneath her feet, William slipped his hand out of hers.

Layla stuffed her chilled hands into the pockets of her cargo jacket. She couldn't help but notice with more envy than she cared to admit that Samantha and Kerry remained hand in hand with their mates.

William was scanning the property with his signature—stoic demeanor—and likely committing every speck to memory. His hair was tied back tightly at the nape of his neck, and he seemed more tense than usual, which really wasn't surprising given what they were about to do.

They'd barely said two words to each other since last night on the porch. She couldn't blame him. She'd been such a bitch and so cold to him. Why the hell should he bother anymore? She kept telling herself it was best.

So why did she feel so shitty?

Although their energy signatures were linked, he'd managed to buffer his somehow. It was as if a steel trap had clamped down over his emotions, and the growing void was unsettling.

The biting wind howled across the ranch, and an enormous, white clapboard colonial farmhouse with black shutters stood directly in front of them. It made Rosie's five-bedroom home look like a tinker toy. However, as huge as the house was, it was completely dwarfed by the breathtaking mountains that loomed behind it. There were two classic red barns with white trim off to the right, with a roomy corral between them that Layla assumed was for their horses.

The place looked like it was plucked out of *Better Homes and Gardens of Montana*—except for the cylindrical steel structure that loomed ominously to the left. It reminded Layla of something you might see in a movie about Area 51 and looked completely out of place amid the sprawling, rustic ranch. The rest of the property, the house in particular, emanated two thick, distinct energy signatures, which she suspected were those of Richard and his wife Salinda. However, the steel building was completely void of energy, and the only word that came to mind was *death*.

"This place is absolutely spectacular," Samantha breathed. "I've never seen anything like it in all my life." She linked her arm around Malcolm's waist. "Seriously, isn't this the most beautiful place you've ever seen?"

Kerry pulled her knit cap over her ears and snuggled into Dante's arms. "Yeah, yeah. It's fantastic," she said through chattering teeth. "I'm freezing my ass off, so can we go in the house and find out how gorgeous the inside is?"

"No," William snapped without taking his eyes off the house. "They're not in there."

"But I can sense their energy signatures coming from the house."

"Their energy is permanently imprinted on their

home. Remember, Richard and Salinda are almost three hundred years old and have been mated almost as long." That stone-cold mask faltered as he tore his eyes from hers. "Our powers increase substantially once we are mated. Everyone is in the Council building. We mustn't keep them waiting."

They followed him to the long silver structure, but when they got about fifty feet away, William stopped dead in his tracks. *Don't move.* Layla's gaze skimmed that imposing figure of his, and she imagined that few people would question him in *any* situation.

Layla stood to the right behind him, flanked on both sides by the others. Layla scanned the area but could find no evidence of anyone other than the six of them. The double doors of the building had to be ten feet tall, and it didn't look like there were handles. How the hell were they going to get in there?

What is it? she asked hesitantly. *Do they know we're here?* In spite of her best efforts to remain calm, her heart was beating a mile a minute and she'd broken out in a cold sweat. She found herself inching closer to William, hoping and praying that she could hold it together.

Where are the guardians? Malcolm's even voice filled their collective minds. *I thought the Council building was always protected by them.*

They're here, William said confidently.

What the hell is a guardian? Layla asked abruptly. She glanced at Kerry and Samantha, who both shrugged.

Don't ask us, girl. Kerry's typically candid tone resonated in Layla's mind. *Samantha and I haven't been at the party that much longer than you have.*

He's right. Malcolm murmured tensely. *I can feel*

them now too. He pulled Samantha into the crook of his arm as his eyes shifted to their clan form.

There are always two guardians who keep watch over the Council when it is in session. William's matter-of-fact tone slid into her mind with irritating calmness. *They also provide additional security for the prince and his family on the ranch. It is a position of extremely high honor among our people*.

There. Dante's sharp tone cut into the conversation as he pointed toward the building. *And there*.

Layla squinted and shaded her eyes from the bright afternoon sun, searching for these *guardians* they were talking about. Irritation crawled up her back at her inability to sense them or see them, and just when she was ready to scream with frustration—she saw them.

On either side of the towering doorways, just above the tall brown grasses, there was a subtle ripple in the air, similar to heat waves coming off pavement in the summertime. Layla sharpened her focus, and her breath caught in her throat when she found two sets of glowing golden eyes staring back through the fluttering brown stalks.

The grasses wavered, and if Layla didn't know better, she'd think she was hallucinating as two enormous tigers stood up from their well-camouflaged hiding spots, finally revealed. Layla's entire body went stone-still, but her heart raced almost to the point of pain.

As the massive, striped beasts stalked toward them side by side, her gut instinct was to run the hell away, or visualize herself back to the safety of the farm. Instead, she steeled herself against the mind-numbing fear and stood her ground at William's side. She would be damned if she was going to run away. No more running.

They won't hurt you. His soothing baritone floated gracefully along the edges of her mind, and instantly relaxed the tense muscles in her neck. *They'd have to get through me first.*

Layla didn't respond, worried that she'd sound as terrified as she felt. Gratitude flooded her as she merely nodded and bit back the bile that rose in her throat, while the exotic guardians moved toward them in unison. Their muscular, gold- and black-streaked bodies moved with unnatural grace, and those glowing eyes didn't move from Layla's face.

The beasts stopped about five feet away and bowed their enormous heads low.

Welcome. I am Dominic, and this is my sister Daniella. The slightly larger tiger on the left spoke first as a low growl emanated from his throat when he touched their minds with his. *The prince and the rest of the Council have been expecting you.*

Three hybrids? A high-pitched female voice drifted from the smaller tiger, and laughter edged her words. *No wonder they called an emergency meeting,* she snarled.

Daniella! His voice blared into their collective minds. Dominic let out a bone-shattering roar, his ears flattened against his thick skull, and his lips curled back to reveal a mouthful of razor-sharp white teeth. *Silence,* he snarled, and his hackles rose as he reprimanded his sister. *Tell them that the guests have arrived.*

Daniella bowed her head low in submission to her brother, but her glowing eyes never left Layla's. *Apologies,* she hissed as she backed up, turned, and stalked to the entrance of the structure.

Layla didn't buy it for a second. *Guardians of who?*

She touched her mind to William's, using the private connection that only he could hear. *That bitch is no fan of hybrids.*

William didn't flinch. *We shall see.*

Forgive my sister's impertinence. Dominic's sharp voice came through loud and clear. *She's new to the position of guardian, and sometimes she forgets herself. Please follow me. They are ready to see you.*

They followed Dominic back to the now open doors of the Council building. Layla didn't take her eyes off Daniella, who stood to the right of the open doors and tracked their every move with the same intensity a tiger in the wild might track prey.

They stepped through the doors, which immediately closed behind them, leaving Dominic and Daniella alone outside to fulfill their duties. Layla was relieved to put some distance between them and the guardians.

The entryway they stood in was wide open, and the curved walls of the steel skin of the building arched over them like a silver rainbow. The black-and-white marble floor stretched out to the white wall in front of them, and there wasn't a stick of furniture, a lamp, or a picture. There weren't any doors or windows either.

Nothing.

It was a white room—barren of everything—except the six of them.

"So what the hell is this?" Kerry asked out loud. She took her knit cap off and smoothed her long dark locks as she looked around the empty, cavernous room. "This place sucks, and I have to tell you, I'm unimpressed."

Dante sighed and linked his arm around her waist. "Tell us how you really feel, princess."

"Sorry, Dante." Samantha raised one gloved hand. "I agree with Kerry. Major suckage."

Malcolm chuckled and kissed the top of Samantha's head. "Suckage? Is that even a word?"

Layla smirked. She liked them better and better by the second. Anyone who could diffuse tension from a situation like this was someone she wanted to hang out with. She glanced at William to see if he was remotely amused by their friend's reactions but he wasn't. He remained perfectly still and kept his sights fixated on the blank white wall.

"So where is everyone?" Layla asked, wondering if she wanted to know the answer.

William looked down at her through the eyes of his clan, and to her surprise, linked his fingers with hers. Those moon-glow eyes zeroed in on her, comforting her, reassuring her, and all without saying a word.

His eyes twinkled, and he whispered, *"Revelamini."*

The floor vibrated beneath their feet as the white wall disappeared into the floor. Layla gasped and looked from the vanishing wall back to William, who looked remarkably pleased with himself.

"Okay, that doesn't suck," she said through a shaky breath.

"That doesn't suck, but *you do*, William." Kerry leaned over and gave him a friendly smack on the arm. She winked at Layla. "Your friend here is full of surprises."

A smile cracked Layla's face. "That is the understatement of the century."

As the wall disappeared, the Council's meeting space came into view. Layla's smile faded. Suddenly, the tigers outside seemed like a walk in the park. The cavernous space reminded her of pictures of lost caves in the mountains of Transylvania or something.

The three couples crossed the threshold and stood at the top of a flight of stairs. Looking around, she fleetingly thought that this is what it must look like from the top of a Mayan pyramids. The steps ran all the way around the four sides of the structure, and there had to be at least thirty steps leading down to what looked like an arena from Greek and Roman times.

I bet thousands of people would fit in here, she mused to the others.

Generations ago, they did. William's voice touched her mind gently. *The clans would gather in this arena once a year, but when the Caedo began to hunt us down, everything changed. The Council has continued to use it for their meeting place, and anyone who stumbles upon the structure would mistake it for a heated barn or a storage facility.*

The rectangular space at the center of the arena was lined with five pairs of raised platforms on either side, and at the far end was what looked like a larger pair of platforms. Behind the platforms at the head of the arena were two enormous carved stone statues of a roaring lion and a snarling tiger.

Despite the size of the mostly empty space, it was quite warm, and the comforting scent of pine lingered in the air.

Where is everyone? Layla touched his mind gently. *I thought they were here?*

They are here, but you won't be able to see them until they want you to. William expanded his thoughts to include the others. *The prince and a few of the elders have the ability to cloak themselves and those around them. It's an advanced visualization ability.*

That's new, Dante said with clear irritation.

No, but it's been kept secret for a reason. He glanced at Layla. *You can imagine how valuable this can be against our enemies, and it's even more valuable to us if they don't know about it.*

What else are the elders keeping from us? Malcolm's voice bit into the conversation, and he pulled Samantha tighter against him. *They lied to us about being able to mate with humans, they kept the truth of the Vasullus from us, and now, they're covering up certain abilities.* He glared at William. *What's next?*

Nothing that I'm aware of. He turned his serious gaze to each and last of all on Layla. *I promise you. You now know everything that I do, but I have a feeling there are more secrets within the Council.*

The six lined up across the top step. Layla squinted as her eyes adjusted to the lower light level. She tried to get a bead on what was waiting for them down in the seemingly vacant arena. Before she could ask William anything, the floor beneath her began to vibrate, and the wall closed behind them.

Panic swamped Layla. She couldn't help but feel like they were being buried alive. She gripped William's hand and was sure she may have actually drawn blood, but in his usual steadfast manner, he stayed the course and remained the calm in the storm.

"William," Kerry asked quietly from the right side of the stairs. "Did you do that?"

"No." William's jaw clenched, and he flicked his

gaze to Layla. "Richard and the rest of the Council are the only ones who can control the environment within these walls."

"Like I said, *major* suckage," Samantha murmured.

"It's game time," Layla said in a strong, clear voice.

The six moved down the steep staircase at a slow and steady pace. As they got closer to the bottom, Layla took in every inch of the arena they were about to stand in. The floors and pedestals looked like they were made of smooth, white marble. Everything was pristine and put together so perfectly, it almost looked as if it had been carved out of one gigantic piece. There were no seams anywhere—it looked as if it was part of the same stone.

The closer they got to the bottom, the more invisible the outer walls became. When she stepped foot onto the snow-white floor and looked up to see how far they'd come, her breath caught in her throat. The walls, doorway, and ceilings had vanished, and they were surrounded by an inky black sky, dotted with what looked like millions of stars.

"Where the hell are we?" Layla breathed as she and the others looked around in awe.

A vaguely familiar female voice drifted through the cavernous room and into the recesses of Layla's memory.

"You are home."

Chapter 17

THE ROOM SHIMMERED BEFORE THEIR EYES, AND seconds later the empty platforms were no longer vacant, and an exotic menagerie was revealed. Layla couldn't help but think of Noah's ark. Two members of each clan stood atop each platform, except for the last pair on the right—it was an elderly man and woman she could only assume represented the Vasullus. She gripped William's hand for dear life as she took in the mind-blowing scene.

"Holy shit," breathed Kerry.

Layla couldn't help but agree with her sentiment. Tigers, panthers, wolves, bears, and falcons lined the left side of the space, and she noted that these animals were larger than any that would be found in the wild. Eagles, foxes, coyotes, cheetahs, and two humans stood on the opposite side and were equally imposing figures.

All of the Council members turned their glowing eyes onto the six visitors with razor-sharp focus, and their energy waves pulsed with strength that Layla hadn't ever experienced. At the head of the arena sat two mammoth lions, and she knew that the male with the thick dark mane had to be Richard, the prince.

She braced herself against the onslaught of their power and willed herself not to pass out. She glanced at Kerry and Samantha and was relieved to see that they looked as stunned as she felt.

Her attention immediately went to the two cheetahs that stood next to the human couple, and an instant sense of belonging embraced her. She locked eyes with the smaller beast and knew that it was Bianca, her aunt—the woman manipulating her life.

"Hello, Bianca," Layla said in a surprisingly strong voice.

Verto. Their collective voices cried out in unison and rang clearly through their minds. The cavernous space sparked with static electricity as all the Council members shifted into their human state. Enormous, polished black armchairs materialized behind them. They all sat regally without saying a word. She noticed that each had a gold ring on the right hand, just like the one Bianca used to create the wax seal.

Silence hung heavily in the air, and the tension grew with palpable force. As Layla's eyes scanned the room, she knew with certainty that there were Purists staring back at her. She could practically taste their hatred. But which ones were they? She prayed that their plan would work and force the haters to come out into the open.

"Step forward, friends." Richard's deep voice boomed through the massive space as he waved them forward.

Layla studied the leader of the Amoveo. His long dark hair was the same color as his mane, but he had large blue eyes, which she suspected was unusual for a member of the lion clan. They smiled back at her brightly, and her nervousness eased.

In a black sweater and a pair of jeans, he was dressed more like a soccer dad than the prince of an ancient race. He radiated power and was one of the most beautiful men she'd ever laid eyes on. Based on his energy, Layla sensed he was an ally.

However, the blond woman to the right of him didn't look as welcoming. Her glowing pale yellow eyes stared down with obvious disdain.

The walk to the other end of the arena felt like forever with the Council members tracking their every move in stony silence. She swallowed her fear and kept her sights set on Richard, the individual she was sure wanted to help.

They stopped about ten feet in front of Richard, and William bowed his head in deference to their leader. "Thank you for calling the Council together, my prince." William's cool, calm voice streamed steadily through the room. "We are honored that you accepted our request for a special meeting."

"It would seem that it's long overdue," he replied as his bright blue eyes flickered over them but lingered on Layla. "After the unfortunate experiences suffered by Samantha and Kerry, I informed the Council members about the Purist activity and made it quite clear that prejudice of that nature would not be tolerated. I must admit that I was quite surprised to learn about you, Layla. I'm not a big fan of surprises." His voice was edged with anger, and he leveled his stern gaze at Bianca. "Care to explain yourself, Bianca?"

All eyes turned to Bianca, who didn't look a day older than she had almost twenty years ago. She was indeed the "social worker" who had brought Layla to Rosie's farm. Tall and thin, her strawberry blond hair was swept up in an elegant French twist, and her glowing, golden eyes looked back lovingly at Layla. She was dressed impeccably in a dark skirt suit and reminded her of an attorney from *Law & Order*.

"Yes, my prince." Bianca rose from her chair and clasped her hands in front of her. "Layla is the daughter of my brother, Francis. His mate was human, and although she was a gifted psychic, she was unable to handle the power of her gifts. Like many of her kind with unique abilities, she succumbed to madness, and eventually death. Francis had heard rumors of other hybrid children, and of the violence that had befallen their parents."

Her voice, soft and melodic, floated over Layla like a warm blanket, and her heart tugged with unexpected emotion. William, sensing her need for comfort, pulled her into the shelter of his body, and stroked her arm reassuringly. He may have only been doing it out of duty, and when they left this place, he may never do it again, but she was grateful for it now.

Bianca's eyes filled with tears as she turned to Layla. "He wanted nothing more than to raise you as his own, but he feared for your safety among our people," she said in a quivering voice. "Francis was poisoned. We still don't know who did it, and our healers tried to save him but nothing worked." Her voice broke with emotion. "On his deathbed, he told me about you, and made me swear that I would find you and keep you safe."

"Safe?" Anger and frustration clawed at Layla. "You have manipulated my life, lied to me, and moved me around like some pawn in a twisted game of chess." Her eyes narrowed, and heat crawled up her back. "Would you mind telling me and the rest of us," she said with a sweeping gesture to everyone, "exactly how you knew where to find a 'safe house' that just happened to have two other hybrid children living in it?"

"*What?*" The baritone voice boomed through the room, and Layla could swear she felt it to her bones. It was the male representative from the Bear Clan, and he was pissed. "There are safe houses for hybrids? This is treason! How dare you keep information like this from the Council?"

"Silence!" the prince shouted and stood. "Artimus, you will hold your tongue."

Layla watched as Artimus's bearded face turned red with anger. His eyes glowed jet black, and his thick, meaty hands balled tightly into fists. He said nothing but sat his hulking frame back into the chair. The woman next to him was younger and radiated a different energy. It wasn't as thick or strong, and she looked oddly familiar.

"Artimus, please," pleaded the young woman next to him.

"Shut up, Marianna," he roared.

"I'd watch the tone you take with my sister." Dante's voice cut through the room and carried an unmistakable threat.

Sister? Layla looked from Dante to Marianna as she put it together. Marianna is the twin sister Kerry had mentioned, the one who took their father's place on the Council.

"Is that a threat?" Artimus growled and flicked his hate-filled sights on Kerry. "Half-breed lover."

Dante growled, and his eyes shifted to the eyes of his clan as Kerry held him back. "He's not worth it."

"Enough! I will have silence." Richard glared at

Artimus. "Do not forget your place." He sat down and turned his serious eyes back to Bianca, who was staring wide-eyed at Artimus. "Answer Layla's question, Bianca. I'd like to hear the answer myself. How did you know where to find this safe house?"

Layla held her breath, and you could hear a pin drop in the place as they all hung on every word. Bianca took a deep breath and gazed around the room. "There have been rumors that several men in Francis's generation mated with humans. One was his childhood friend from the Timber Wolf Clan, James. They confided in one another about their unusual mates and heard rumors of others. When James was killed by the Caedo, Francis kept track of his mate and their twins, Raife and Tatiana." She smiled at Layla. "Before my brother died, he told me where to find them."

"Are there other safe houses?" Richard asked intently, and his eyes flickered bright blue. "Do not lie to me, Bianca." Layla shivered from the threatening tone, and in that moment, there was little doubt of his strength.

"I have only heard rumors, your majesty." She dipped in a low curtsy. "I swear it to you on the honor of the Cheetah Clan."

"Honor?" Artimus spat. "What the hell would the Cheetah Clan know about honor? Your brother bred weakness into our race with a feebleminded human, and you helped cover it up." He rose from his seat and glared at the six of them. "And these three—" He pointed at the men accusingly. "They disgrace their clans by doing the same damn thing with these half-breeds."

"Artimus," Richard warned. "Sit down."

"No," he bellowed. "I will not sit down. I am sick and

tired of keeping my mouth shut, and so are the others."
He turned his dark eyes to Dante. "You know who had
honor? Your father! Brendan gave his life to keep our
race pure, free of human blood, and look what you did?
You hooked yourself up with a half-breed."

"You bastard," Dante growled.

"What?" Marianna stood and looked frantically
from Artimus to Dante. "You said Daddy died protecting Samantha!"

"Ha!" Artimus laughed loudly and leered at Samantha
as Malcolm pushed her securely behind him. "Protecting
her? He wanted to wipe her off the face of the earth.
Your father died honorably trying to snuff out the half-
breeds before they could spread like a disease through
our people."

"Dante, is this true?" she pleaded. "Daddy was
a Purist?"

"Yes," Dante replied. "I didn't want you to know
what he'd done and how he shamed our family." His
features softened. "I'm sorry, Marianna."

"The only thing you should be sorry about is mating
with that thing," Artimus spat.

A bone-shattering roar ripped through the room, silencing everyone.

Richard had shifted into his lion and stood on the platform, looming largely over the room. His magnificent
mane framed his glowing blue eyes, and his muscular,
feline body covered in tawny fur dwarfed the woman
sitting next to him.

No one moved.

I will not tolerate further outbursts. Richard scanned
the room, his head moving almost imperceptibly as his

powerful voice touched their collective minds. *I have long suspected that there was dissension on the Council, but I prayed I was wrong. If our race is going to survive, we must embrace this evolutionary change, or we will die out. Pure-blooded Amoveo mates seem to be fewer and fewer with each generation, and if we do not learn to adapt, then it will be our undoing.* He sat on his haunches, and his long tail curled around him. *I will ask this question only once. Is there anyone else on this Council who shares the same opinion as Artimus?*

"I am not alone." Artimus stood and whispered the ancient language. The chair behind him vanished as he shimmered and turned into the most enormous grizzly bear that Layla had ever seen. Artimus stood on his hind legs, swiped his massive, clawed paws outward, and bellowed into the air. *We will not allow you to muddy our ancient bloodlines and permit the destruction of our people.*

In a rush of static electricity the room erupted with roars, growls, screeches, and the haunting howl of a wolf as the rest of the Purists revealed themselves in a chorus of dissent. William, Dante, and Malcolm pulled their mates into their arms and looked around in horror. Artimus was most definitely *not* alone.

In addition to Artimus, both members of the Falcon and Eagle Clans screeched their objections, the females from the Coyote and Arctic Wolf Clans both growled down at them, hackles raised with clear disdain, as did the male representatives from the Fox, Tiger, and Panther Clans. The last to shift was the female representative from the Lion Clan, the one who'd been shooting Layla daggers from the moment she'd walked in.

The tension was dangerously high as the Council members still in their human form stood to face the others. Layla glanced at the Vasullus family members, and to her surprise, they remained seated and oddly calm amid the anxious situation.

Richard jumped to his feet and snarled at the lioness next to him. *Traitor.* His voice rumbled low and menacing.

Veronica growled and crouched low, with her tail switching behind her. *You are the traitor,* she hissed. *What kind of a leader allows his people to destroy themselves and knowingly weakens their race? If it were up to you, we'd all breed with humans, until we were nothing more than they are—weak and pathetic.*

Your time is over, Richard, Artimus bellowed. *The true believers, the pure-blooded Amoveo, follow me now. You can keep the half-breeds and your theories of evolution, because the only one who is going to be extinct around here is you.*

William's body tensed, and just when Layla thought that it was going to be World War III and fur was going to fly, the Purists uttered the ancient language and vanished into thin air.

———

William's heart thundered in his chest as he held Layla's shaking form in his arms. She was spooked, and he couldn't blame her. Dante and Malcolm clung tightly to their mates as well and exchanged concerned looks with William. The arena had gone hauntingly quiet, and the sight of the abandoned platforms made his heart sink. Only half the Council members remained.

Richard shimmered, shifted to his human form, and

cursed loudly. William watched as his wife, Salinda, who was heavy with child, went to his side and wrapped her arms lovingly around him, sobbing against his chest. Her fellow Tiger Clan member had left with Artimus and the others. William didn't know what was worse. The Amoveo divided as a whole or the clear division within the clans themselves.

"Your Highness." It was David Vasullus who finally broke the silence. "You should know that you have the full support of the Vasullus family." His somber gaze wandered over them. "We know what it's like to lose our mates or to not find them at all. You three men are lucky to have found your other halves. Hybrid or pure-blood... a mate is not a gift to be squandered."

The elderly woman next to him stood and linked her arm through his. "I always thought Artimus was a troublemaker," she said through sympathetic pale blue eyes. "I know this is difficult, Your Highness, but it's better this way."

"Better, Georgina?" Richard asked incredulously, while he cradled his wife in the crook of his arm. "The Council has dissolved, and it looks like we have a civil war on our hands. How on earth is this better?"

"At least now, our enemies are out in the open." Layla's voice cut into the conversation, and William looked at her with pride. "The lines have been drawn, and it's time for people to choose a side. No more hiding or wondering where people stand."

"I couldn't have said it better myself," Georgina said with a wink to Layla. "She's right, Your Highness. It's much easier to fight the enemy if you know who they are."

Bianca stepped down from the platform and made her way to William and Layla, who stiffened at her approach. He touched her mind with his. *It's going to be alright.*

"I'm so sorry, Layla." Bianca's light brown eyes were filled with sadness. "I wish there had been another way, but at the time it seemed like the right thing to do. I hope you'll forgive me and your father for keeping you in the dark for so long."

Layla said nothing but shrugged.

"He loved you, you know." Bianca smiled, and one large tear rolled down her face before she could brush it away. "More than anything, he wanted to keep you safe long enough to find your mate, so you could explore your full strength and know true happiness." She flicked a glance at William. "I'm so glad that he found you."

William's throat tightened with emotion, and he brushed his hand down Layla's back. She was here, but for how long? Would she ever truly give herself to him and be his mate in the true fashion of the Amoveo, or would she refuse?

"Bianca." Layla stilled in his arms, and he watched as Bianca braced herself for what Layla was going to say. "I have to thank you for bringing me to Rosie's farm. I'm still not convinced that lying and hiding things the way you did was right." She let out a slow breath and stuffed her hand in the pocket of her jeans. "But the truth is, for all the lack of control I've had over my life, the craziness and uncertainty… growing up on the farm with Raife and Tati really was a gift. So thank you for that."

"You are welcome." Bianca turned to Richard and

bowed her head. "Your Highness, if it's alright with you, Michael and I would like to go back to our clan and inform them of the latest developments."

"Yes," Richard said evenly. He gazed upon the remaining loyal Amoveo solemnly. "All of you must spread the word to your clans. Purist or Loyalist. Now is the time to decide which side of the fence you are on. Loyalists will always have my protection, and if anyone is threatened, they can seek refuge here at the ranch with Salinda and me." His mouth set in a grim line. "Go now, and I expect a report from each of you by the end of the week as to how your clans respond."

"As you wish," Bianca said with a deep curtsy. She turned to Layla. "I do hope you'll allow me to stay in touch with you." She smiled. "I would like to get to know my niece."

"Sure." Layla gave a curt nod. "I guess you're the only blood relative I have left."

"That's hardly the case. We have a large family, and I would love for you to meet them."

"Yeah, well, I wonder if they'll all be as eager to meet me," Layla said skeptically. "It wouldn't be outside the realm of possibility that some of the Cheetah Clan members are Purists."

Bianca's face fell. "I—well—I'd never think it was possible, but after what we all just witnessed, I suppose anything is possible. Either way, I hope you'll let me know when you and William are ready to meet the others."

"The future is up to Layla," he said smoothly and cleared his throat. He wasn't exaggerating. He was leaving all of it up to her and would not under any circumstances make the move to bind them together until she told him that's what she wanted. "Safe journey home."

Static filled the air as Bianca and the remaining Council members vanished—except for one—Marianna.

Dante's sister stepped down from the platform, and her eyes were latched firmly onto her brother and Kerry. Her dark wavy hair spilled over her narrow shoulders, and she nibbled nervously on her lower lip.

"Our father died because of all of this," she said through a shaking breath. She looked around at all of them but lingered on each of the women. "Everything is falling apart, Dante. Our mother is dying, and she'll be just like one of them soon," she said with a nod to the Vasullus.

"I know this is difficult," Dante said gently.

"You don't know anything." Her voice shook with anger. "All you care about is *her*." She pointed accusingly at Kerry. "I don't want any part of this. None of it. Do you hear me?" Her eyes shifted to glittering black diamonds. "I'm going back to New York, and you know what? I don't care if I ever find a mate. Not if it means dealing with shit like this. You can all go straight to hell—just keep me out of it." She uttered the ancient language and disappeared.

"I guess I won't be having Christmas with *her*," Kerry mumbled.

"She'll come around." Dante kissed the top of her head and rubbed her back reassuringly. "I'll have Pete keep an eye on her and make sure she stays out of trouble."

"Oh, that'll work," Kerry said with pure sarcasm. "He's an ex-cop, *and* he's human. She's not going to want to have him around for a second."

"That's probably a good idea, Dante." Richard and Salinda stepped down from the platform hand in hand. "Marianna was the other Bear Clan Council member, and something tells me that Artimus is going to do his best to get her to join his cause." His sad eyes examined everyone in the group. "I have a sinking suspicion Artimus won't like the fact that she didn't leave with him and declare her allegiance to the Purists."

"Pete was instrumental in helping defeat the Purists in New Orleans," William explained to Layla. "He's one of few humans who know about us, and he's considered part of the Vasullus family now, just as Rosie will be."

"We need to come up with a plan," Richard said to the group grimly. "You can be assured that Artimus and his followers have one, and they won't stop until they've wiped out anyone who disagrees with their philosophy. I'd feel better if we had more information about some of the other hybrids. I fear that finding and exterminating them will be his first move."

Layla raised her hand. "Excuse me, but I may have something that could be of use." All eyes landed on her as she removed the worn leather diary from the inside pocket of her coat. William hadn't a clue that she'd brought it with her, and he wondered what else she was keeping to herself.

Are you sure Raife and Tatiana will be alright with this, Layla? William whispered along the edges of her mind. Layla simply nodded and kept her attention on Richard. *Raife is the one who suggested it.*

"Raife and Tatiana's mom kept a diary about her courtship with their father. I didn't think there was anything of use, but last night Raife showed me something."

William's brow furrowed as he watched her gently open the frayed book to the inside of the back cover. With extreme care, she peeled back the fabric lining, gently pulled out a yellowed, folded paper, and handed it to Richard.

The tension in the room was thick enough to choke on.

"It's a list." She glanced from Richard to William. "A list of Amoveo men who had hybrid children. At least that's what we think it is. Both of our fathers are on it, as well as Kerry and Samantha's, and there are five other names."

"These men are all dead." Richard read the list, his face a mask of concentration. "Most of them were killed by the Caedo."

"At least that's what we've been led to believe," Malcolm said somberly. "Perhaps the Caedo have been responsible for far less than they've been given credit for."

"And in case you all forgot, until very recently, my father wasn't dead," Kerry chimed in. "He was living as a human—Vasullus—but my mother *was* killed by the Purists." She sighed heavily and put her head on Dante's shoulder. "At least, that's what we were told."

"We have to find them," Salinda whispered and clung tighter to her husband. She looked at the rest of them through sorrowful eyes. "We have to find their children—the other hybrids—before Artimus does."

"What do these numbers and letters next to their names mean?" Richard squinted and looked closely at the faded ink.

"Raife thinks that they may be the number of children they had, and the letters look like abbreviations for states.

Raife and Tati have an MD and the number two next to their father's name—they were raised in Maryland, and there are two of them. Kerry and Samantha have RI and the number one by their father's names—they were raised in Rhode Island, and both were only children."

"Thank you for sharing this with us, Layla. You'll have to extend my gratitude to your siblings for sharing such a personal thing with us." Richard took her hands in his and kissed them with the regality one would expect from a prince. "It gives us a solid place to start."

Layla's energy waves pulsed with pride and satisfaction, which had William feeling relieved. She smiled, and he could tell that she felt a new kinship and sense of belonging to their people. Even if she never chose to bond with him, he knew she'd have the protection of the prince. As long as she was safe… that was all that mattered.

"I think we should go back to the house, take stock of the situation, and get a game plan. We need to have a better idea of how much divisiveness we have within the clans themselves," Richard said.

Everyone nodded. They had gotten some answers, and most of their enemies had revealed themselves, but the future of their race remained unclear. William glanced over his shoulder to the empty arena below. He couldn't help but wonder if this was the beginning of the end.

Chapter 18

THE FRESH SMELL OF SOMETHING BAKING WAFTED through the old farmhouse and made William's stomach rumble as he threw the few items he had with him into a small duffel bag. The others had left last night when they got back from the ranch. Malcolm was eager to get his pregnant wife back home and out of harm's way. Dante and Kerry left for New York to try and get Marianna to listen to reason, but based on what he knew of her, that was going to be no easy task. She hadn't chosen a side, which meant she was fair game for Artimus and the Purists.

He looked around the quaint room, and his gaze lingered on the bed he'd shared so briefly with Layla. Images of her soft, sexy body writhing in ecstasy beneath his flooded his mind, but he squashed the memories quickly, knowing that to linger would only make things worse. William closed the door to the room but couldn't shut the door on his feelings, although Layla seemed to have had no problem doing it.

He came into the kitchen to find Sylvia puttering away and fussing over Raife, who was scarfing down what looked like a delicious breakfast of pancakes and bacon. The two seemed to have picked up where they left off all those years ago, and he did his best to squelch the jealousy that reared its ugly head.

Sylvia, coffee pot in hand, smiled shyly at William. "Can I get you a cup before you leave?"

"No," he said. "Have you seen Layla this morning? I have to be going, but I'd like to say good-bye."

"You're really leaving? Just like that, huh?" Raife looked at him through narrowed eyes and swallowed the food in his mouth. "Layla's not here. She split with her camera early this morning."

William's jaw clenched. She left? She knew he was leaving this morning and hadn't even come back to say good-bye. He didn't want to get into a pissing match with Raife, but the truth was that he didn't think he'd be able to keep his emotions in check.

"Where is Rosie?"

Raife shook his head. "She's in the living room, resting."

"Thank you."

"Hey, bird boy," Raife called after him. "I never figured you for a quitter."

William stopped dead in his tracks as anger, frustration, and desperation clawed at him. "I'm not the one who quit," he said without turning around. "Layla cornered the market on that."

Bag in hand, William found Rosie bundled up on the couch, reading a magazine in front of a crackling fire. She had the color back in her cheeks, and aside from a large bandage on her head and a sling on her arm, she looked like herself again. Richard had sent an Amoveo healer to visit Rosie in the hospital, and needless to say, her speedy recovery baffled the human doctors.

"Are you gonna stand there starin' at me all day, or are you gonna come in here and talk to me?" She didn't even look up from her magazine.

"I came to say good-bye." William rounded the end of the couch and gave a cursory glance to the chair that he and Layla had enjoyed so much. He cleared his throat and turned his full attention to Rosie. "I'm going back to Richard's ranch in Montana. I'll be staying there for a time, while we try and sort things out. We still have several other hybrids to find."

"I see." Rosie placed the magazine on her lap and peered at him over the edge of her glasses. "Where I come from, we call that running away." Rosie waved him off. "Bye-bye."

William's mouth set in a firm line, and he struggled to keep his eyes from shifting. "I am not running away." Anger crawled up his back. "Layla has made it clear that she is not interested in binding her life to mine, and I am not interested in forcing her. I have told her how I feel." His voice rose with frustration. "I don't see what else there is to say."

Rosie pursed her lips and made a sound of understanding. "I see."

William placed a quick kiss on Rosie's forehead. "Thank you for welcoming me into your home. And thank you very much for everything you have done for Layla. Tell her…" He trailed off, unsure of what to say.

"I think I know what to say." Rosie picked her magazine back up. "You go on now, and have a safe trip." Without looking at him, she licked her finger and flipped the page. "I'm sure I'll be seeing you around."

William reached out in search of Layla's energy signature, but was unable to connect with her. Emotions clogged his throat as he realized she was blocking him and must be intentionally hiding from him. Loss, emptiness, and despair flooded him as he reconciled the fact that she wasn't going to stop him from leaving. He'd fooled himself into believing that she wouldn't let him go, and now the disappointment just might crush him. Fighting back the flood of bleak emotions, he uttered the ancient language and vanished.

Camera in hand, Layla trotted up the steps of the house and kicked off her boots before heading into the kitchen in search of the source of the delicious smell. She hit the doorway and screeched to a halt when she found Raife and Sylvia cleaning dishes side by side at the sink. She watched them and found herself envious of how oddly at ease they seemed with one another. He washed the dishes and passed them to her, so she could dry them. It looked like they'd been doing this for years, opposed to a day or two.

How did they step back into each other's lives so seamlessly?

"It's not polite to stare," Raife said over his shoulder.

"Sorry," Layla mumbled. She grabbed a banana from the fruit bowl on the table.

"Would you like some pumpkin bread?" Sylvia asked with a genuine smile. "I just made it this morning."

"No." Layla shook her head and held up the banana. Having Sylvia as an ally, and from the looks of things, as a possible sister-in-law, was going to take some getting used to. "I'll just stick with this."

"Layla," Sylvia said hesitantly. "I'm sorry for everything. My father… the way I behaved… all of it." Tears filled her blue eyes. "I hope you can forgive me."

Layla looked from Sylvia to Raife. "As long as you're good to my brother, then you and I are square."

"Thank you." Sylvia gave her a nod and smiled at Raife, who winked at her warmly.

"You just missed him." Raife turned around and leaned against the edge of the counter. "William just left."

Layla paled, and she swallowed the bile that rose in her throat. "What?"

"He split." Raife tossed the sponge back into the sink but kept a watchful eye on her. "I'm surprised. I really thought you two were gonna stick, but he said that you quit on him."

Heat flashed in her cheeks. "*I quit?* He said that *I'm* the one who quit? That arrogant son of a bitch," she said as she fought the tears. "He's the one who left without saying good-bye."

"Layla Nickelsen," Rosie barked from the living room. "You get your skinny ass in here, and stop cussing in my kitchen."

Raife smirked. "You're in trouble now."

"Oh shut up." She slammed the banana back into the bowl. She heard Raife chuckling as she stalked out to the living room.

Layla sat on the arm of the sofa with her arms crossed and struggled to keep from crying. "William left," she whispered.

"Yes, he did." She tossed her magazine on the table and waved Layla over to her. "Come here." She patted the edge of the sofa near her.

Layla complied and sat next to Rosie as she took her hand in hers. "Layla, I have one simple question." Rosie's gray eyes looked earnestly at her. "Do you love him?"

Layla's eyes filled with tears, and she nodded as they rolled down her cheeks. "Yes."

"Then, honey, why wouldn't you tell him? Fate or destiny, whatever the reason... that man loves you." She squeezed her hands tightly. "He *loves* you, Layla, and you love him. So what the hell is the problem?"

"I'm scared." Layla squeezed her eyes shut. "He says he loves me, but he never said the bonding rite." Her face reddened at the idea of discussing sex with Rosie. "He could've said the words and bound us together, but he didn't." She lifted one shoulder and looked down.

Rosie burst out laughing and clapped her hands. Layla wiped the tears off her cheeks and looked at her as if she'd lost her mind. "What are you laughing at?"

"You, ya silly girl." Rosie shook her head, let out a long sigh, and folded her hands on her belly. "The man told you he loves you, and I'm guessin' he showed you too." Rosie gave her a knowing look that sent her cheeks aflame with embarrassment. "Why wouldn't he say those words? Why wouldn't he just say the bonding rite? *Think* about it for a minute."

Layla looked at Rosie through confused eyes, and then the realization hit her like a tsunami. Her eyes grew wide, and a smile cracked her tear-stained face. "Oh my God," she breathed. "Of course." Layla laughed and jumped off the couch. She smacked her forehead with one hand. "God, I'm *such* an asshole."

"Well, you said it, not me." Rosie smirked and watched as all the pieces fell into place.

"I have to go to him." She ran her hands through her tousled curls. "Oh shit! Where is he?"

"He went back to Richard's ranch in Montana."

Layla ran over, hugged Rosie, and rained kisses on

her weathered face. "I love you so much, Rosie." She giggled. "Thank you."

Layla stood in the center of the room, closed her eyes, and did what William taught her. She envisioned the wild beauty of the ranch, which was imprinted in her memory. The smell of pine and the clean, crisp, cold air filled her nostrils as the enormous clapboard house and towering mountains came into focus.

"*Verto*," she whispered.

In a rush of static and a flash of light, Layla was standing on the ranch, and the icy Montana wind rushed over her briskly. She hugged her coat tighter around her and ran up the flagstone path to the entrance of their home, but the low, deadly growl of a tiger brought her to a screeching halt.

Going somewhere? Dominic's rumbling baritone flooded her mind.

Layla turned on her heels and found herself face to face with the mammoth tiger. Even on all fours, he was almost as tall as she was, and the muscles that rippled beneath that striped fur left little doubt to how much damage he could do in a short time.

"Hello, Dominic." She scanned the area. "Where's Daniella?"

Dominic growled, whispered the ancient language, and shifted into his human form. Like most Amoveo men, he towered over her at well over six feet tall, and was a solid wall of muscle. He had cropped black hair and was dressed in combat fatigues with a dagger tucked in his belt. The man looked like he'd stepped out of an ad for the army or special forces. Needless to say, he was a badass.

"My sister claimed the side of the Purists," he said tightly. His yellow-gold eyes burned down at her brightly. "I am the only guardian now."

"I'm here to see William." She held her ground, ready to shift into her cheetah. "Is he here?"

"William is upstairs." Salinda's sweet voice floated down like a breath of fresh air. "Thank you, Dominic."

"Your Highness," he said with a bow.

Layla headed up the steps while Dominic erupted into his tiger form and stalked out to the fields. Shaking from a touch of adrenaline, Layla stepped into the front hall and breathed a sigh of relief.

"I had a feeling we might be seeing you sooner rather than later." Salinda closed the door, smiled, and rested her hands on her pregnant belly. "William is staying on the third floor." Her warm brown eyes glinted at Layla knowingly. "It's private. Go right up. I know he'll be very happy to see you, and I, for one, am thrilled that you're here." She scooped up her purse and shrugged on her coat. "Now you make yourself at home. I have an appointment at the healer, belly checkup, and so on. Richard is meeting me there, so you two will have the place to yourselves. As you saw, Dominic is guarding the property, so rest easy."

Layla grinned. "Thank you, Salinda." She bounded up the steps two at a time as Salinda vanished.

She gripped the mahogany banister, breathless by the time she reached the landing of the third floor. Trying to catch her breath, Layla ran her fingers through her unruly red curls in an effort to make herself presentable.

She shucked her coat, draped it over the newel post at the top of the steps, and straightened out the V-neck sweater she'd thrown on that morning.

She moved slowly down the hallway and peered into the rooms on either side, but the office and what looked like the sitting room were empty. At the end of the hallway was one more door that was open just a crack. Layla entered and found William standing at a tall oval window with his hands clasped firmly behind his back in his signature stance.

"Why are you here?" he asked coldly without even turning around. "You made it perfectly clear this morning that you want to be left alone."

"What are you talking about?" Layla asked with genuine confusion.

He glanced over his shoulder. "Your energy signature was completely cut off from me." William turned to face her, and the look on his face broke her heart. "That was a clear enough signal for me."

"Cut you off?" Layla hooked her thumbs into the back pocket of her jeans. "Are you referring to this morning? When I was out shooting pictures of the farm?"

"Yes." William's brow furrowed. "But I don't see what that has to do with anything."

"Well, counselor, you didn't look at all the evidence." Layla closed the distance between them in deliberate steps. "When I get focused on my work, I shut out everything else, and all my energy, thoughts, feelings—everything that I am—is pointed at whatever it is I'm shooting. So I wasn't shutting you out intentionally, I was absorbed in my work, but now that I know it has the side effect of cutting you off, I'll have to be more careful."

Her body wavered inches from his, her gaze skimming that devastatingly handsome face.

"So you see, William." Layla took a deep breath, and her breasts brushed against the hard planes of his chest. "I wasn't blocking you or avoiding you. I couldn't avoid you if I tried."

She ran her hands up his muscular arms and linked them behind his neck. His body hardened beneath her touch, and she felt him struggle to keep control.

Layla pulled his hair free from the ponytail he wore and tangled her fingers in his silky hair. To her delight, his eyes shifted to their clan form and glowed down at her with the unmistakable glaze of desire.

"I can't avoid you, William, and you sure as hell can't avoid me. You can't make me fall in love with you and expect to get away with it." She nipped at his firm, warm lips and rasped her tongue along the tiny hurt. "You're buried deep. Under my skin and in my heart," she said seductively.

He murmured her name, captured her lips savagely with his, and dove deep. Passion raged as he explored the dark cavern of her mouth. Hands tore blindly, and their clothing fell away in a tangle of arms and legs. He picked her up easily and placed her on the bed. Breathless and panting, he covered her small body with the length of his, buried his face in the curve of her neck, and breathed her in. Layla shuddered beneath his ministrations and moaned as he kissed and nibbled his way back to her mouth.

William settled himself between her legs and drove into her hard and fast.

Layla gasped with pleasure as he plunged into her

with strong strokes. He held her to him and took one rosy nipple into his mouth as he filled her time and again. Layla whispered his name as pleasure coiled deep inside. She wrapped her legs around his waist and held his head to her breast, urging him faster.

Knowing that they were approaching the peak, she reached out to him with her mind as he sank into her, and in that moment, openly gave William everything.

Nos es unus. Materia pro totus vicis. Ago intertwined. Forever.

As she touched her mind to his and uttered the ancient mating rite, the world exploded in a cavalcade of pleasure and blinding lights. They cried out in ecstasy and toppled over the edge of oblivion together.

Spent, sweaty, and exhausted, William rolled gently off Layla, but promptly pulled her naked body against his and nestled her into the crook of his arm. They lay in a tangle of limbs—hearts pounding, bodies shaking—and it was several minutes before either said anything. Layla chewed her lip nervously and ran her finger along the white scar on William's chest.

"I guess you're stuck with me now," she said through heavy breaths.

William propped a pillow under his head and looked down at her, while he played with her red curls. "It would seem so." He smiled, and his brow furrowed. "Where on earth did you learn the mating rite?"

"Kerry and Samantha told me what it was." She turned on her belly and rested her chin on his chest as she looked at him coyly. "Is it okay that *I* said it and not you?"

"Is it okay?" He laughed loudly and took her head in

both hands. William sat up, pulled her to him, and kissed her firmly. "It is more than okay, Firefly." He brushed her cheek with his thumb.

"I love you, William." She took his hand in hers and kissed his palm tenderly. Her heart swelled with love, and for the first time, she was exactly where she longed to be. Looking into his moon-glow eyes, she knew she was home. "I choose you," she whispered. "I choose you and me. Forever."

Watch for

UNDONE

next in The Amoveo Legend series
By Sara Humphreys,
Coming May 2013 from Sourcebooks Casablanca

Acknowledgments

Thank you just never seems to be enough, and whenever I write the acknowledgments, I'm worried that I'll leave someone out. The truth is that just about everyone I deal with on a daily basis should be thanked. They have to tolerate me and my annoying habit of stuffing a hundred things into one day. My husband and children, as always, are at the top of the list. They support me, love me, and inspire me to be better every day.

I'd like to extend my thanks to my agent, Jeanne Dube, for knowing just what to say and exactly when to say it. Thanks to Deb Werksman, Cat Clyne, and Susie Benton for their editorial brilliance, and for the much needed words of encouragement in my moments of self-doubt. The Sourcebooks art department continues to create spectacular covers that capture the heart of the story. Many thanks to Danielle Jackson for her super-fab publicity efforts and putting together a stellar blog tour for every book.

Many thanks to the Community Relations Managers at Barnes & Noble who have been consistently supportive with my book tours and work hard to make each a success. Especially to Kelly at my local CRM at B&N—you rock! Sheila—you're still the best beta reader ever!

A big shout out to all of the angels on the street team... you gals are the best! Thank you for sharing your excitement about the series.

Thanks to the folks at the Rustic Inn down in Maryland for letting me take tons of photos of their place and for answering all my questions. Thanks to Tom Emory, my cousin and Woodbine resident, for sending pictures of different local joints, which helped me narrow it down and select the kind of spot I was looking for.

Last, but not least, thanks to the Fleury family for hosting the big reunion at Woodbine Farm every five years. At the 2010 reunion, inspiration struck, and the plot for *Untamed* was born. I hope you'll feel that I did the old homestead justice.

Dream on...

About the Author

Sara Humphreys is a graduate of Marist College, with a BA degree in English literature and theater. Her initial career path after college was as a professional actress. Some of her television credits include *A&E Biography*, *Guiding Light*, *Another World*, *As the World Turns*, and *Rescue Me*.

She is the president of Taney Speaker Training, which specializes in public speaking, presentation development, and communication skills. She has trained executives at Verizon, Bristol-Meyer Squibb, Westchester County, and the United States Navy. Her speaking career began with Monster's Making It Count programs, speaking in high schools and colleges around the United States to thousands of students.

Sara has been a lover of both the paranormal and romance novels for years. Her sci-fi/fantasy/romance obsession began years ago with the TV series *Star Trek* and an enormous crush on Captain Kirk. That sci-fi obsession soon evolved into the love of all types of fantasy/paranormal: vampires, ghosts, werewolves, and of course, shapeshifters. Sara is married to her college sweetheart, Will. They live in Bronxville, New York, with their four boys and two insanely loud dogs. Life is busy but never dull.

You can find information about upcoming books on her website www.sarahumphreys.com.

Untouched

by Sara Humphreys

—⁓—

She may appear to have it all, but inside she harbors a crippling secret...

Kerry Smithson's modeling career ensures that she will be admired from afar—which is what she wants, for human touch sparks blinding pain and mind-numbing visions.

Dante is a dream-walking shapeshifter—an Amoveo, who must find his destined mate or lose his power forever. Now that he has found Kerry, nothing could have prepared him for the challenge of keeping her safe. And it may be altogether impossible for Dante to protect his own heart when Kerry touches his soul...

—⁓—

Praise for the Amoveo Legend series:

"Sizzling sexual chemistry that is sure to please." —*Yankee Romance Reviewers*

"A moving tale that captures both the sweetness and passion of romance." —*Romance Junkies*, 5 blue ribbons

"A well-written, action-packed love story featuring two very strong characters." —*Romance Book Scene*, 5 hearts

For more of the Amoveo Legend series, visit:

www.sourcebooks.com

Unleashed

by Sara Humphreys

***What if you suddenly discovered
your own powers were beyond
anything you'd ever imagined…***

Samantha Logan's childhood home had always been a haven,
but everything changed while she was away. She has a
gorgeous new neighbor, Malcolm, who introduces her to the
amazing world of the dream-walking, shapeshifting Amoveo
clans…but what leaves her reeling with disbelief is when he
tells her she's one of them…

And shock turns to terror as Samantha falls prey to the deadly
enemy determined to destroy the Amoveo, and the only chance
she has to come into her true powers is to trust in Malcolm to
show her the way…

***Get swept away into Sara Humphreys's glorious
world and breathtaking love story…***

For more Sara Humphreys, visit:

www.sourcebooks.com

Discover a new LOVE

Are You In Love With Love Stories?

Here's an online romance readers club that's just for YOU!

Where you can:

- **Meet** great *authors*
- **Party** with new *friends*
- **Get** new *books* before everyone else
- **Discover** great *new reads*

All at incredibly BIG savings!

Join the party at DiscoveraNewLove.com!

A SEAL in Wolf's Clothing

by Terry Spear

———

Her instincts tell her he's dangerous…

While her overprotective brother's away, Meara Greymere's planning to play—and it wouldn't hurt to find herself a mate in the process. The last thing she needs is one of his SEAL buddies spoiling her fun, even if the guy is the hottest one she's ever seen…

His powers of persuasion are impossible to resist…

Finn Emerson is a battle-hardened Navy SEAL and alpha wolf. He's a little overqualified for baby-sitting, but feisty Meara is attracting trouble like a magnet…

As the only responsible alpha male in the vicinity, Finn is going to have to protect this intriguing woman from a horde of questionable men, and definitely from himself…

———

Praise for Terry Spear:

"High-powered romance that satisfies on every level." —*Long and Short Reviews*

"Hot doesn't even begin to describe it." —*Love Romance Passion*

For more Terry Spear, visit:

www.sourcebooks.com

Kiss of the Goblin Prince

by Shona Husk

—⁓—

The Man of Her Dreams

He is like a prince in a fairy tale: tall, outrageously handsome, and way too dark for her own good. Amanda has been hurt before, though. And with her daughter's illness, the last thing she needs right now is a man. But the power of Dai King is hard to resist. And when he threads his hands through her hair and pulls her in for a kiss, there is no denying it feels achingly right.

In a Land of Nightmare

After being trapped in the Shadowlands for centuries with the goblin horde a constant threat, Dai revels in his newfound freedom back in the human realm. But even with the centuries of magic he's accumulated, he still doesn't know how to heal Amanda's daughter—and it breaks his heart. Yet for the woman he loves, he'd risk anything…including a return to the dreaded Shadowlands.

—⁓—

For more of the Shadowlands series, visit:

www.sourcebooks.com

Enslaved

by Elisabeth Naughton

—~~—

GRYPHON—Honorable, loyal, dependable…tainted. He was the ultimate warrior before imprisonment in the Underworld changed him in ways he can't ignore.

She calls to him. Come to me. You can't resist. But Gryphon will not allow himself to be ruled by the insidious whispers in his head. And there's only one way to stop them: kill Atalanta, the goddess who enslaved him. But with so much darkness inside, he can't be sure what's real anymore. Even the Eternal Guardians, those who protect the human realm and the gods, want to exile him.

Finding Malea is like a miracle. Somehow he doesn't feel the pull of the dark when she's near. And he's determined to keep her as near as possible, whether she wants him close or not. But she's a temptation that will test every bit of control he has left. One that may ultimately have the power to send him back to the Underworld…or free him from his chains for good.

—~~—

Praise for Enraptured:

"A spellbinding and wickedly sexy thrill ride that turns the heat up. Ms. Naughton continues to rock the Greek Mythology world with another entry in her brilliant Eternal Guardian series." —*Bitten By Paranormal Romance*

For more of the Eternal Guardians series, visit:

www.sourcebooks.com